LINDOW END

A Novel

Christine Pemberton

REX PUBLISHING
2001

Published in 2001 by
REX PUBLISHING
First Floor
The Rex Buildings
Alderley Road
Wilmslow
Cheshire SK9 1HY
Tel: 0845 0909102 Fax: 01625 530900

ISBN 0 9540391 0 6

This novel is a work of fiction and the names, characters and events
portrayed in it are the work of the author's imagination.
Any resemblance to actual persons, living or dead, is entirely
coincidental. Only the landscape is real and even that,
overtaken by time, is changing rapidly.

Acknowledgments

I thank Katherine Frank for her enthusiasm, advice and encouragement during the final stages of writing this book. Thanks also to my brother for working his magic on my original dark old photograph of Lindow Moss.

CP

SECTION of PEAT BOG on LINDOW COMMON

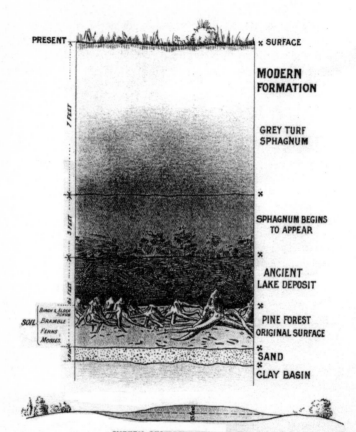

SKETCH SECTION ACROSS BOG

J. C. PRESTWICH Del.
OCT. 1884.

CONTENTS

"Our oldest element is a dark one, now scattered up and down through the population, and only gathered into a little nucleus here or there .... "

Quoted by William Norbury in a lecture entitled 'Lindow Common As A Peat Bog - Its Age and its People', delivered to the Cheshire & Lancastrian Archaeological Society in 1884, and reproduced in its entirety as an Appendix to Lindow End

1
Summer 1983

On the last day of his first month on the moss he suddenly found himself staring down at a dead man. He knew it was a man because of the moustache and beard. A dark brown dead man with a small winged insect crawling out of his left nostril. With unusual presence of mind Barry pressed the emergency button and the conveyor shuddered to a halt.

Lindow Moss was all right when the machinery was running. As soon as it stopped there was something spooky about the ensuing silence. It hung like a thick blanket, broken only by the distant howl of the wind which sounded across that dark landscape, even on the stillest days. Now, as his terrified eyes fastened onto the face, resting peacefully upon its peat cushion, his mind suddenly retched up the partially digested remains of too many video nasties.

The rest of the body remained entombed within the wedge of peat. A sharp needle of fear stem-stitched up his spine. As it stabbed into the follicles of his spiky bleached hair, his scalp lifted fractionally. *Bogey Man! The Bogey man will get you!* He heard his kid brother's hoarse whisper across the darkness of their shared bedroom. Was it there now, hovering close by? The soul, the spirit, whatever they called it, was it there, waiting, ready to get him?

Throughout the centuries, peat had been taken from the moss under the common right of turbary. In the past men had sweated and ached to provide for their families, each digging his quota of the peat that had fuelled countless hearths and provided the heat to cook food for the family. Common right and communal back break had long since ceased. Today it was a commercial enterprise. Lindow was still exploited for its peat, but modern technology had been brought into play, hacking deeper, brutal and violent, until the earth shuddered. The pits and trenches left in the wake of the diggers filled with dark water which oozed from the scars and formed black acidic pools, as if the disturbed land wept for its lost repose.

To his surprise, Barry Doyle had enjoyed his first taste of employment. It was good to be out in the open, working beneath a fine August sky with no lessons, no books, no teachers breathing down the back of his neck. The moss was worked by real men, men of his own kind and he liked their bad language and rough humour. On Friday afternoons, after the pay packets had been distributed, they knocked off early and allowed him to tag along with them to the local pub.

For the first time in his short life Barry discovered a flicker of ambition. He longed to drive the main digger, that wonderful lime green Hy-Mac which rose powerful and dominant over the damaged landscape, cratering the ground as it sliced out gigantic slabs of peat, lifting them effortlessly skywards before tipping them back to earth as easily as the little compressed blocks of tobacco flake that his Dad kept in a tin box to make roll-ups. Ken, who operated the Hi-Mac, laughed loudly when Barry, eyes shining with enthusiasm, confided his new found aspirations.

'But they're supposed to be training me.' Barry argued indignantly.

'This machine's worth a bloody fortune lad. Nobody's going to let a lad like you play about on it.'

'I'm here to learn. "All aspects of the job", that's what it said. That's right, isn't it, Mr Kirkham?'

'Just shut it and get on with sorting that lot.' replied the foreman irritably, so Barry quickly turned his attentions back to the conveyor, sifting though the passing blocks of freshly dug peat as the belt rolled by.

His hands were already pleasingly rough, the stubby fingers stained dark brown since he refused to wear the gloves they had provided. At the end of the line, the loads tipped into the waiting bogeys, to be transported along a series of narrow gauge rails to the sorting sheds. Here the peat was shredded and packed, ready for dispatch. Barry's job was to remove anything embedded in the freshly dug slabs which might cause damage to the shredding machinery. His days were spent dragging free old timbers, large roots and half rotted tree stumps. It was repetitive work and sheer boredom would have quickly driven a brighter boy to distraction, but Barry seemed ideally suited to the task. He enjoyed rummaging through the heaps of compressed peat hunting for debris and was perfectly content, that first summer out of school, sifting and sorting beneath a clear blue sky. Earning a living.

And now this. Barry had only encountered dead people in films. In the flesh he had come across squashed rabbits, run-over cats, a stiff fox, birds reduced to a flattened mess of sticky feathers. He had studied such remains closely, finding a morbid fascination in the grey beans and bloodstained entrails that tumbled from the split fur of small carcasses. For years he had thought that 'human bean' was some sort of reference to these complicated entrails, until the day his error was held up for class ridicule by one sorely tried English teacher. This dead person was different and it frightened the daylights out of him. With thudding heart he began to run for the safety of the packing sheds.

Geoff Kirkham glanced through the glass partition of his tiny office as the lad entered, ashen faced and trembling.
'What is is, Barry? Has there been an accident?'
Gulping for breath, Barry shook his head and gesticulated wildly towards the moss. 'Come quick, Mr Kirkham. Quick, it's on the conveyor. Hurry, please come!'
Kirkham stared at the terrified lad and pulled him into the

office.

'Calm down, lad. Get your breath back - here, sit down. Now tell me slowly. What's on the conveyor? Have you left it running?'

Barry shuddered and shook his head. 'No, I stopped it.' He stared at the foreman with wide eyes and Kirkham saw him swallow nervously. 'It's a body. It's bloody horrible. I pulled away this wedge of peat and there he was. I saw his face. It's a black man - a Paki. A dead Paki. Buried in the peat.'

Kirkham's sharp features creased into a frown.

'You're not making a lot of sense, Barry. Slow down. Tell me again.'

'Come with me. Come and have a look.' implored Barry, 'Don't make me go back on me own, Mr Kirkham. He's there, on the conveyor. In the peat. A dead Indian bloke.'

Kirkham got up from his desk immediately. 'Well don't just sit there!' he snapped, 'Come on, get a move on!'

Geoffrey Kirkham knew a lot more than the average foreman about preserved corpses. His knowledge had grown with the job, a bizarre, first hand knowledge which had accumulated during the twenty five years he had been employed on the moss. Supervising the peat cutting operations had provided Geoff Kirkham with a reasonable wage and several rare insights into some ancient traditions. Although he never spoke of such matters, he knew all about the annual sacrifices and ritual killings which had formed an important part of the pagan Celtic calender.

Now, as he stood alongside the stationary conveyor with the reluctant Barry Doyle, one glance told him all that he needed to know. Fumbling beneath the chin of the corpse, he probed into the leathery recesses of the throat and gave a muted exclamation of satisfaction as his searching fingers encountered the encircling garotte. The foreman turned to Barry with a relieved smile and gave the boy a paternal pat on the shoulder. Barry backed away from his touch.

'No problem, Barry. You come back to the office with me. I have to make a phone call and then we need a little chat, you and me.'

**

'So you do understand?'

Kirkham handed Barry a mug of strong tea, to which he had added a small slug of whisky from the bottle in his desk.

'There, get that inside you, lad, it'll settle you down. It was a nasty little shock, but it's over now. Best forgotten. You know that old saying - least said, soonest mended? Good advice that. No need to dwell on it. Like I was saying, you do understand, don't you?'

Barry nodded dully, cradling the mug in his dirty hands. He gulped at the hot liquid and felt the whisky stab somewhere inside his chest as it travelled down. Kirkham watched him closely, wondering if the lad's obvious stupidity was going to prove to be the advantage that he hoped.

'So we're both going to forget all about this. You never saw it, never saw anything. It never happened - and not a word to anybody. Right?'

'Shouldn't you ought to report it to somebody?' mumbled Barry, after a lengthy silence.

Kirkham's nostrils quivered fractionally and then his lips pursed in irritation.

'Let's try again, Barry. Listen to me - and listen very carefully. Perhaps you didn't take it all in properly. I've already explained that these bodies turn up from time to time. When we report them, it holds up the job. It costs the business a lot of time and money. Disrupts the schedule. Over the years we've handed over three corpses to the authorities. All we ever get in return is the police, followed by the forensic chaps and the press. Next thing you know we've got members of the public hanging

11

around, trying to nosy into the site. After that it's a team of archaeologists crawling all over the place for weeks on end. All bad for business. We're here to extract peat, not to entertain a media circus.These corpses, Barry, including the one you found today, are so old that it doesn't matter any more.'

Barry's eyes grew larger.

'Doesn't matter? What d'you mean, doesn't matter? How can you say a body don't matter?' Barry swallowed nervously, beginning to wonder if Mr Kirkham was involved in some terrifying mass murder cover-up.

'They're older than Jesus Christ, Barry! And that's old, believe me. Look at it this way. Nobody's going to catch the murdering devils that did 'em in, are they? So you just have to shrug your shoulders and toss 'em back into the moss, back where they came from. They're best left in peace.'

The foreman unscrewed the cap of the whisky bottle again and poured a generous measure into his own mug of tea. There was none for Barry this time. They stared at each other in silence. It was Barry who looked away first.

'If you want me to put it another way - you do want to keep this job, don't you?'

Suddenly alert, Barry looked up and nodded. 'Yer not going ter sack me? That's not fair Mr Kirkham. It weren't my fault. Honest.'

Kirkham smiled reassuringly and pressed his advantage.

'Come on, Barry, calm down. I'm not holding you to blame, not at all.' He spoke gently and then got to his feet. 'But it might be a different matter if you don't keep your trap shut. Right, if you've finished that tea we'll get back to work. Get that blasted slab of peat loaded into an empty bogey and we'll truck it across to - let me see.' He crossed to the large site plan pinned on the office wall.

To the trained eye this plan provided a complete history of the site excavations to date. A large scale map of the moss had been overlaid with a grid which reduced the entire area into small sections. Carefully numbered and dated, the various diggings were colour coded with tiny flags. A little forest of green flags denoted early diggings which had been exhausted and subjected to infilling. Brown flags identified those areas currently being worked, whilst the next sections due for excavation were marked by yellow flags. Geoff Kirkham suddenly realised, for the first time, that the green flags vastly outnumbered the brown and yellow ones. Pushing this unsettling thought aside for later, he stabbed his finger at one of the brown flags.

'Here, this will do. E3's about due for infill. Do you know where it is, Barry?'

The youth nodded, trying to appear helpful.

'Good lad. Right, get back to the conveyor and tip that blasted slab into a bogey. Truck it down the lines to E3 and I'll be waiting there with the Landrover. We'll get that poor bleeder tipped back where he came from and no one's any the wiser. Just between you and me, this one.' he ended conspiratorially, and suddenly produced a crumpled ten pound note which he stuffed clumsily into Barry's shirt pocket. 'Bit of a bonus, lad.' he said, softly, 'Make up for all the upset. Help you to forget it. All over and done with.'

Since it was Friday the plant shut down at four o'clock. A few minutes later, eager to go their weekend ways, the workers were congregating around the office to collect their wage packets and clock off. Geoff Kirkham led the digger operator over to the site plan, where a red flag had replaced the brown one previously marking Pit E3. A red flag signified priority infilling. He tapped his forefinger on the section.

'Change of schedule for Monday morning. Take the Hy-Mac across to that eastern section first thing, Ken. Get that exhausted pit filled in.'

Ken opened his mouth to say something, but Kirkham

13

intervened. 'Don't ask.' he warned, shaking his head.

As the early evening sunlight cast hazy rays over the flat, disturbed landscape Lindow Moss tried to settle back into brooding silence, but the peace was constantly broken by rustling sounds. Air currents and small wind pockets continued to pursue their restless, erratic courses, quartering the terrain like hungry predators. And as dusk slowly turned to darkness the underlife stirred, stretched and took possession. All manner of whispering things emerged from secret places to claim the old nocturnal rites of passage.

At E3 a young brown rat scrambled over the high stacks of debris which had been tipped along the edges of the pit in readiness for infilling. Having reached the ridge of the heap he paused, ears cocked, listening intently. Silhouetted against the night sky his long whiskers twitched nervously and the thick pelt of fur suddenly rose in an untidy ridge along the course of his back. After a moment he urinated and then clawed his way inside the heap. As the rat vanished from sight a large clod of peat rolled silently downwards, landing with a tiny splash in the bottom of the pit.

2
Entertaining Lydia

It was the quiet time at the Drover's Arms, the usual early evening lull which followed the workers' homeward drift after celebrating the start of the weekend. It would be at least another hour before the the bar began to fill with the Friday night regulars. Only a handful of stragglers remained; a couple of committed drinkers and those with no real home to beckon.

Lydia Pendle was seated at her usual table in the darkest corner of the lounge bar. She finished her customary bar snack, lit a cigarette and continued to observe the youth from behind the shelter of her Manchester Evening News. Obviously underage, he was now slumped miserably on a high, uncomfortable stool, head propped on one bare, tattooed arm which rested on the counter of the bar. During the time it had taken her to eat, Lydia had watched him travel from the bravado of inebriation to depressed intoxication, aggressively and noisily refusing to leave when his companions had started to disperse. She smiled to herself, recalling her father's tales of his early days in Calcutta. 'The three stages of drunkenness - Peacock - tiger - pig.' His thin shoulders had been shaking with laughter. 'That's how the Bengali house boys used to keep each other posted. They would pass the whisper down the line, whilst their British masters were busy enjoying themselves.'

This young man was definitely moving out of tiger and heading rapidly towards pig. His hair had been rendered lifeless by repeated applications of bleach, which had turned his mid brown thatch to a glowering and offensive shade of marmalade. Unnecessary attempts at shaving had inflamed the clusters of pimples decorating his chin and the lobe of his left ear, which had been pierced several times, sported a collection of studs and rings. Picking and shredding a damp beer mat he stared miserably at his empty glass. Young and drunk and vulnerable, thought Lydia and wondered why. She left her seat and crossed to the bar.

'Here, try one of these.' She passed him a cigarette but he had trouble lighting it. She took from him, lit it and handed it back.

'The usual, Miss Pendle?'

She nodded and the barman poured half a lager.

'And whatever this young man is drinking.'

The barman gave her a warning glance. 'I think he's had enough.'

The youth turned troubled eyes upon his unexpected patron. Then he slid his glass clumsily across the bar and asked for a whisky. Lydia nodded to the barman.

'Had a bad day?' she inquired kindly. 'It usually helps to talk about it. I expect you're working at the moss?'

The hand holding the cigarette trembled as he stared glassily at the old girl, wishing that she would go away. When the whisky arrived he gulped it down too quickly and began to splutter.

'I gotta go now. Thanks, missis.'

Clumsily he lurched towards the door.

She spotted him at the back of the car park, being noisily sick behind a low hedge of yellow potentilla bushes. Reversing the car, she drove slowly across to where Barry Doyle leant weakly against a concrete post.

'Get in, I'll give you a lift.' She leant over and opened the passenger door. 'Come on, you look ill. I'll take you home.'

Barry hesitated and then scrambled into the car. He stank of vomit and she quickly wound the window down.

''You'd better tell me where you live. What's your name?'

'Barry.' His pale eyes suddenly filled with tears of resentment. 'I daren't go home, me Mam'll kill me if she catches me like this.'

Lydia turned out of the car park. 'Then we'd better get you sobered up.' she replied briskly. 'I'm going to take you to my house and we'll get some strong coffee into you.'

Too unwell to offer more than the feeblest of protests, Barry closed his eyes and gave himself over to suffering.

At the time of this encounter with Barry, Miss Lydia Pendle was in her late fifties with two more years to complete on the local paper, to which she had devoted most of her working life. Having already planned out her approaching retirement, she greeted the prospect with pleasurable anticipation. Throughout the preceding years she had concentrated on her research, collecting and collating vast amounts of information. Some of this she had stumbled upon during the course of her work, but the major part had been unearthed with dogged singularity during whatever free time was available.

Intuitive and uncompromising, she had passed her private life wedded to the dark, secret places, probing into depths both distant and mysterious in her urge to investigate. The processes of death, renewal and regeneration became her obsession. How could it have been otherwise? *"You fall under the rule of Pluto, Guardian of the Underworld'*, said each and every one permitted to cast her natal chart, merely confirming what she already knew. For Lydia had been born under the sign of the scorpion - an unforgiving creature whose tail carries the most bitter of stings.

At the outset she had enrolled for extra-mural courses. Seminars, summer schools and residential weekends on early history and related subjects; religion and mythology, archaeology and etymology. These studies had propelled her down the trackway towards paganism. Choosing to remain aloof and uncommunicative, she had lingered on the perimeters of all these groups, listening intently. Gathering and arranging, expanding her knowledge, all the while taking careful notes and keeping her own counsel. Later, when these possibilities had become more or less exhausted, she had switched her attentions to the margins, where the less academic branches of this strange cabal flourished.

Making her way cautiously through this exotic hinterland she encountered altruism and avarice, both amateur and professional. Some with a true gift, others merely out to make a fast buck. By this time peeling back the layers had become her way of life. She journeyed on, down through the dark ages. By-passing the Normans and the Angles and the Saxons, she devoted a great deal of her attention to the Romans. Then, inevitably, she arrived at the Celts. Here, feeling very much at home, she settled and it was here that she had remained.

Thin and sallow, Lydia was an earnest and formidable looking woman who favoured well cut tweeds, good brogues and a soft brimmed trilby styled hat, the latter worn at what she considered to be a slightly rakish angle over her wiry grey hair. She was well known and respected around the small Cheshire town whose stories and events she had faithfully recorded each week for almost forty years. There were no friends, just hundreds of acquaintances, all alphabetically listed in her bulging contacts book. All there to be used whenever she needed them. Questioned, quoted and discarded. Out of all those names which had been harvested during the long years of interviewing, there had only been one that really mattered. Just one person with whom she had actively striven to establish an association. It had not been easy, chipping away at that armour plated indifference. Only in recent times had her perseverance had been rewarded.

There was a hard, survivor's look about Lydia Pendle which was strangely at odds with her pretty stone cottage. Poor, poorly Barry Doyle, oblivious to the anomaly, followed her hesitantly, a lamb to the slaughter. She ushered him through the creaking gate and led him up a narrow pathway which wound between flower filled borders. When they reached the cottage porch he leant heavily against some trellis that half supported the old Albertine rose on its rambles up the front wall. A scattering of pale pink petals drifted to the ground. Lydia unlocked the door and Barry stumbled after her into the dimness of a narrow hallway, redolent with the clashing aromas of cats, air freshener and the sweet perfume from a precious looking bowl of pot pourri on a small side table.

Lydia took him into the front room and motioned him towards a chintz covered armchair.

'Now, Barry, you just make yourself comfortable in here while I get you a good strong coffee. Lots of sugar? Right.'

He gripped the arms of the chair tightly and stared around the room, trying to stop it from rippling. Too ill, too tired to question why he should be there, he listened to the sounds of running water, a kettle gathering steam, cupboards opening. His head began to pound.

Lydia returned with strong coffee and a bottle of pain killers.

'Here, take a couple of these, and drink this mineral water - all of it. It will help, it really will. Get lots of water down you. Dilute all that booze you've taken on board.'

He did as he was told, all the while staring into the empty fireplace in moody silence. She brought the mug of coffee over to him. 'Have you lost your job?'

He shook his head, wincing at the pain this caused.

'Look, lady, I don't know why you're going to all this trouble for me. I'd best be off. I've not even been home yet.'

'Where do you live?'

'River Street.'

'Down near the church? Well that's not far. Can't be more than ten minute's from here, once we've got you fit to walk in a straight line. Just relax until you feel a bit better. The fresh air will help. You'll be as right as rain by the time you reach home.'

She sat down in the opposite chair and smiled reassuringly.

'Listen to me, Barry. I can see that something's troubling you. It usually helps to talk things over, you know. Why don't you tell me what's wrong, and we'll see if we can sort it out together.'

The look of torment which suffused his face aroused her curiousity even further. The lad was clearly very frightened of something.

'Are you working at the peat diggings?'

He straightened his shoulders slightly.

'How did you know that?' Surprise had lifted his monotone a fraction.

Lydia smiled reassuringly. 'I've seen you in the Drovers the last few Fridays. I recognised some of the chaps you were with. You've not been working there very long, have you? Just left school?'

Barry nodded, miserably.

'And don't you like your job? Aren't you getting on very well there?'

'I liked it, I really liked it. Better than I thought, but I don't want to go back again now. Not after that.' He lapsed back into silence.

'Not after what, Barry? What happened today?' She watched intently as he suppressed a shudder.

'Nothing.'

'Something's upset you or you wouldn't be in this state. What's the matter?'

The boy bit his lip

'Well?' she persisted.

He inclined his head, staring at the carpet and gave a long sigh. Lydia waited. Finally he looked across at her helplessly.

'It's no good keep asking me. I daren't speak to anybody. I promised not to talk about it, not to no one.'

'Promised Mr Kirkham?'

He stared at her suspiciously.

'How d'you know that?'

'Oh, I know Mr Kirkham very well.' said Lydia, airily, 'I know quite a lot about Geoff.'

'Well you can go and tell him that I said nowt about anything then. You trying to lose me my job? Is that your game?'

Time for a swift change of tactics. She got to her feet.

'Just excuse me for a few minutes, Barry. You sit back and relax, give those pills a chance to get to work. It's time to feed my cats and then I'll make some more coffee.'

After she had left the room he rested his head against the wing of the chair and closed his eyes, relieved to find that the accompanying blackness had ceased its sickening spin. He could hear her voice, slightly muffled, coming from the kitchen and wondered if she was telephoning Kirkham. Beyond caring, he was almost asleep when someone slammed a car door on the road in front of the cottage, making him start. He leaned forward, listening. There was nothing. Just the painful rhythm of the thudding somewhere inside his head, which was suddenly joined by a whirring noise which he recognised as the sound of an electric can opener. He closed his eyes again. Something brushed against his calf.

The cat was surprisingly strong, weaving around his legs and thrusting its muscular body against his denim clad calf. He bent to push the creature aside. As it opened its mouth in protest he caught a strong whiff of fish. The cat suddenly bounded onto the arm of his chair and fixed him with an unnerving gaze, holding him against his will. Preventing him from - from something. Barry pressed himself back into the chair and for a few seemingly endless seconds was lost, drawn irresistibly down into the glittering amber discs that beckoned, dragging him into their centre as they steadily dilated, glowing like lamps in the darkening room. He stared helplessly as the pupils began to retract, reducing from blackest ovals to the merest of slits as the shutters came down. The cat was purring loudly, its entire body vibrating through the chair arm, making the moment seemed like eternity.

Lydia Pendle was watching silently from the open doorway.

'All the way from Cairo.' she said, softly. 'No wonder they worshiped them.'

Poor Barry felt his scalp begin to prickle for the second time that day. He tried to press himself even further back in the chair.

'Get it away from me.' he pleaded, not daring to move. 'I don't like cats.'

Lydia's laugh sounded slightly sinister.

'We know that, don't we, Pharaoh?' She scooped the cat into her arms, cradling its head against her throat. 'There, my little soldier, my lovely, lovely Pharaoh.'

She crooned to the creature in her cat voice, thicker and more resonant than the tone she reserved for people. It clung to her, claws lightly embedded in the shoulders of her jacket as the long, whip-like tail flicked rhythmically against the swell of her stomach. Her face suddenly softened as she ran a soothing hand down the silvery, charcoal spotted pelt.

'There's a beautiful boy.' she whispered, walking towards the door. Her voice changed instantly as she addressed herself to Barry.

'Sorry about that. He's really such a dear old softy, but he knows that you don't like him, you see. He knows a great deal more than you or I. I wasn't expecting you to be afraid of him, a big lad like you! He was just curious. We don't get many visitors, you see.'

'No bloody wonder.'

As Barry started to rise from the chair Lydia shook her head.

'Sit down, Barry. Just stay there whilst I put Pharaoh back in the kitchen, then we'll continue where we left off. You can't go until you've had some more coffee.' she added, firmly. 'You don't want your mother to know you've been drinking, do you?

22

I'll be back in one moment.'

Straining his eyes in the deepening gloom, Barry stared unhappily around the room. He was beginning to feel very uneasy. He had somehow lost track of time and wondered exactly how long he had spent in this chair. A large desk stood beneath the window, its shadowy bulk filling most of the wall. Alongside the dim outline of a typewriter he made out a white gleam of neatly stacked foolscap sheets. Beside the typewriter, silhouetted against the leaf patterned wallpaper, his gaze alighted upon the head.

It was life sized, a crudely fashioned lump of dark grey stone. And more eyes, which seemed to grow towards him through the darkness, burning with a completely unnerving luminosity. As he blinked the face suddenly leered, lurching towards him. It was that face. With its eyes open. The face from before. No longer peaceful, but definitely the face he had been trying to forget. He grasped the chair arms until his knuckles grew white and still the eyes continued to hold him. The atmosphere in the room changed, became charged, filling with the hot fry of electricity, followed by a static flash of emerald. The pounding inside his head was accompanied by the loud groan of his protesting stomach as it ridded itself of the accumulated gases of fear. Too much fear for one day. Too much for a sixteen year old to handle.

The overhead light came on and Lydia crossed the room with more coffee.

'My goodness, Barry, you are jumpy. I really had no idea that Pharaoh would upset you so much. I've shut him away, he won't bother you again. Now, you take this and drink it whilst it's hot.'

She sat down opposite him, with her back to the window. 'Tell me what's frightened you so, Barry. You can tell me about it. I promise you, whatever it is, it won't go any further. I won't tell a soul. Trust me.'

He pointed silently to the stone head. Now that the light was on he could see that it was a stupid, childlike thing. Lydia got up and walked to the desk.

'You're attracted to the head, are you? Let me show you.'

Lifting it from the desk, she brought it over to him, running a bony forefinger over the dome of the forehead and down the wide stone nose.

'Here.' she held it towards him. 'He comes from Glossop, up in the hills, but he's lived here with me for a long time now. An old woman let me have him, because I promised to look after him. They were digging the back garden over when they found him. She was just a little girl, but she remembered watching while her grandfather lifted him out of the ground. Isn't he beautiful?'

She stroked the stone cheek. 'You won't know what this is, so I'll explain. This is what is known as a votive offering, Barry. A tricephalic head. He's got three faces. They were carved out of the stone more than two thousand years ago.' Smiling, she began to turn the head slowly in her hands. 'Look - another face, and another. So that you can't escape from him. Here, take a closer look.' Suddenly she thrust the head towards him and he pulled away. Her lips curled into a strange, satisfied smile.

'Yes.' Her voice dropped to a half whisper. 'You can feel it, can't you? It's still there, even after all these centuries, Barry. Still as strong as it ever was. The forces haven't grown old and weak, Barry, they've travelled down through time. They are still amongst us, all around. Don't listen to those who tell you otherwise.'

He shoved the head away. 'Just get it away from me. It's - it's worse than the cat.'

He buried his head in his hands and lapsed into silence. Lydia remained over him, motionless, cradling the head in both hands. 'I have to take care of it, Barry. It's under my tutelage - I am the guardian.'

Still too frightened to move, Barry stared up at her. 'Please, take it away.' he begged. 'I don't want it anywhere near me. You're bleedin' potty. Let me out of here.'

A flicker of annoyance darted through her facial muscles before she regained her composure. She watched as the dry-mouthed boy tried to swallow.

'Calm down. You're just suffering from the after effects of too much alcohol. It upsets the brain chemistry for a while. There's nothing to get alarmed about. A good night's sleep and you'll be fine again. There we are. See - he's back on his desk. Now, just let me pour you another coffee and you can tell me what happened today.'

Lydia now brought into play the finely honed interrogation skills perfected by forty years of experience. Within half an hour she had extracted the full story, including the precise location of E3. Afterwards, as the room fell silent, Barry was suddenly horrified.

'Christ, lady, Kirkham will kill me for this.' Sobering rapidly and feeling utterly wretched, he buried his spiky hair into his hands. 'Now I've gone and lost the only job I could get. I'm done for. What am I going to say to my mam? What's she going to say? She'll play hell with me.'

Lydia tutted soothingly, a sound which belied the gleam of excitement in her eyes.

'Now then, Barry, stop being so gloomy. You're not going to lose the job. In fact, I'm pretty sure that your job is safer than ever, as long as you put today's events completely out of your mind. What you've told me won't go beyond these four walls. It's our little secret and I'm sure it's done you good to get it off your chest. It was better to talk to a grown-up about it than to go blurting it out to one of your mates. You can trust me, Barry. You've had a nasty experience and it's shaken you up. You're a brave young man. You're mother would be extremely proud of you if she knew how well you've coped with what happened this afternoon. You were suffering from delayed shock. That's what made you start to imagine things - hardly surprising after an awful experience like that. You'll feel better now, now that you've shared it with me. No need for you to worry anymore, you must forget about it all. Pretend it never happened.'

'That's what Mr Kirkham said. He gave me a tenner to help me to forget about it.'

Lydia opened her handbag.

'And I'm giving you twenty. Here, take it.'

Barry stood up, took the proffered note and stuffed it into his jacket pocket. Thirty quid in one day! Thirty quid to keep quiet. No, ten to keep quiet and twenty to spill the beans. The fleeting vision of a squashed cat floated back into his mind and he pushed it aside quickly.

'You'll not tell anyone I talked? You promise?'

'Stop worrying about it, Barry. I won't say anything to Geoff Kirkham. Scouts' honour.' Lydia replied with mock seriousness. 'Take yourself off home and get a decent night's sleep. It's over and done. In the morning it will all seem like a bad dream and that pit will be filled in on Monday morning. What time did you say they start?'

'It's early at this time of the year. Before eight, usually.'

'Don't think about it any more.' repeated Lydia, walking him down the path. 'You enjoy your weekend. Buy yourself something nice. A special treat. You deserve it.'

She leant against the gate, watching until he had turned the corner.

Back indoors, she cleared away the cups and returned to the sitting room, closely followed by her cats. She closed the curtains and switched on a table lamp before turning out the main light and then she stretched out on the settee and lit a cigarette. The cats jumped up and lay alongside her.

Unusual cats, spotted cats of ancient lineage, each bearing the mark of the scarab upon its brow. Sacred cats, rare and

26

expensive pyramid cats, descended from the cat gods of the Nile. And more, much more than that. They were carefully chosen companions who brought a little warmth into her solitary existence, making the emptiness bearable. Aloof and independent, the qualities which she most admired and had striven to develop within herself. Cats were the most wonderful of creatures. Receptive to every nuance of mood, they watched over her. But never fawning. Not like dogs.

They lay against her now, perfectly still. Lydia smiled fondly, and her face softened. Any one of her colleagues and associates would have been surprised if they could have seen her then. Relaxed, lost in thought, waiting for it to be late enough.

Hours passed. Towards midnight she gently detached herself from their embrace and got to her feet. Crossing to the tray on the sideboard she poured herself a generous measure of Scotch. Switching on the small lamp beside the telephone she checked the time, and then started to rummage through her briefcase for the contacts book. Lips pursed, she began to leaf quickly through the battered notebook, running her finger down the chaotic pages until she finally found what she was looking for. She finished the whisky and poured another. Another glance at the clock, a slight hesitation and then Lydia picked up the telephone and began to dial the precious number.

3
November 1997

It was cold and wet, still only Wednesday and his forty eighth birthday, none of which did anything to ameliorate Andrew Thrower's deepening sense of depression. His wife had left three weeks ago, and the realisation that this might be something more final than the melodramatic gesture he had initially assumed was beginning to hurt. After the postman had been it had taken all of two seconds to open his cards. The one from his mother in Long Eaton had contained a ten pound note and the other, post marked Manchester, arrived with his sister's best wishes and one biro kiss. Sitting now at his desk, he fingered the folded tenner in his pocket and turned to the racing pages, which is how Trevor Stephens found him when he came back into the office nearly an hour later.

A newspaper man through and through, Stephens had come to the Gazette from one of the dailies, where he had been employed as a sub editor for several years. He wore light grey suits, enlivened by a consistently bizarre selection of ties, spectacles with perfectly round lenses which imparted a certain owlish quality and the same schoolboy haircut, minus the Brylcream, with which he had begun his first day at the Grammar school. Well liked, he first invoked disbelief - at his size - followed by affection, followed by a great deal of respect, once the office staff had seen him lose his temper, something which, since he was a tolerant and fair minded man, happened only rarely. But when it did the atmosphere in the office became charged as the perpetrator of any serious misdemeanour was subjected to a very public dressing down, be it a member of the staff or some complaining member of the public with an ill founded grievance. Then it was all over and forgotten, with Trevor ungrudgingly reverting to his normal avuncular self.

No one, including Trevor, had managed to figure out why he had stayed on for far longer than he had originally planned. Somewhere along the line he must have decided to settle for a reasonably quiet life in the once prosperous little commuter town, but he never could manage to pin-point the exact moment.

The affluent boom of the sixties had seen the blossoming of expensive shops and by the early eighties the town had boasted one of the most exclusive shopping streets to the south of Manchester. By the end of that decade yuppie money and yuppie manners had been followed by a terminal case of yuppie flu and the once proud High Street collapsed. Family businesses which had flourished for several generations gradually disappeared. The cheese shops, the old fashioned grocers and the cavernous and excellently stocked wine emporium closed down, one after the other. The highly respected bookshop - every town gets the bookshop it deserves, and Wilmslow had a good one - hung on for another year or so, and then that, too, gave up the unequal struggle. Windows were boarded over and a forest of For Sale signs appeared on each side of the street. With no sign of any imminent recovery the little town had taken on a desperate, decaying air of failure, from which indignity it was only now slowly making a partial recovery.

Even so, the rambling and discreetly screened abodes still abounded on the edges of town. Solid properties these, built to the highest of Victorian standards by the affluent classes, when cotton was still king of Manchester. The social structure may have been irrevocably altered by two world wars, but Wilmslow had ignored the changes as best it could. Clinging on to its reputation as smart commuter country for the Manchester businessman, only in recent years had it succumbed, with small, up-market developments beginning to mushroom in the over-generous grounds of the original mansions, from which these new estates took their names. Trevor Stephens had recorded this decline, and the rippling effects upon the local inhabitants, every week for more years than he cared to count.

'So how did it go?'

Andy abandoned the lists of runners and flipped open his notebook.

'Sorry - nothing very melodramatic for you, Trev. Accidental death. Didn't take as long as I'd expected. FINGERS must be feeling relieved. One of my contacts told me a couple of days ago that that's what they were hoping for. God only knows what can of worms a suicide or open verdict might have opened. It was pretty low key, even for an inquest. Not many there. The deceased's sister - only living relative, and a woman called Susan Jackson, who was his housekeeper. They both identified the body.'

He began to read aloud from his notes. 'The pathologist's post mortem report: The body of a well nourished male aged about 60. There were no external signs of violence. There had been some minor ante mortem capillary haemorrhage, possibly due to the onset of minor apoplexy. Internal examination revealed no evidence of disease and the organs were found to be normal in appearance for a man of this age. The cause of death was found to be asphyxia due to drowning. The time of death is placed at around 4.30am.'

'Is that it?' Trevor looked surprised.

Andy nodded. 'Yep. Swept under the carpet, all nice and tidy.'

'Watch it.' said Trevor, sternly. 'So they've released the body?'

'I was just about to ring the undertakers' to check out the arrangements.'

'That's what I thought.' said Trevor, removing Andy's Racing Times out of temptation's way. 'So what was he doing out on Lindow Moss at that hour?'

Andy shrugged his shoulders. 'Who knows?'

And who cares, he thought as he began to dial the undertakers' number.

On the morning of the following Tuesday, Trevor Stephens entered the editorial office, raised his hat politely to the two girls and tossed it with a practised hand on to the waiting hook of the coat stand.

'Good morning, ladies. Everything all right?'

The two girls exchanged glances. Neither spoke. Once he had squeezed his enormous bulk behind his own desk, he glanced around the room and noted the two empty ones. Sophie Tate waited.

'Is Andy out interviewing?'

'He rang in.' said Rachel. 'He's not well - flu, he thinks.

Trevor rubbed his chin, removed his spectacles for a moment, examined each lens in turn, replaced them and began leafing through the papers which spilled forth from the tray on his desk.

'This leaves me with nobody to cover the Rush funeral.' he said, eventually. 'I can't do it myself, I've got a meeting straight after lunch. What about Keith?'

Sophie shook her head. 'No chance, he's out on interviews all morning and then he's going straight on to cover the council meeting. I doubt he'll be back in the office much before four. And I've got lunch with someone from one of the major advertising agencies today. I can't put that off, I've been trying to get them interested for months. Not that I'd know how to write up a funeral anyway.'

Trevor grinned. 'I wouldn't dream of asking you to, sweetheart. I'm trying to run a newspaper here, not 'Hello' magazine. I thought you were looking particularly stunning this morning. Nice jacket.'

The sarcasm was lost.

'Glad you like it.' said Sophie, whose middle aged lover was involved in the expensive and therefore exclusive end of the rag trade. 'One tries to rise to the occasion. It's hardly funeral gear, anyway.' She flashed him a wide, appreciative smile, displaying perfect teeth.

'Hardly.' said Trevor, with the merest trace of malice. 'I don't think they get much peacock blue silk at Macclesfield Crematorium.'

Rachel suppressed a giggle.

'You've run out of choices. You'll have to send Rachel.' continued Sophie. 'Who knows? This could be her big break. The opportunity she's been waiting for.'

Rachel Mackenna had settled in well at the job and Trevor, having already decided that she showed promise, found himself feeling slightly protective towards her. She was around the same age as his own daughter, and the mixture of youthful enthusiasm and the desire to please was familiar. He was also fully aware of the need to overcome the nervousness of inexperience. Given the right coaching, Rachel could become a valuable asset. Innocence and apparent lack of guile could turn out to be a blessing in disguise. Petite, with a boyish, elfin quality which belied her commitment to the job, it was reasonable to assume that most potential interviewees would respond kindly to her queries. Maybe she could get more out of today's mourners than Andy.

Trevor turned to his fledgling. 'Well, do you fancy a challenge, Rachel? It would be good experience for you to get outside the office for a change. This is front page material, with photographs, so Neil Carver will be going. I'll ask him to take you with him. We need a couple of quotes from Rush's work colleagues and then I'll help you with the write-up when you get back. Everything needs be handled with great tact. No prying questions.'

'I've got the obituaries to finish - including Dr Rush's - and I haven't even made a start on Coming Events. Then there are two advertising features and that short piece on the Scouts.' She smiled shyly, slightly apprehensive. 'If you think I can do it, I wouldn't mind. I could stay on late if it would help.'

'Bless you, my child,' said Trevor, with mock seriousness. 'There's commitment for you, Sophie.' He got up and crossed the office. Resting one vast buttock on the edge of Rachel's desk he continued, kindly, 'You'll be fine. I'll run through it with you now, tell you the sort of things you need to ask, who to look out for. I know one or two chaps from the FINGERS crowd who are fairly approachable. They're bound to be there. Listen to what they're saying. Take some notes and we'll cobble something together when you get back. Neil will be taking photographs as the cortege arrives, but you don't need to attend the actual service. Wait until they come out before you speak to any of them. And find out where they're holding the wake. You and Neil could tag along if you get the chance. There's bound to be someone from one of the news agencies around. Probably someone Neil knows. This funeral is sure to get some coverage in the serious dailies. Sophie, ring down and ask Neil Carver to come up to see me.'

**

As they left town the rain was bouncing off the pavements and the only people on the streets were the ones who had no choice in the matter. A few minutes later they were passing through Alderley village, which had also fallen victim to the deluge. Neil Carver dropped into low gear for the steep climb up Alderley Edge, heading for Macclesfield. Rachel stared silently through the window.

'Is this your first time out for the paper Rachel?' asked Neil, for something to say.

'Well, it's my first proper assignment. I've never had anything really serious and important before. My only other outside job was to report on the local Cat's Protection League fund raising day. I was pretty nervous then, so you can imagine how I felt when Trevor asked me to go to this. He says it's going on the front page.' She fidgeted with the cover of her notebook. 'I hope I don't mess up.'

'There's nothing to it.' said Neil, reassuringly. 'Stick with me, kid and I'll make you a star.'

He winked at her kindly and she began to relax a little.

'Have you been to lots of funerals, Neil?'

He laughed. 'I suppose I have, over the years. I've never really thought about it. It's a ghoulish profession, newspaper photography. I only get to photograph a funeral if it's the result of some tragedy - or if the deceased is a local 'name'. This one's pretty important, because it combines the two. Trevor will probably be able to milk it for weeks. Today is going to be a good opportunity, Rachel. It could set you on your way. He's quite impressed with you, you know.'

Rachel flushed with pleasure. 'Really?'

'Really.' said Neil.

'I've never actually been to a funeral before.' confessed Rachel. 'You have now.' Neil drove through the tall wrought iron gates into the winding drive leading to the crematorium buildings and turned into the adjoining car park. When the mourners from the previous funeral began to disperse and return to their vehicles Neil got out of the car.

'Come on Rachel, we're on next.'

Beneath black umbrellas subdued crowds were already gathering in small, sombre groups. As they approached the crematorium entrance Rachel studied them curiously. Smartly dressed people, plenty of them, who all appeared to know each other. Silver haired men in dark suits, black ties and shoes that you just knew had been polished properly, army fashion, which included the bit underneath the instep. A lot of navy blue cashmere overcoats and wives with expensive hats and silk scarves, looking terribly elegant, whilst the laboratory and clerical staff kept discreetly to one side. No one was talking. Rachel took a deep breath and forced herself to ignore the feelings of intimidation which were starting to surface.

'Here it comes.' said Neil, softly. 'I have to get to the front.'

Despite the communal display of savoir faire, the entire gathering instinctively shrank back almost imperceptibly as the hearse crawled slowly by. It was followed by a large black Daimler, with tinted windows. As the two cars came to a halt in front of the crematorium steps, Rachel skirted the edges of the rapidly forming crocodile and joined her colleague.

The undertaker's men were already unloading the coffin. Four bearers moved silently forward to take delivery. From the second car emerged Barbara and Charles Whitehead, their two grown sons, and Ursula Rush. Suddenly a middle aged woman and a thin old lady, who may have been her mother, appeared, working their way through the waiting ensemble. Poorly dressed in comparison to the others, both looked visibly distressed and ill at ease. Barbara Whitehead glanced round and embraced the old lady. The pair got into line behind the family mourners and followed them slowly into the chapel. Rachel turned towards the rest of the entourage and noted exchanged glances and raised eyebrows. Watching them shuffle silently into the crematorium she suddenly realised that the sinking sense of intimidation had vanished of its own accord.

'Rachel, come and meet Flynn, from the News Agency. Don't trust him - not as far as you can throw him.'

'Thanks, Carver. I'll do the same for you sometime.'

Flynn was in his thirties. Tall and thin, with messy hair, untrimmed beard, and a black Ferrari jacket which had seen better days. One shoulder appeared to have dropped beneath the combined weight of an impressive array of photographic paraphernalia.

'Hi, Flynn.' said Rachel, and then, turning to Neil, 'Who are the chief mourners? I noticed you were photographing them.'

'Sister, brother-in-law and the two nephews. The brother-in-law is Charles Whitehead, senior partner in a highly successful legal firm. Barrister extraordinaire.'

'And the other woman?' she persisted.

Neil grinned at Flynn, 'See what I mean? We're talking embryo newshound here. Don't mess with her.'

'News puppy.' corrected Rachel. 'So who is she? Come on, Neil, you've got to help me out here. Tell me.'

Neil shook his head. 'I'm not sure, but she's definitely not 'other woman' material. If you're asking me to make an educated guess I'd say she's probably the ex-wife.'

'I thought he was a loner? I didn't know there ever had been a wife. How long since they divorced?'

Neil shrugged his shoulders. 'Years ago, I think. You'll have to make some discreet enquiries. She's probably turned up today to see if there are any pickings.'

'Cynical as ever, Neil.' said Flynn.

'You'd expect her to attend her ex-husband's funeral.' said Rachel, defensively. 'It would have looked bad if she hadn't. And the pair behind them? Where do they fit in?'

Neil shook his head. 'Not very well, from where I was standing. I can't help you on that one, Rachel. I haven't got a clue.'

The funeral cars pulled off, turned round somewhere and parked up some distance away. The drivers got out and leant against their vehicles.

'Ought I to go over and talk to them?'

'You could ask them to see that you get a list of mourners. Tell them to fax it through.'

'And what about the others? Should I try to speak to them when they get back to the car park? I don't know what the form is. Will they be too upset?'

Neil shook his head. 'I shouldn't think so.'

'Everybody's usually glad that it's over.' said Flynn. 'Unless you're a close relative it's a bit like being let out of school. Best not to bother the family, but the FINGERS chaps will be all right. You'd do better to come along to the wake. That's where

I'm off.'

'Where is it?' asked Neil

'Bollin Lodge - usual bar and buffet thing. Why don't you follow me down there and we'll get settled in before they arrive. It will give Rachel a chance to mingle. She'll get a much better reception once they're indoors with a glass of sherry.'

'You go on ahead, Flynn. I need a couple of shots as they come out.' Neil looked at his watch. 'Another ten minutes or so. We'll still be able get there ahead of the pack. See you in the bar.'

Rachel stood to one side as the funeral party emerged. First came Barbara Whitehead, going through the motions, dabbing the corners of her eyes with a scrap of white lace and clutching the supporting arm of her husband. They were followed by Ursula Rush, alone and self contained, face pallid and tight lipped beneath the wide brim of her hat. Next, red eyed and snuffling into a damp tissue, was the poorly dressed woman, who came to a sudden halt to the top of the steps, forcing the rest of the exiting mourners to fan out around her. As Rachel watched the old woman appeared and placed a comforting arm around the hunched shoulders of her companion.

'There, love, don't take on so. Don't go upsetting yourself again. You heard what the vicar said. You'll forget all this, given time, and only remember the good things. Let's get you home now, away from all these people.'

Barbara Whitehead was waiting for them. 'Are you joining us for something to eat, Lillian? And Susan, of course. You must both come. I'll find someone to give you a lift.'

'No thanks, Mrs Whitehead. It's best if we don't. I think it would be better if I get our Susan home.' The old lady took Barbara to one side. 'Oh, I'm that sorry about your poor brother, Mrs Whitehead. It was such a lovely service. Are you sure you're all right?'

'Bearing up. One has to.' She smiled stoically. 'I'll be very glad when today is over.'

'You can see what a state she's in.' whispered Lillian, glancing back. 'Would you mind if I stayed over with her tonight? I don't want to leave her on her own in that - there, not while she's so upset. It was a lovely service.' she repeated.

**

'Honestly, an orange juice will be fine, Flynn. Really.'

'Just get the girl a juice Flynn, there's a good chap, and make mine a half.'

Whilst Flynn was at the bar Neil turned to Rachel, who was checking the list of queries that Trevor had compiled.

'All right, Rachel? Just give them chance to settle down and then I'll hang on here with Flynn for half an hour while you go and do your thing.'

Flynn returned with the drinks and a plate of sandwiches. The noise levels were already beginning to rise from the room where the wake was in progress.

'You go and help yourself from the buffet, Rachel. It's the best way to get chatting with them.'

'Wish me luck then.' Picking up her notebook she made her way through the reception area towards the Styal Suite. Flynn watched her go.

'Bit of all right, isn't she?'

'Poor kid, I feel sorry for her. Stephens has chucked her in at the deep end. Way out of her depth with that tight lipped team. Right, now it's my turn to get them in - same again?'

Rachel grabbed a plate and surveyed the long table. Under normal circumstances she would have enjoyed such a splendid buffet, but today she had little appetite. She helped herself to a couple of tiny canapes and was just steeling herself to gatecrash the wake when someone tapped her on the shoulder.

'Hi! Should I know you?'

He was tall and slim. Intelligent blue eyes, half hidden by an overlong tress of toffee coloured hair which kept falling

38

forward across his face, holding out the promise of something far less formal than the black tie and dark suit proclaimed. Rachel thought him quite handsome, in a slightly arrogant way. He held out a cool, sensitive hand and took hold of her's in a grip which was polite but firm. A real smoothie, that's what her mother would have called him.

'Julian - Julian Whitehead. Ought I to know you?' He smiled down at her, waiting for a reply.

Playing for time, she put the plate down and shook hands. 'Rachel Mackenna.'

'Did you work with Uncle Vinny?'

She shook her head. 'No.'

'A long lost cousin I never knew existed?'

She laughed and shook her head again.

'Good, I'm glad we're not related. Well, do I get to find out why you're here?'

Rachel looked uncomfortable.

'Oh dear, I wouldn't like you to think that I'm intruding. I work for the Gazette. I'm actually covering for a colleague who is off sick. I don't want to cause any upset, but I'm responsible for the obituary. I hope you don't mind.'

'Mind - why should I mind? It's a relief to find someone who doesn't remember the war years.' He removed a couple of glasses of wine from a passing tray and handed one to Rachel.

'I really shouldn't. I'm here to work.'

'Go on, one won't hurt. Oil the wheels. Why don't we sit down over there?'

Rachel followed him to the empty table.

'Would you mind if I asked a few questions about your uncle?'

She mentally cursed herself. Not the right way to start an interview, giving him a chance to refuse. What she should have said was "I just need to ask you a few questions".

'Not at all. How long have you been with the paper?'

'I'm supposed to be asking the questions.' said Rachel, firmly.

'But since you ask, just few months. I'm still training. It's important that I get everything right today.'

'I'm away at university. Just came home for the funeral.'

'What are you studying?'

'Law. It's what the old man wanted. My older brother rebelled and went into banking instead, so I felt under an obligation. It's turned out to be a hard slog. Anyway enough about that. What sort of things do you need to know?'

'Age?'

'Twenty six.' said Julian.

'Not you ....' She stopped. He was laughing at her.

'Sorry, no more teasing. He was fifty nine, divorced, no kids, impossible to live with and totally reclusive. Absolutely brilliant in his own field and totally useless at everything else. One of the most boring men you could ever meet. We didn't see much of him after Aunt Ursula left. Mum used to make him come to us for Christmas Day, but even when we were kids Simon - that's my brother - and I, we could always tell that he wasn't enjoying it. He couldn't wait to leave. To be honest, I don't think he'll be greatly missed. Oops - I hope you're not intending to quote me.'

Rachel shook her head. 'No, don't worry. But I've got to come up with something.'

'Mum was always fond of him, of course. She worried about him a lot, but he really shut her out after Aunt Ursula cleared off. I suppose you could say that he just lived for his work. They say that no one's irreplaceable, but that research department will never find another Vincent Rush.'

'Something else. I saw a sad little woman at the crematorium. She seemed terribly upset - in tears. There was an elderly lady with her. Do you happen to know who they are? They didn't quite seem to fit in with the rest of the mourners.'

'That would be Mrs Jackson, his housekeeper. Been with him for years. I really don't know much about her. My mother could probably tell you - in fact, I seem to remember it was Mum who got her the job in the first place. She was with her mother, Lillian. Lillian used to clean for us full time until she got too long in the tooth. She didn't want to pack it in altogether and I think she just comes in a couple of times a week now. My mother has always been very fond of old Lillian. Look, I think Simon needs rescuing. I have to go and circulate.' He got up. 'Not that I wouldn't prefer to sit here and talk to you, but I'd better do the family bit and mingle.'

'I need to get a quote from one of his colleagues.' said Rachel. 'Do you know any of them? I was wondering who would be the best person to ask.'

'Come on, I'll introduce you to Frank - Frank Newbolt.' Julian stood up. 'His wife has been a close friend of my mother's for years. And I suppose Frank was the nearest thing Uncle Vinny had to a friend. He should be good for a few words.'

The interview was short and distinctly chilly. Not a therm of warmth. Restricting his comments to the purely professional, Frank Newbolt had some highly praiseworthy things to say about the deceased. It all sounded a little too pat, almost rehearsed. If this was the closest that Vincent Rush had ever got to finding a friend, he must have been an intensely lonely man. Rachel, not daring to interrogate further, took careful notes. Driving back with Neil later, she read them through.

"Vincent Rush was the most widely acclaimed specialist in his chosen field and his contributions to the advancement of techniques remain unrivalled, to this day. His input has been considerable. He published several papers and amongst his peers he will always be regarded as the founding father of molecular biology. When he agreed to work for the company virtually unlimited resources were placed at his disposal. This included his own research unit. He will be sadly missed."

She shook her head. 'It's like a carefully prepared press release.'

'That's precisely what it is.' said Neil. 'Were you expecting something more?'

'The only tears at that funeral were shed by the housekeeper. Everyone seemed quite jolly by the time they got to the wake.'

'Well, that was your first funeral. That's the way wakes are. People are really relieved when the service is over. It was perfectly normal - a reassertion of life. No weeping and wailing and gnashing of teeth.'

'Oh, I see. I hadn't thought about it like that. Neil, I didn't like to ask Frank Newbolt, because its really something I ought to know, but what is FINGERS? I know it's all classified and highly sensitive, but what goes on there, exactly?

Neil gave her a sidelong glance. 'Who knows? It stands for Forensic Industries Genetic Experimental Research Station. Vincent Rush was their top man.'

4
Susan

The Saturday morning following the funeral found Charles and Barbara Whitehead sitting in silence at opposite ends of the long pine table which dominated the centre of their enormous kitchen. Barbara began to clear away the breakfast plates. Her husband remained immersed in the financial section of the the newspaper. She stood for a moment, staring out through the window. November sunlight, thin and hazy, filtered through the almost bare branches of two ornamental maples standing sentinel beside the tall wall which screened the perimeter of their property from the narrow lane leading into the heart of the park. She turned back towards Charles, tight lipped, her eyes slightly narrowed so that the tiny creases at the corners were emphasised.

'More coffee?'

'Just a drop.' said Charlie, without looking up, 'Then I'll make tracks.'

'I don't see why you need to dress so formally, Charlie. Are you deliberately setting out to intimidate the poor woman?' She returned the percolator to its stand. 'Why won't you let me come with you? Vinny was my brother. You're even trying to exclude me from this, just like everything else.'

Charlie folded the newspaper neatly and placed it down.

'Don't start again, Barbara. Don't you think I would rather be spending my Saturday morning on the golf course?'

'Susan is terribly upset,' she persisted, 'without you turning up looking as if you've come straight from chambers. How do you think she'll feel when she finds you knocking on the door? She's totally defenceless, poor thing.'

Charles Whitehead sighed. 'I've already told you, this is a delicate matter which needs to be handled professionally. It looks better if I go to talk to her alone. I need to explain everything properly, go through it with her so that she understands the situation. I don't think she's very quick on the uptake, from the little I've seen.'

He stood up and put on his jacket.

'Should I ring and let her know you're on the way?.'

Charlie shook his head. 'No, I prefer to catch her unawares. I want to take a good look around.'

His wife followed him out to the garage. 'Charlie, be nice to her.'

'I'm always nice.' said Charlie, starting up the Daimler. 'See you later.'

Barbara returned to the kitchen. She was halfway through loading the dishwasher before she realised that she had forgotten to ask Charlie to collect his suits for the following week from the dry cleaners. Better catch him before he got to Vincent's. She dialled his car phone several times and received the all too familiar sound of the engaged tone. Returning the receiver to its cradle, she sat down at the table and took another cigarette from the almost empty packet.

So much to cry about and not a tear to shed. All dried up. Brittle. She found herself wondering what one was supposed to do instead. Her gaze roamed around the kitchen; the Twenty-K-Plus kitchen, courtesy of Alexander Crick and Charlie's guilty conscience. If one happened to live in South Manchester's stockbroker belt at that particular moment in time, a Crick-designed kitchen was something to aspire to, as many husbands had already discovered to their cost. Handsome limed units, state of the art appliances, a floor of hand made ethnic tiles costing the earth; the precious resource of some struggling third world country. For a moment her mouth altered into a tight little smile of triumph as she remembered Charlie's snort of derision when he had seen the estimate.

'Good God, Barbara, we've got the Staffordshire Potteries just down the road. Choose local tiles, for heaven's sake, they'll be far more reasonably priced than these damned things.'

He had picked up the sample, running a finger along the edges. 'They're awful things - rough as ....'

'They're supposed to be like that.' Barbara had interrupted quickly. 'And they haven't been sealed and waxed yet. They look quite different after they've been treated. They're hand made, you see. Ethnic. Laid out to dry in the hot sun before they go into the kiln, so they take on a distressed look. That's what gives them their charm and individuality.' she added, quoting Alexander Crick verbatim. After Barbara had relayed Charlie's criticisms, the great designer himself, adept at overcoming spouse opposition, had arrived to point out that Staffordshire tiles, which were commercially produced in vast quantities, would always lack the cachet of Mexican Saltillos.

'And the Saltillos are very reasonably priced. Were Mrs Whitehead to have opted for Antique Reclaimed, we'd be talking at least double.'

Even successful barristers have their Achilles tendon. At that point Charlie had withdrawn from the fray, leaving Barbara and Alexander Crick to get on with the redistribution of his funds.

Her gaze now settled upon the yawning dishwasher, with its cargo of eggy plates and dirty pans and ringed cups. Overcome by a sudden urge to kick the thing she got up and rammed her foot hard against the gleaming door, which shut fast, smooth and silent, without complaint.

Charles Whitehead was trying to recall when he had last visited Medlar Hall. It must have been years ago, he suddenly realised, not long after Ursula had left. And she'd been gone - he did a quick calculation - it must have been around 1982. Strange that she hadn't remarried. Probably went against the grain of her feminist principles. Maybe she had turned? Life with Vincent Rush would be enough to drive any woman dykey. He pulled into the sweeping curve of a tree lined driveway, following it round to the side of the property, and parked within the long shadow cast by the high gable end of the north wing. He got out and stood for a moment, briefcase in hand, glancing up at the towering edifice. It was not as he remembered. The thick straggles of creeper which had once run rampant, all but obliterating the windows of the upper floors and suckering themselves on to the guttering, adding to the general air of gloom and neglect which had settled over the old place like a shroud, were now vanquished, barbered into good behaviour and neatly pruned back from the lintels. The wide flight of steps leading to the entrance were freshly swept, and the two huge urns on their stone plinths, once choked with weeds, now boasted elegant dark green balls of carefully clipped yew. The solid oak door shone with recently applied varnish and the verdigris lion's head knocker had been polished so that it now glinted brassily at him as he reached forward to rap it. Contrary to expectations, Medlar Hall was well maintained and in an excellent state of repair.

He heard footsteps padding down the hallway and a moment later the door was opened fractionally. He recognised the look; a momentary flicker of surprise, replaced by apprehension, before she smiled politely.

'Mr Whitehead.'

'Good morning, Mrs Jackson. I hope I haven't called at an inconvenient time. May I come in?'

She opened the door properly.

'Yes, of course. I've just got back from taking Mum home. She stayed over with me since the funeral. Come through. I'll get some coffee.'

Her face was plain, unadorned by makeup and framed by mousy hair which hung lankly to its owner's shoulders. She had a worn, downtrodden look which invoked in him not sympathy but extreme irritation, and he experienced a primitive urge to stamp on her. What in God's name had Vincent been playing at, having this ghastly little drip hanging around the edges of his domestic arrangements?

'Later.' said Charlie, taking charge.

He followed her down the hallway. 'I think we need to have a little chat. Shall we go through to the lounge?'

She led the way, held open the door and hovered uncertainly until he had entered.

Charlie glanced round quickly; time only for a fleeting impression of the galleried landing with its heavily carved rails, the oak panelling shining like glass. A smell of beeswax and turpentine mingled with the sweet scent of pot pourri which emanated forth from the body of an enormous 'famille rose' punch bowl. The room was dominated by a massive fireplace which owed its inspiration to the arts and crafts movement. The hearth was enclosed by a huge brass fender while a surround of exquisite tiles in subtly faded turquoise continued up the chimney breast, interrupted by a border frieze of twining convolvolus before continuing to ceiling level. Two large pre-Raphaelite paintings hung in the recesses. Above the faded oriental carpet a delicate crystal chandelier trembled discreetly, refracting joyful prisms of morning sunlight. Tall French windows led out into the old walled garden.

He sank into the Chesterfield and laid his briefcase beside him, suddenly realising why Ursula Rush had reappeared on the scene. The house, he had to concede, was a credit to Susan Jackson.

'Your mother taught you well, Mrs Jackson.'

Susan nodded. 'She did, Mr Whitehead. She showed me how to take a pride in caring for beautiful things. To cherish them, to do justice to the craftsmen who made them. It's taken me years, but gradually, room by room -' her voice tailed off and she fell silent, watching cautiously as he opened the briefcase.

'Do sit down, Mrs Jackson, there's no need to look so worried.' Susan perched on the edge of a chair, leaning slightly forward as he began to shuffle through the sheaf of documents. Eventually she summoned the courage to speak.

'I suppose you've come to see when we're leaving. I haven't had chance to organise anything yet, it's been such a shock, I wasn't able to think straight. The police kept coming back asking more and more questions, and I couldn't really tell them very much.' Her eyes filled with tears and she blew her nose noisily. 'It was all so sudden, I just don't know what we're going to do. I'm going down to the Housing Department next week.'

He was watching her intently. Either she was an excellent actress, which he doubted, or she genuinely had no idea. He passed one of the documents over to her.

'Here, you'd better take a look.'

Her hand trembled as she unfolded the pages. After a few minutes she glanced up.

'This is Dr Rush's will. Why are you showing it to me? I don't understand.'

'It is a copy of the will, Mrs Jackson. It's yours to keep. You're entitled to have it. Study it at your leisure. I've come here this morning to explain the implications. Firstly, I'm sure you will be relieved to learn that you don't have to leave here, certainly not for the present. Apart from some small legacies, Dr Rush has left the bulk of his estate in trust. Under the terms of the will you can remain here until the legatee comes of age.'

And who is the - who get's the estate?'

'Your son, Mrs Jackson. On Benjamin's twenty first birthday Medlar Hall becomes his, together with substantial investments and endowments. Those were Dr Rush's wishes.'

He watched her reactions closely; incredulity followed by disbelief. Her jaw dropped. He waited in silence.

Susan began to fill up with tears again. 'But I don't understand.'

she sniffled.

'It is perfectly clear. He intended that your son should inherit everything. He has made adequate provision for you to continue here. The trustees will release funds to you as and when they are required, to enable you to maintain yourself and the boy and to continue with the upkeep of the Hall. You are an extremely fortunate woman, Mrs Jackson.'

'When was the will made?' asked Susan.

'Some ten years ago. The date is stated at the beginning. Just a moment, I can tell you precisely.' He put on his spectacles and perusing his own copy of the will, read out the date, which brought on more tears.

'That was just after Brian died. Why would he do that?'

Charles Whitehead looked at her over the top of his spectacles. 'I thought you might be able to tell me.' he said, quietly.

Susan's face began to burn. Tiny beads of moisture erupted across her forehead and as he watched a scarlet rash began to mottle her throat. She put her hands to her reddening face.

'Are you all right, Mrs Jackson?'

She looked up, embarrassed, and nodded.

'Yes, I'll be fine in a minute. It's just my age.' she explained, apologetically.

It was Charles's turn to feel uncomfortable. He cleared his throat. 'Can I get you something - a glass of water, perhaps?'

'No, it'll pass off in a few minutes. It's got worse just lately, it must be all the upset. It happens all the time.'

Charles, who had no desire whatsoever to be drawn into an exchange concerning the havoc being wreaked by Mrs Jackson's hormones, cleared his throat and rummaged unnecessarily in the briefcase. When he looked up again she was relaxing back in the chair. Her colour had returned to normal and for the first time since his arrival she made proper eye contact.

'Mr Whitehead, I have to tell you here and now that there was never anything going on between me and Dr Rush, if that's what your thinking. On my life. On my son's life.'

Her glance did not waver and Charles, well versed in the art of using his eyes as a weapon, now found himself in the unusual position of being the first to look away.

'We never - I wasn't implying that there was.' he replied, realising that he was beginning to sound defensive. 'Vincent must have been extremely fond of the boy. We're rather surprised, my wife and I. We both find it rather strange. We never thought that he cared about anything or anyone, apart from his work.'

'He didn't, but he always took a keen interest in Ben's welfare. Even more after Brian died. When I tried to thank him he said that Ben was the nearest thing that he'd ever have to a son. I thought he was just being polite. I never expected this. I can't take it in.'

'Where is Ben, Mrs Jackson?'

'He's away. At school.' She reddened.

This time he felt sure that it had nothing to do with 'her age'.

'But today is Saturday, Mrs Jackson.'

'I know. He's at boarding school. He was very unhappy once he got to middle school. Ben's not a good mixer and there was some trouble. Bullying. It got really bad and he grew more and more nervous. Dr Rush thought he'd be happier at a private school.'

'So Dr Rush was paying the fees?'

She nodded uncomfortably. 'I know how it must look - what you must be thinking - but it wasn't like that. Dr Rush insisted that I sent Ben. I just wanted to do what was best for my boy, so I took Dr Rush's advice and went along with it. I miss having my son here with me, Mr Whitehead, I really do. I can't wait until he's back for the Christmas holidays.'

'Why don't we have that cup of coffee?' suggested Charles. 'Give you a few minutes to think about everything. I'm going to take a look around now.'

He followed her through the dining room and into the passageway which, he now recalled, led to the kitchen and laundry room and out towards the rear of the house and the old coaching sheds. Halfway along the passage he paused before a door and put his hand out to try the handle.

'That's Dr Rush's study, Mr Whitehead.'

'I know.' replied Charles.

'I don't think you should go in there. He only let - I mean, he never allowed anyone to go inside unless he was present. He wouldn't even allow me in to clean. It's all in a mess.'

Charles looked at her sharply. 'So you have been into the study, then?'

Susan flushed again. 'I had to let the police take a look. They insisted. There was nothing I could do to stop them.'

'I need to see what's in there, Mrs Jackson. There's a vast amount be sorted out here. If you could just leave me to get on with it please, and then we'll have that coffee.'

He watched as she walked off towards the kitchen.

In stark contrast to what he had seen in the rest of the house, the study exuded the dingy, gloomy atmosphere of many years of neglect. Charles Whitehead shivered and crossed to the ornate iron radiator. It was almost too hot to touch, yet the study felt distinctly chilly. He glanced round the dusty, book lined room wondering where to begin and crossed to a squat Victorian partner's desk, the tooled leather surface of which was all but obliterated by untidy piles of books, files and loose papers. Rising incongruously from the midst of this mess was an impressive looking computer with a dirty screen and an extremely grubby extended keyboard. Charles, who held an unconfessed aversion for computers and had thus far in his career managed to avoid any actual hands-on involvement with the things, touched it gingerly and then abandoned the idea. On the wall behind the desk tall shelves housed a dusty assortment of early medical instruments and a long row of apothecary jars. This collection was worthy of any museum but Vincent Rush had lost interest in it long before his untimely death. Charles's eye travelled upwards to the distant top shelf, way out of reach, which was empty save for a huge lidded jar of green glazed earthenware. Truly ugly, it was embellished with masses of ornate gilt scroll work. Across the bulge of its inelegant body it bore the word **LEECHES** in heavy black lettering.

The room now seemed even colder than when he had first entered. He bent down and switched on the single bar electric fire standing in the narrow hearth of a cast iron fire place. A strong smell of scorch pervaded the room as the heat worked through the thick coating of dust which choked the glowing bar. After a moment he turned it off again.

The floor was littered with papers. More spilled forth from mounds of document wallets stacked in untidy heaps against the walls. He looked up at the grey strands of thick cobweb which had been painstakingly interwoven, as if the weavers had formed a co-operative with the express intention of totally obliterating the ceiling in order to trap and return earthward the stale, dead smell that lingered in the atmosphere. He pushed an old leather armchair aside, revealing the mouldering remains of a takeaway meal, still in its foil container. Feeling faintly sick, he shut the door on the study and made his way up the main staircase, from which a rambling network of panelled passages led to the various wings. The second floor had originally contained six bedrooms, each with its own dressing room. The three bedrooms at the far end of the main corridor had been turned into the housekeeper's living quarters. These were clean and tidy but, furnished in a humbler and shabbier style, contrasted sharply with the discreet opulence he had encountered downstairs. Charles made his way back to the galleried landing, which provided a bird's eye view of the principle room and leant over the rails. On a small mahogany chest of drawers lay a fan of magazines of the non-glossy variety - back dated women's weeklies and a television guide, together with the current issue of the Gazette, which lay face up, Tuesday's funeral dominating the front page. Mrs Jackson, it would seem, did not restrict herself to her own quarters. Still, who could blame her? He drew back quickly as the lounge door began to open and Susan Jackson entered, carrying a tray. Descending the stairs quietly he reentered the room.

'Did you find what you were looking for, Mr Whitehead?' asked Susan, placing his coffee, with a shaky hand, on a low side table.

'Not really. It's quite chaotic but I'd be grateful if you left things as they are. Don't touch anything in the study until I've had a chance to sort things out. There's a lot that needs to be gone through, but no immediate hurry. I'll have to come back when I've got more time.'

He drank the coffee quickly and looked at his watch. 'I must go now.'

'So what happens next?'

'Well, someone will be coming here to make an inventory. Everything has to be listed and assessed for probate. You'll be contacted about that nearer the time. Normally this would all be reasonably straightforward, but unfortunately -' He hesitated for a second.

'What is it?'

'Mrs Rush is considering contesting the will. She has taken advice and is seeking counsel's opinion. You are going to have to do likewise. If she decides to proceed everything will be frozen. It could take a long time.'

'But she hasn't been here for years. I've never met her once, not in all the time we've been here. She never kept in touch with Dr Rush. He told me that himself, a long time ago. Surely he would have mentioned it in the will if he wanted her to have anything?'

'It's more complicated than that. The coroner's report and the inquest verdict will slant things in your favour. She would have been in with a better chance if they had returned verdict of suicide. Then they would have argued that he was of unsound mind. As things stand -well.' He shrugged.

'Could she still win?' asked Susan, showing him to the door.

'Mrs Jackson, it is not my place to get involved. As a member of the family I am not in a position of detachment. My first concern is for Barbara and our own boys. Blood runs thicker than water, as they say. Anyway, at least you can forget about the Housing Department. I suggest you arrange to see a solicitor - I can recommend someone, if you like.'

'No thanks, Mr Whitehead. I'll deal with this on my own. I just need some time to think things over.'

'You will need to take legal advice. It is in your own interests that you do so. Good day to you, Mrs Jackson. I'll be in touch.'

He shook her hand formerly and was halfway down the steps when she called to him.

'Mr Whitehead?'

He turned, impatient, irritated, anxious to be off. 'Mrs Jackson?'

'It isn't always.'

He raised a questioning eyebrow. 'What?'

'Thicker than water.' said Susan, closing the door.

5
Monday

Andy Thrower was already in the office, feet up on the desktop, browsing through last week's edition when Sophie and Rachel arrived. He glanced up as they entered.

'Hi, you two.'

'Hello, are you better?' Rachel took off her coat and sat down.

'If he was ever ill.' said Sophie. 'Probably bunked off to go to Haydock.'

'Behave.' said Andy. 'I didn't get out of bloody bed till Friday.'

'And how's the poor lady?'

Andy chose to ignore the remark. 'See you've been rubbing shoulders with the FINGERS crowd, Rachel.'

'Trevor sent me. I had to do it, Andy, there was no one else free to cover for you.'

Sophie looked up. 'Usurped by a younger woman. Feeling threatened, are we?'

'Not at all. Shut it, Sophie. You've done a good job here, Rachel. Thanks. It must have been a bit unnerving for you.'

Something in his tone roused her curiosity.

'What do you mean?

He shrugged. 'Nothing. Just that Trev dropped you in at the deep end on your first time out. Close ranks, that lot.'

Andy fell silent.

'Do you know anything about a lad called Benjamin Jackson?' asked Rachel, eagerly.

'Don't think so.'

'He's inherited the lot, apparently, but the ex-wife is contesting the will. That's the whisper around the local pubs."

Andy stood up. 'Listen, I'll catch up with you later, Rachel.

Trev's left a load of messages on my desk - evidently extracting his revenge for the time off. I've got an interview with the people who have taken over the old cinema building at half past nine, followed by yet another bloody opposition meeting about the second runway.'

Rachel, whose sympathies lay with the protesters, said nothing. Andy grabbed a bunch of keys from the desk and stuffed them, together with a new note pad, into his coat pocket. 'I thought he might be a bit off with me for covering that funeral. He was all right about it, wasn't he? He's nice, once you get to know him.' said Rachel

'Yes, Andy's OK.' Sophie put the phone down. 'Except for his fatal flaw. I shouldn't tease the poor sap when he's having such a rough ride, but sometimes I just can't help myself.'

'What's the matter with him?'

'His second wife has just walked. Still, who can blame her?'

'Why did she leave?

'Same reason as the first one.' Sophie lowered her voice a fraction. 'Andy can't walk past a bookmaker's doorway. Haven't you noticed the way he's always nipping out? You can always tell when he's lost - which seems to be most of the time. I once spotted him coming out of that one on Water Lane, white as a sheet. Looked as if he was about to throw up. Andy's a nice enough chap but no woman is going to put up with that sort of behaviour for ever. I don't think he sees much of his kids, either. They moved out of the area when the first Mrs Thrower remarried. He's been gambling for so long he's out of control. Can't stop, even if he wanted. Not a day goes by.'

'Poor Andy, I had no idea.' said Rachel. 'How old is he?'

Sophie shrugged. 'Too old to alter. Late forties, I suppose. He's been here a long time, nearly as long as Trev, I think.'

'Does Trevor know about it?'

'Everybody knows, but they don't mention it. Neither must you, Rachel. Andy isn't bad at his job, it's the one thing he's managed to hang on to. He'd probably have been offered sub-editor a long time ago, but his problem makes him - well, it places him in the 'not quite respectable' file.'

'And what about Keith? Any gossip about him?'

Sophie shook her head.

'No, Keith's above reproach. Takes life very seriously. He's got ambitions, wants to carve out a career in serious journalism. This is just a stepping stone along the way. I don't think he'll stick around the local rag for much longer. As soon as he gets a better offer he'll be off. Play your cards right and there's a good opportunity for you here, Rachel - if that's what you want.'

'I want.' said Rachel and went off to laser print some more editorials to add to the heap already accumulating on Trevor's desk.

That afternoon Rachel acquainted Trevor with the rumours which had started to circulate regarding Ben Jackson and the Rush will.

'That's interesting. You know something, Rachel? I've got a feeling in my waters about this business. It could turn out to be the iceberg that sank the Titanic, right here on our own doorstep. Maybe we should start gathering whatever facts we can ferret out before events overtake us.'

'Do you think we could be on to something?' asked Rachel, trying to sound casual.

'Maybe. It's as well to be prepared. Have you cleared the decks for today?'

'More or less.'

'In that case, how do you fancy a bit of research? Go down to the archive room and see what you can dig out from files.'

'What am I supposed to be looking for?'

'Anything on Rush and FINGERS. The Jacksons .....' he suddenly stopped.

'What is it Trev?'

'I've just remembered that Lydia had a FINGERS contact, but I can't recall his name - actually I don't think she ever told me. Always played things close to her chest, did Lydia. I wonder how she's doing - must be getting a bit long in the tooth by now.'

'Who's Lydia?'

'One of your predecessors, my dear. The formidable Miss Pendle. One of the strangest women you could ever meet.'

He stopped rather abruptly.

'When would you like me to start from?'

'Around 82/83 - perhaps a bit earlier. Begin from when Rush took up his appointment at FINGERS. There'll be something in the files about that. And pop into personnel on your way down, Rachel. See if they've got a contact number for Lydia Pendle. I know she's not living on Chapel Lane anymore. Check if there's a more recent address.'

Trevor turned his attention back to the editorial column and found recollections of Lydia creeping in, spoiling his concentration, as if all the intervening years had dissolved, elbowed aside by that first day in the editor's office. The open plan workplace had not yet been thought of and he remembered sitting on the opposite side of this very desk, in Nicholls' private office, discussing the staff with the departing editor on the eve of his retirement. Edwin Nicholls had taken him one by one through the list of employees, providing his assessments of their strengths and weaknesses.

'And finally, we come to Miss Pendle. You may think me impertinent, Mr Stephens, but I have always believed that knowledge is power. If one knows, one understands. If one understands, one learns to deal accordingly. It is a simple but important principal and vital if one is to get the best out of the team and treat them with fairness. The case of Miss Pendle illustrates my point admirably. Something which happened many years ago, the unpleasant events of one single afternoon, have shaped her into the person you will shortly meet.'

At this point Edwin Nicholls had paused for a moment, as if wondering whether to continue. Leaning across the desk, he lowered his voice.

'This is, of course, in the strictest confidence.'

'Of course. You have my word.'

'Lydia had been with the paper several years by then. She must have been about twenty five or twenty six, and what they used to call 'left on the shelf'. I don't think she'd ever had a boyfriend. Rather a serious sort of girl. Very committed to her work, always eager to progress. Disaster struck in the early part of - now let me think.' He paused, pursing his lips. 'It was the year after the Festival of Britain, so that would make it '52. There was a bad 'flu epidemic and that particular day I was extremely short staffed. Lydia, who had recently learnt to drive, eagerly volunteered to step into the breach. I made the mistake of allowing her go off alone to cover a story. Something trivial. I cannot even remember the details, but it was some distance away.' He frowned as the story continued to elude him.

'With some slight misgivings, I gave her the use of my car. As it turned out, my qualms had been well founded, because afterwards, instead of returning to the office, as she should have done, Miss Pendle impetuously decided to drive to the hills. I know exactly where she went. A strange, inhospitable location dominated by the bleak moorland wilderness. Leaving the car in a rutted lay-by, she set off to follow one of those narrow tracks that wander ever deeper into that wind swept desolation. She had not ventured very far into this landscape of boggy tarns and trickling streams when a strange fellow materialised, emerging suddenly out of a small plantation of young conifers.

She blames herself for what happened, of that I am certain. Her native inquisitiveness, that nose for a story. The need to impress her editor. Yes me, Mr Stephens. Seeking to impress me, Miss Pendle quite deliberately turned aside and trudged across the heather and the cotton grass, working her way towards him. I will spare you the sordid details. You can guess what happened next. Upon her return she told no one but myself. She seemed strangely fatalistic about the whole dreadful business. Convinced that the episode was entirely due to her own folly, she would not permit me to report the incident and refused to do so herself. Since that day the doors of her emotions appear to have remained closed. She began to enhance the plainness of her appearance, concentrated upon her chosen career with renewed fervour and remained at home, the dutiful daughter, caring for each of her parents in turn, as it became necessary. And all the while, that dreadful experience has simmered, eventually reducing itself to a hard little knot of contempt for the male species, which she conceals rather skilfully.

As you will see, she effects a brisk, militant stride, swinging her arm in an attitude which broaches no nonsense, and chooses to ignore the unkind comments of the younger members of staff, who have no knowledge of the events which turned Miss Pendle into the person to whom you will shortly be introduced. Nature always compensates, Mr Stephens. In Miss Pendle you are getting a highly intelligent woman and a valuable member of staff. An excellent and dedicated reporter. I trust you will respect this confidence, Mr Stephens. I pondered long and hard before deciding to speak of the matter. I decided that I must hand over my authority in the knowledge that I have done my best to explain Miss Pendle's eccentricities. I owe her that much.'

With the benefit of hindsight, Trevor had come to realise that this long conversation, all those years ago, had taught him something fundamental. Edwin Nicholls had passed on a valuable lesson from which had sprung Trevor's reputation as 'everybody's uncle'. With a faint smile he turned his attention back to his column.

Rachel knocked on the door of the personnel office and entered. The girl at the desk looked up from her computer.

'Hi, Trevor has asked me to check if you've got an address for one of the old reporters, Miss Pendle. I think she retired about twelve or thirteen years ago.'

'Hang on, I'll check the lists.'

The girl began to scroll through the files. 'Here we are. Pendle - Lydia, is it?'

Rachel nodded.

'The last address we've got was Chapel Lane.'

'No, she's moved from there.' One of the older woman looked up. 'If you're trying to locate Lydia, I think she's in one of the local nursing homes. Went in a few months back, poor old duck. Nobody to look after her. I can't imagine her fitting in very easily.'

'Did you know her, then?' asked Rachel.

The woman nodded. ''As much as anybody ever knew Lydia. A queer fish, kept herself to herself. But she was quite a character and she'd been with the paper so long that she'd become part of the furniture.'

'Is she ill?'

'I would imagine so. There's no way Lydia Pendle would choose to give up her independence.' The woman smiled. 'She wasn't the type to go gently. I bet she had to be dragged there kicking and screaming. Poor old Lydia.'

'You don't happen to know which home she's gone to?'

'No, but I can try to find out. I think it might be that big place in Mobberley but I would have to check. Who want's to know?'

'Trevor.' said Rachel. 'I think he wants to send her a Christmas present.'

'I'll find out and get back to you. Rachel, is it? Leave it with me.'

'Thanks. Do you have the keys to the archive room? I need to check something for Trevor.'

The woman got up. 'Have you been down there before?'

Rachel shook her head.

'I'll come down with you and show you the classification system, otherwise it will take you the rest of the day to find your way around.'

She led the way to the basement, unlocked a door and turned on the lights.

'Which year are you interested in?'

'I think I need to start around 1980 and work my way forward. I'm not sure exactly what I'm supposed to be looking for.'

'You're not going to manage that before home time.' said the woman, waving towards the lines of shelving closely packed with enormous files which went back to the 1870s. 'At least they're not on microfilm. That would make it even harder for you. Now the photocopier is over here. I've switched it on so you can just run off copies of anything you need. Drop the keys back into my office when you've finished. I'm Dorothy, by the way. I'll let you know when I find out Lydia's whereabouts.'

Apart from a brief and sympathetic report concerning his involvement in a minor traffic accident towards the end of 1983, when he was charged with driving without due care and attention, pleaded guilty and was fined, with his licence revoked for twelve months, Rachel found nothing of great interest relating to Vincent Rush. After that incident he appeared to have maintained the lowest of profiles.

She turned back to a 1981 article concerning the development and continuing expansion of FINGERS and suddenly noticed that it had been the work of Lydia Pendle.

'Today Forensic Industries Genetic Experimental Research Station is a far cry from the comparatively humble complex of small laboratories and kennel blocks which sprung up piecemeal within the grounds of an old mansion house in the heart of our local countryside, following the end of the Second World War. Set deep within rolling parkland, careful tree planting keeps the entire complex well screened from pubic view. Following those well publicised threats of disruption during the late Seventies from the more militant elements of the ALF (*Animal Liberation Front - Ed.*), the security arrangements are now first rate. Over the last decade the FINGERS development has become virtually self contained, with its own power generating system, major incineration facilities, impressive library and a luxurious hospitality suite in which corporate visitors from around the globe are hosted. With a massive on-site leisure complex, generously subsidised by the American parent company, the FINGERS workforce has little reason to venture off site in search of recreational pursuits.'

Rachel smiled to herself, diverted by the typesetting error which had managed to evade the careful eye of the proof reader, and found herself wondering whether Miss Pendle had found it equally amusing. Probably not. So far no one had mentioned Lydia and a sense of humour in the same breath.

The piece had been written at the time of the opening of a second research unit, which coincided with the appointment Vincent Rush. At the comparatively young age of 42, he had just arrived as Head of Research. The feature was accompanied by a small photograph of the new boy, an unprepossessing looking individual with a thin, clean shaven face, around which pale hair straggled untidily. The eyes, also pale, peered myopically from behind the thick lenses of metal framed spectacles as he stared unsmiling into the camera. He looked so much younger here that Rachel felt almost able to relate to him. In the only other picture she had seen, a more recent portrait which had been supplied to accompany the obituary, the bearded face had been deeply lined, the muscles tense. In both he appeared unfriendly and unapproachable. Well, he certainly was now, she thought ruefully. As in life, so in death.

She made copies of both these reports before returning the files to their shelves and removed two more. Patiently she turned page after page of subsequent issues, which offered valuable insights into the march of progress of the by then rapidly expanding town, but provided no further information concerning Dr Rush. She was just about to abandon her task for the day when she spotted a photograph of Lydia Pendle at the top of a double page spread announcing the start of a new feature:

Man in his Landscape - Reporter Lydia Pendle will be exploring our surrounding countryside to report upon local myths and legends associated with ancient sites and local beauty spots. She begins her series from the ancient beacon site on Alderley Edge.

The articles were well written and contained some interesting observations. Natural curiosity appeared to have evolved into something more intense as the author's delving took her into ever stranger regions. She explored the tantalising clues long buried within the folk lore and race memories which she had unearthed, carefully analysing the ways in which they had translated themselves into fairy tales of magic and superstition. As the series progressed the writer appeared driven by the need to discover that core of truth which lay at the heart of these mysteries. The series proceeded with such confidence and authority that Rachel began to get the impression that Lydia Pendle had felt almost there, but had never quite arrived. She had certainly travelled to the fringes, to the brink of - something. Her fascination with the unknown, the forgotten, the unrecorded was clearly evident. Rachel was so immersed that she jumped when the door opened and Trevor entered. 'Rachel, do you know what time it is? We're waiting to lock up.'

'I'm sorry, I lost track. I came across this series Lydia Pendle wrote on local earth mysteries. They're really interesting.'

Trevor frowned. 'One of my more embarrassing errors of judgment. I should stick them back on the shelf, my dear. I had to axe them after a few weeks.'

'Why? They're fascinating.'

'They weren't suitable for the Gazette. Didn't go down at all well. Caused a lot of trouble.'

'What sort of trouble?

Trevor closed the file and returned it to its correct position on the shelf. 'We received several letters of objection. A number of our more orthodox readers became very upset about the content of one or two of the articles. In fact, one of the local vicars grew quite incensed. Some of the older members of his congregation had complained. 'Leave the mysteries to the Creator'. You know, that type of thing. There were a lot of comments along those lines. I should never have let her get away with it.'

'What was Lydia like?'

'She dabbled - dangerous stuff. Ended up letting it take over her life. She really believed in it. Poor lonely Lydia and her precious cats. If she'd been born three hundred years earlier she'd have been burnt at the stake.'

'And how did she react when you cancelled the series?'

He shrugged. 'Well, she took it on the chin. I suppose she had to. She wasn't about to put her job on the line. We remained on good terms. I don't think she went home to stick pins in my photograph. She realised she'd overstepped the mark. Not that it stopped her, mind you, she carried on digging and delving in her own spare time. I think she was planning to write a book when she retired. 'The Pagan Pantheon' - that was her dream. I'm surprised that it never came to anything. She was always so dogged and obsessive about it, I was quite expecting a review copy to land on my desk, but it never did. Come on, Rachel, get your things together. You can come back later in the week, but don't get sidetracked with Lydia Pendle's nonsense again. Enough for today. Sophie's already gone. I told her that I'd give you a lift home.'

6
Friday

At the time of his death in the autumn of 1987, Brian Jackson's swarthy good looks had long since disappeared and he was almost ugly. Below vacuous eyes the accumulated debris of his drinking had gathered within the cartilage of his nose, forcing pores to expand as the epidermis thickened to accommodate his excesses. Maybe Bacchus himself had stamped this award of merit upon the bulb of Brian Jackson's nose. He certainly sent him out for the final time on that wild and stormy night.

It was long after closing time when Brian and his two friends piled into the old van. The driver gave a loud belch as he cursed the worn wiper blades which scraped noisily and ineffectually against the glass of the windscreen. He drove slowly until they reached the back lanes and then the van gathered speed, bald tyres spinning dangerously over the wet surface. Squeezed together in the front seats, the two passengers cheered loudly as the driver brought the skidding vehicle back under control.

'Let's have some music.'

Brian leant forward and fiddled with the radio.

'Not that late night easy listening crap.' said Sam Parker, turning his attention from the road. 'Find the rock n roll station.' When he glanced back to the road, the old stone bridge was careering towards them. Sam went for the brake pedal.

The last thing that Brian Jackson saw was a large white bird, wings outstretched. Buffeted by the wind, it dominated the parapet, blinking in the headlights. As they collided with the stonework the van's rusty sills concertinaed and the bodywork collapsed into a jagged, crumpled shell. The terrible noises from within the wreckage continued for a time and then, save for the low howling of the wind, there was silence.

Hours passed. It was getting towards the end of the night shift when the headlights of a cruising patrol car picked out the damaged stonework and just growing light when the grim faced sergeant walked up the front steps of Medlar Hall and rapped the lion's head knocker.

If there is any compensation to be gained from clinging on to the loneliness and unhappiness of an unsatisfactory marriage, it must surely come with the unexpected demise of one's spouse, when the bereavement is, perhaps, a little less painful. If only there had been something honourable to cling to - a trace of self sacrifice, maybe, or even a terrible illness which they could say afterwards had been bravely borne. But no, there had been nothing heroic about Brian's end. Sordid and embarrassing, it had merely echoed his life. Tacky, self centred, a squandered waste, anaesthetised by alcohol. This was the way it felt for Susan Jackson as she adjusted to the realisation of her sudden widowhood. She shed her tears both in public and in private, but only she knew which of them fell from grief and which from a sense of propriety.

**

It was not until Friday afternoon that Rachel had an opportunity to return to her perusal of the archives. Today she had decided to concentrate on finding anything relating to the Jackson family. The latter pages of the 1987 file rewarded her with the following headline.

TRIPLE DEATH AT BLACKSPOT BRIDGE

A commonplace accident, the result of excessive intake of alcohol and an unroadworthy vehicle. Having spent the evening in a heavy drinking session, visiting several of the local pubs, Samuel Parker, James Turner and Brian Jackson had been discovered dead at the scene by a passing police car, several hours, according to the police surgeon, after the van had skidded out of control and impacted with the bridge. No other vehicle appeared to be involved.

The three funerals were reported in a later edition. Rachel made a copy of the Jackson obituary, which was unusually brief and informed the Gazette readers that the deceased had left a widow and young son. His address was given as Medlar Hall. Family mourners included Mrs S Jackson (widow), Mrs J Jackson (mother), Mr & Mrs Stuart Jackson (Brother & sister in law), Misses EM and TS Jackson (Nieces), Mr Anthony Jackson (Brother) Mr & Mrs Alan Burgess (Sister & brother in law), Mr J Jackson (Nephew), Mrs Lillian Bayliss (Mother in law).

When Rachel returned the keys to the office a note had been left for her.

'Dorothy's gone to the dentist.' said the girl, handing it over. 'She asked me to give this to you. She forgot when you were here earlier. It's the address you were asking for. Dorothy said would you remember her to Lydia if you get to visit her.'

'Thanks. I certainly will.'

She returned to the editorial office and left copies of the Jackson reports in Trevor's in-tray.

'Any luck?' asked Sophie as Rachel returned to her own desk.

Rachel shrugged. 'A bit, but I don't think it's anything very relevant. I found out how Mrs Jackson came to be widowed. I get the impression that Mr Jackson must have had a drink problem. He'd been out with a couple of drinking chums. They crashed the van on the way home. Their alcohol levels were off the clock.'

She handed Sophie the copies she had made. Sophie glanced at them briefly and handed them back.

'I think I vaguely remember it.'

'Sophie, you know those articles that I was telling you about? The ones written by Lydia Pendle? Well, one of them was on dowsing and she mentions something about accident blackspots. She reckoned that they're usually at places where water courses are sited beneath the road. There's a theory that they create a build-up of electromagnetic forces which can affect the steering. I mean, this accident was right on the bridge. The brook runs right underneath.'

'Well of course it does. That's why the bridge was put there in the first place.' Sophie stabbed a well manicured finger in the general direction of the photocopies. 'What you've got there is three pissheads in a nail of a van that should never have been on the road. An accident waiting to happen. Honestly, Rachel, you're trying too hard.'

Rachel flushed and returned to her desk in silence. After a few minutes Sophie glanced across at the bent head and experienced a flicker of guilt. Poor, thin skinned Rachel. She got up and went across. 'I'm sorry Rach, I didn't mean to upset you. Listen, I'm calling into the wine bar after work. Everyone stops off on Fridays. Come with me. Go on, just for a laugh. I won't be staying very long. We're going out tonight and I'll need to get ready.'

'I'm not sure. I really ought to get home.'

'Why?'

'Well - no real reason, I suppose. Habit - I'm just used to going straight home after work. The cats will need feeding.'

'Come on, Rachel, just listen to yourself. We all need to chill out sometimes. The cats aren't going to starve if you're an hour late with their Whiskas. Anyway, I insist. I want to buy you a drink and I won't take no for an answer. You've got to get a life sweetheart, you're only here once.'

Rachel glanced up from her papers and suddenly realised that this was Sophie's way of trying to make amends. Not wanting to hurt her feelings she reluctantly agreed. 'You're probably right. I'll come. Sophie, what's a nail?'

Sophie gave her a strange look. 'Something you bang with a hammer? Something you paint red?'

'No - I mean that van - the one in the accident. You said it was a nail. What did you mean?'

Sophie began to laugh. 'Oh that! It's just motor trade jargon for a car that's not fit to drive. I never really thought about it, but I expect it's slang for coffin. You know, a coffin nail.'

Sophie drove at an alarming speed to the prettiest of the neighbouring villages, where the predominantly elderly residents enjoyed dignified retirements centred around the church, the golf course and the cricket club. In between shopping for non-essentials in a leisurely, untrammelled fashion they exercised their retrievers and walked their little toy dogs around the village green. In the daytime the discreet and gentle murmur of old money created a relaxing, if slightly stifling air of shelter from the storm, a little refuge of carefree solidarity and reassurance. Once darkness fell the ambience changed dramatically as the new money arrived, en route to the cluster of smart restaurants and thriving country pubs, shrieking its head off beneath the thatched roofs and the black and white Cheshire timbers. Sophie parked her little white sports car at an outrageous angle outside the wine bar and scrambled out, showing more leg than skirt.

'Come on, Rachel. Have you locked your door?'

Civitavecchia - commonly known as Chivs - had long since established itself as the place to be seen. Already festive, the wine bar was tastefully decked with the latest in subtly understated decorations. Positioned to either side of the entrance, matching trees - topiaried twins - hosted plump cherubs trailing golden ringlets, ushering one into the porchway where necklaces of tiny white lights were artistically festooned. Vivaldi concertos for mandolin and harpsichord played in a continuous loop, providing a suitably *classico ma non troppo* background to the conversational buzz.

Initially frequented by the offspring of successful families from the locality, it had quickly become a favourite watering hole for Cheshire's smart set. Nowadays it tended to attract stylish singles and people involved in various branches of the media - generally those whose careers were either yet to wax or in imminent danger of waning. On the fringes of this in-crowd lurked a handful of ageing roués, adrift and rapidly running to seed, who surveyed the talent with an intensity verging on desperate. Girls gathered at the tables in anticipatory groups, studying form with the single minded dedication of prospectors en route to the Yukon.

Sophie returned from the bar, followed by an attractive young waiter bearing a tray with two enormous wine glasses, the rims of which had been seasonally sugar frosted, and an outrageously expensive Chablis, its bottle still dewy with condensation.

The waiter poured generous glasses.

'Cheers - here's to chilling out.' Sophie offered Rachel a gold tipped menthol cigarette. Rachel shook her head. 'No thanks, I don't.'

Sophie laughed and asked the people at the next table for a light, which someone produced with alacrity.

'So, what else do you do, apart from scurry on home to feed the puss cats?'

Rachel shrugged. 'Read, go to the cinema sometimes. Visit friends.' Spoken aloud it all sounded horribly sad and boring, which it wasn't. 'Sophie, you must let me pay my share.'

Sophie flapped a disdainful hand. 'Don't worry about it. My treat. Anyway, I put it on Steve's account.'

She was looking beyond Rachel, her eyes raking the throng.

'Rachel, I've just spotted someone over there. I must go and say hello. Will you be all right for a minute? Back in a sec.'

Before Rachel could reply, Sophie got up and pushed her way through the crush of drinkers, towards the bar. Abandoned on unfamiliar territory, Rachel glanced around, feeling awkward and excluded. Unable to purchase admission, since

71

the price of acceptance remained a mystery, she was now beginning to wish that she had followed her instincts and gone straight home. After a few moments someone's mobile phone rang and she found herself eavesdropping as a middle aged man lied noisily as to his whereabouts. After he had escaped from this interruption he caught her eye and winked. Rachel looked at him reproachfully and turned away. Somewhere behind, out of her line of vision but within easy earshot, the bones of some absent friend's relationship, which appeared to have degenerated into something which threatened to turn ugly, were being picked with rapacity. She sighed and took a long gulp of wine, wondering how to extricate herself from this dazzling parallel universe.

After what seemed like an age, Sophie suddenly reappeared. 'It's Jules! Just got back from Uni. They get about five weeks vacation over Christmas. - can you believe that? Jammy devil. Haven't seen him for months. He's coming over in minute.'

'Who is he?'

'Oh, one of the old crowd from years ago. We all used to go around together - pop concerts, razzing off to Abersoch with somebody's speedboat hitched to one of the cars, parties when the parents were away. Great times. You know, kid's stuff.'

She looked at Rachel severely. 'Or maybe you don't. It was called fun.'

'Before Steve?'

'A long time before Steve.' Sophie smiled, rather wistfully. 'Here's Jules now, I'll introduce you.'

Rachel turned round in her seat. Julian Whitehead was making his way through the drinkers towards their table.

'Is that him?' whispered Rachel.

Sophie nodded. 'Quite a dish - this could turn out to be be your lucky night! He's really nice.'

'Sophie, don't you know who he is?'

'I told you, I've known him for years. Haven't you been listening to a word I've said?'

'I already met him. His mother is Vincent Rush's sister. I talked to him after the funeral.'

Before Sophie could reply Julian Whitehead arrived at the table, hand outstretched. 'I thought I recognised you. It's Rachel, isn't it?' He turned to Sophie. 'How do you two know each other?' And then, before Sophie could reply, he tapped himself on the forehead. 'Of course, I'd forgotten.You're at the Gazette, Soph, aren't you? How long have you been there now?'

'Too long.' said Sophie. 'They gave me a pay rise and put me in charge of the advertising department. Has its perks, I get taken out to some decent lunches. Listen, I've really got to split now. Steve and I are going out.'

Rachel began to put on her jacket.

'Why don't you stay, Rachel. Let me buy you another drink.'

Rachel shook her head. 'No thanks, I've got to go, too. Sophie's dropping me off.'

'I'll give you a lift, later.'

Sophie's eyes gleamed. 'That's a good idea. Go on Rachel - all work and no play etc.'

Rachel sat down again.

'Sorry I've got to rush off and leave you.' said Sophie. 'I need to top up my tan with a quick sunbed. It's fancy dress night. We're going to the Midwinter Ball.'

'And who will you be going as?' inquired Julian

Sophie rose to her full height, stretched her arms and piled her long blonde locks high on her head, revealing an enticing strip of bronzed midriff with a hint of navel.

'Who do you think?' she grinned.

'Silly question' said Julian. 'Still the same old tease, Sophie. Have fun.'

After Sophie had departed he turned his attention to

Rachel. 'Let me get you another drink. White wine?'

When he came back Rachel said 'So you know Sophie?'

Julian laughed. 'Everybody knows Soph. One of the local glitterati - although at least she has an IQ to match her aspirations, which is more than you can say for most of them.' He gazed round the crowded wine bar. 'Probably just as well, it looks as though she's got a lot of rising competition.'

Rachel followed his glance. Most of the girls were uniformly waxed, polished, varnished and glossed. Between frequent trips to the powder room to re-apply lip gloss and exchange progress reports, they floated and flirted amongst the tables.

'Do you reduce all females into stereotypes?'

'Only the ones that have been round the block a few times. Sophie's all right - heart of gold and gusset to match.' He watched with some amusement as Rachel blushed.

'Enough of them. Tell me about your week. I assume you're still hacking for the newspaper?'

Rachel nodded. 'It's a busy time. We're trying to line up stuff for the issue between Christmas and New Year, so I'm writing a lot of filler features, because Trevor - he's the editor - Trevor says it's always the most difficult issue to get out. Unless there's some major incident, which isn't very likely, it will be mainly January sales features, the drink-driving figures and bad weather stories. Pretty boring stuff. And you?'

'I got back from Uni a couple of days ago. It's not very easy trying to pick up the social threads around here. I've been away off and on for four years, so I've lost touch with the old crowd. They're either loved up or working away - It's quite a schitzo existence between Uni and home. I used to go out with my brother, but he got engaged recently and I don't intend to spend my vacation playing gooseberry.' He smiled at her. 'It's really nice to bump into you again. Would you like to go on somewhere else?'

Rachel shook her head. 'I need to be getting home.'

'Is someone waiting for you?'

She nodded and he looked so crestfallen the she began to laugh. 'A couple of cats,' she explained, 'who haven't been fed since breakfast time.'

Julian shook his head. 'Well I think that's the first time I've been upstaged by moggies. Come on, Rachel, enjoy yourself, its the season of goodwill and all that. It sounds as though you've had a trying week. It would do you good to release a few endomorphines.'

'I'd better buy myself a big box of chocs then.'

He laughed. 'Not exactly what I had in mind. I was thinking more on the lines of another bottle of plonk and some loud house music. We could go on to Weirdstones.'

For those who liked to make a night of it, Weirdstones had become the next port of call after the wine bar.

'That's the best offer I've had all day.' Rachel heard herself flirting before she knew it. 'But it's not really my scene, I'm afraid.' she added, hastily. 'I need to get home. I have to see to my cats. Perhaps you could drop me off on the way? I live quite close to the station.'

'Sure, I'll give you a lift.' He politely held out her jacket.

Rachel's flat formed part of a large converted house situated on a quiet side road.

'Any chance of a coffee?' asked Julian, opening the car door for her. Seeing a look of unease flit across her features he added, lightly, 'Trust me - I'm a law student.'

Caught in the crossfire between sexual chemistry and the opportunity to discover more about Julian's strange uncle proved too much even for Rachel's cautious disposition. She hesitated and then led the way to the front door.

'All right, you can come in for a coffee.'

'Seriously, you'll be quite safe, Rachel. And it's a bit early to pitch up at Weirdstones. Things don't get going much before eleven.'

He followed her down the wide hallway, waiting while she unlocked a second door which sported the number two in brass, together with a mail box to which had been taped a small card bearing her surname. As she switched on the lights two slinky grey cats materialised and proceeded to roll around the floor whilst she fussed them.

'They behave more like dogs than cats. Are they always so pleased to see you?'

Rachel nodded.

'Do you live on your own?'

'Sort of. Dad's away a lot. His work takes him overseas for long stretches.

'What does he do?'

'He's a civil engineer. He helps me out with the rent and stays here when he gets back. He and Mum were divorced about six years ago. My sister moved down to Swindon, because of her job. She's older than me. When Mum remarried I felt it was time to move out, so Dad found this place. He's coming to spend New Year with me.'

He glanced around quickly. 'Nice and peaceful - and lot more comfortable than the wine bar.'

'Let me take your coat.'

'Don't you get lonely?'

'Not at all.' said Rachel, firmly. 'Sit down, while I see to things. You can choose some music - if you can find anything you like. It's all on that shelf by the fireplace. I'll be back with the coffee in a few minutes.'

Interested to discover more about its occupant, Julian wandered around the room, realising at a glance that Rachel had done the best that she could on a shoestring budget. The old sofa had been given a facelift by the addition of a cotton throw and some cheerful cushions. A couple of modern chairs and a low table completed the furniture. Against one wall, surrounded by pine shelving which sagged in the middle, due to the weight of books it supported, an ex-school desk accommodated a long outmoded computer with a tiny screen. The remaining walls were hung with a collection of museum and gallery posters advertising Manchester and London exhibitions long gone. A large, brightly coloured rag rug covered the pine floorboards between the settee and the fireplace, where a battered pair of Staffordshire dogs stood guard, one at each end of the mantelpiece. Between them a small porcelain clock and a silver framed photograph of Rachel with an older man, whom he presumed to be her father, jostled for space amongst wooden candlesticks, overflowing letter rack and two greetings cards. Plants trailed, climbed and cascaded around the room and he had to set one vast specimen aside in order to inspect Rachel's collection of cassettes. A lot were classical - his hostess appeared to favour string quartets. Mixed amongst them he found a wide ranging selection of mainstream blues, soul and some classic rock albums. Julian paused, undecided. Suddenly realising that he had been set a difficult task he found himself strangely anxious to make the correct choice. After some deliberation he settled hopefully for The Best of Eric Clapton, not too loud. After a couple of tracks Rachel came back into the room, accompanied by both cats. She passed his coffee and sat on the chair opposite and they talked, easy and spontaneous so that they lost track of the time.

'We could leave the car and walk round to the club.' he said later.

'Sorry, I've had enough socialising for one evening. You go.' He shook his head. 'Not on my own. I prefer to stay and talk to you.'

'How are things at home?' asked Rachel. 'I mean, how's your mother? Has she got over the funeral?'

Julian frowned. 'I think so. She doesn't say much, but she seems to spend a lot of time looking out of windows. Mind you, she always did. Too much time on her hands.'

'There was no foul play suspected, then?'

Julian gave her a look which bordered on the derisive, causing Rachel to wonder if she was pushing her luck.

'Don't start letting your journalist's imagination run away with you. He drove himself to Newgate. There were no other fingerprints on the car, except for Mrs Jackson's, which is not surprising, since it was her car he took. Uncle Vinney didn't have his own transport. He gave up driving years ago, when they finally managed to persuade him that he was a menace to other road users and placed a chauffeur driven limousine at his disposal.'

'Maybe he was going to meet someone?'

'At four in the morning? On Lindow Moss? I should say that was highly unlikely.'

'Why would he go wandering out to the moss in the middle of the night.?'

Julian shook his head. 'I wish I'd got a fiver for every time I've been asked that over the past few weeks. He was a strange man. Simon and I never got to know him. I think he just got some bee in his bonnet, went chasing off down Newgate and lost his way. Have you ever been to Lindow Moss? It was a filthy night and pitch dark. He must have stumbled into one of the excavations. You can drown in a few inches of water, you know. It was an accident.'

'It was Halloween' said Rachel.

'And the wicked witch got him? I think not. Anyway, you're wrong. It was the first of November. Mrs Jackson told the police that he went to bed around eleven the previous night. She never heard him get up again. Her son was home for half term and he went to the bathroom just after two o'clock. He said her car was still parked on the drive. He saw it from the window on the landing when he put the light on. It's all in the police statements. Dad's seen them. Now, can we please change the subject?' He patted the sofa. 'Come and sit next to me.'

7
Saturday

Unsettled by the unexpected events of the previous evening, Rachel slept badly and awakened far too early for a Saturday. Finding it impossible to go back to sleep she drew back the curtains to reveal a chilly December morning. As the sun began to rise white rimes of frost glinted from roofing tiles and pavements. Over breakfast, she studied a large scale Ordnance Survey map of the area and plotted the shortest route to Lindow Moss, which proved to be much nearer than she had realised. By way of the back roads and lanes, thus avoiding the town centre, it was no more than three or four miles distant. That was, she decided, still too far to walk, because there and back would take up much of the day.

She dressed quickly and went out to the communal shed at the back of the house. With difficulty she eventually managed to extricate her old bicycle, which had lain forgotten and abandoned, from the lawn mowers, ladders, garden tools and general clutter which had accumulated around it. Wheeling it round to the front of the house, she pumped air into the tyres and wiped clean the dusty seat before returning indoors for the map. She tucked her leggings inside her stoutest boots, covered her head with an unflattering but sensible woollen hat, and pulled on a pair of gloves. Then she pedalled out into Brooke Lane, freewheeling downhill in a fast and exhilarating north westerly direction. Cold air stabbed spitefully into her nostrils and at Brookfield Bridge she stopped to watch the early golfers, who were already wheeling their paraphernalia of clubs and irons down from some distant bunker. She checked the map. Next left. Gravel Lane to Nursery Lane. She traced the route cutting through the suburban streets and lanes towards the edge of the common. Somewhere along here should be the left hand turn in to Newgate. These names had suddenly taken on an exotic and slightly macabre aspect and she cycled towards them with the rising expectation usually reserved for imminent arrival at some famous landmark, part known but never seen. She passed a signpost for Lindow End and stopped to buy a carton of juice at a little corner shop. She found Julian intruding into her thoughts whilst she was drinking it through a bendy straw. She glanced at her watch. Almost eleven o'clock. Twelve hours since he'd taken her phone number and she'd waved him off. She was still busy thinking about him when she reached the next turn and had to brake to a wobbling halt in the gutter.

This narrow country lane led ultimately to the council tip, after which it quickly petered out into an ancient bridleway, disappearing into a gloomy and neglected tangle of undergrowth and struggling birch trees. Rachel dismounted and began to push the bike down the rutted track. There was something faintly creepy about this gloomy corridor, overhung with leafless birches and hemmed by deep ditches. It continued straight and unswerving, towards a perfect circle formed by the trees whose interlocking branches heralded the entrance to the moss.

Rachel's mood for adventure was diminishing with every step. The air grew steadily colder and she found herself wishing that she had not come to the moss by herself. From a distant rooftop came the faint sounds of cooing doves. Something moved in the undergrowth and she spotted a reddish brown wren, flitting mouselike amongst the lower branches. Disturbed, its panicky, typewriter chatter of alarm pierced the tension. She pressed on, finally passing beneath the leafless arch onto the edges of Lindow Moss. Before her stretched a vast, tormented landscape, desecrated by the diggers. The total absence of green came as a shock.

Abandoning the bike against a spindly birch tree she stood quite still, listening. No bird song, no suggestion of life. Nothing moved. Silence without stillness. It was an awful place. Deep pools of dark brown bog water had collected in menacing cauldrons and around the edges white heads of cotton grass shivered in the wind, framing the velvety brown bull rushes rearing skywards. She shivered and forced herself forward into the black, disturbed landscape. Freshly dug peat had been heaped high, left to dry out alongside the trenches from whence it had been extracted, creating geometric black rows which ran over the moss to some distant vanishing point. Bitter gusts made her eyes water as she walked forward into the wind.

She followed the bogey tracks, narrow gauge metal rails which had been laid over the surface of the ground. Now she could hear the sound of water again, cascading in fast, foaming torrents down into the trenches. The ground was littered with huge stumps and the recently unearthed roots of ancient trees. Centuries buried within the moss had imbued them with the handsome colour and sheen of over ripe plums and they lay, dead and distorted, silhouetted against the skyline. She walked on, wondering if there was such a thing as a truly evil place. This one certainly leached bad vibrations. Her eyes travelled over the surface of the ravaged terrain and she found herself forcing back a rising disquiet. Suddenly there came a distant rumble which grew steadily louder. She looked up, shielding her eyes against the light, as the plane came into view, high, ethereal sunlight silvering the wing tips as it banked steeply, gathering height. Lindow Moss lay beneath the flight path.

After it had vanished she watched the lingering vapour trails, until they, too, finally dispersed and the silence seemed even more immense. As she moved deeper into the moss the surface grew iron hard. Peppered with grey dapples of frost the peat was unyielding, no longer springy underfoot. Rachel slithered on thin sheets of black ice, which covered the track in treacherous patches of deceit. She stopped, half afraid to go any further, and surveyed the hostile panorama with a growing sense of unease. Reaching a point where the bogey tracks changed direction, she turned east and made her way towards a wide track of compressed peat. Caterpillar tyres had made solid ripples, leaving the impression of a beach at low tide and the walking became easier. Suddenly she came to a metal bridge, a small portable thing, little more than a ramp, which had been laid across one of the main ditches. Beyond, a few yards distant, a massive, bright yellow digger dominated the skyline. She was just about to walk towards it when the cab door opened and someone shouted to her. The man jumped down and began to walk quickly towards her. As he drew nearer she could see that he was carrying a baseball bat. Rachel remained completely still, waiting, and he slackened his pace, stopping on the opposite side of the metal ramp. He stared across the culvert, weighing her up suspiciously.

She looked back at him coolly, placing him in his early thirties. Short and stocky, with a weather beaten face, he was dressed in workman's clothes - a worn checked shirt, donkey jacket with panels of fluorescent orange and a woollen hat not dissimilar to her own. His muddy steel capped boots began to clump across the bridge and she stepped back as he jumped down on to the trackway.

'Good morning.' said Rachel, trying to sound confident.

'Sorry - thought you were a lad. We've 'ad trouble before. Tea leaves. They come messing around the vehicles, seeing what they can pinch. If they don't find nowt they damage the equipment instead. Addicts usually, on the lookout for something they can sell on.'

He paused, staring quizzically. 'So what brings you here? I can see yer not dog walkin'. Just come for a nosy? Not expecting to find anyone around on a Saturday?'

Rachel forced a smile. 'Do you work here?'

He nodded. 'Doyle. Barry Doyle. I drive that digger over there.'
Detecting a trace of pride, Rachel tried to look suitably impressed.

'Gosh - I'd be terrified. It must take some nerve to be in charge of a great earth mover like that.'

'Not when yer've been given the right training.'

She held out a gloved hand, which was ignored. 'I'm Rachel Mackenna.'

'You a reporter?'

'That's very clever of you, Mr Doyle. Yes, I work for the Gazette. I wanted to take a look around. How did you know that?'

Doyle laughed. 'Well now, you don't look like somebody from the police and I can't think of anyone else as'd be wanting ter wander round this god forsaken dump on a Sat'day morning.'

'Well, I hope you don't mind. I wasn't expecting anyone to be working today. I'm just trying to find out a bit more about the Rush death. Some background material. I'm glad I've found someone here to talk to. Do you happen to know who found him?'

Barry Doyle nodded. 'Yer looking at 'im. Look, I can't 'ang about 'ere chopsin'. Am knocking' off now. I've finished for the day. Taking' me lads ter the match this afternoon. Am going' back ter the sheds to get me things. It's bloody freezing out 'ere.'

'Would it be all right if I walked back with you?' asked Rachel.

'Suit yer self.'

'Will you tell me about it?'

He looked away from her and they trudged along in silence for a while before he spoke.

'Not much to tell. Knew something were up right after I'd clocked on. I'm usually the first to arrive and I'd seen the car at top of the track - yer do get courting couples down 'ere, but they don't stay till that time in the mornin'. Wasn't parked proper,

83

just skewed across top of track, like, with the driver's door 'anging wide open. So I went up to look, thinkin' as 'ow there might be somebody inside. There wasn't, of course, but keys were still in and the lights 'ad bin left on. Battery were nearly flat by then. So I comes back on ter moss and set off over ter the digger. I was nearly there when I spotted the body - it were lyin' face down in that pit.'

'That one over there?' asked Rachel, following his gaze.

He nodded.

'It's a long way in to the moss. How far, do you reckon?'

'Well over a mile from the track. There's not a man 'ere as'd go wanderin' round this place in the dark. An' we all know it like the backs of us 'ands.'

'What did you do?'

'Well, I knew straight off that 'e were dead. There was nothin' I could do for 'im, like, so I went back ter the office and told me boss. He called the police and then we waited.'

He unlocked the office door.

'They all turned up, police surgeon, ambulance chaps. Taped whole area off and spent rest of the day crawling all over the show. Later on their photographer bloke came. Then we all 'ad to go to the office to give statements. Didn't get much work done for a couple of days. We've 'ad a few reporters nosin' round. Course, 'e were a big noise weren't 'e? Read about 'im in your paper. It all came out at that inquest. They read out my statement.' he ended, importantly.

'It's a strange place, this. I'm glad I saw you.'

'Stranger than you think.' said Barry Doyle. 'Still, yer get used to it. D'you work with Loony Lyd?'

Rachel stared at him. 'Who?'

'The daft old bat. That Pendle woman.'

'Oh, I know who you mean. No, she retired a long time ago - she's well into her seventies now. Do you know her?'

Barry Doyle gave an odd sort of laugh.

'She frightened the crap out of me once, when I were a bit of a kid. Didn't walk down her end of Chapel Lane for months. What's 'appened to her then? Still livin' in that creepy cottage?' Rachel shook her head. 'She's in a nursing home. Went there about six months ago. As a matter of fact, I might be going to visit her soon. They usually send her something for Christmas - from the paper, you know. I'll tell her you were asking after her.'

'Shouldn't bother.' said Barry Doyle. 'Only met her the once. It were a long time ago - like I said, I was just a kid. She'll not remember me.'

When she got back Julian's car parked in the road outside her flat. Hot and sticky from peddling uphill, it was with mixed feelings that she realised he was sitting inside in the driver's seat. Not wishing to be seen at less than her best, she pulled the woolly hat down so that it half obscured her face, lowered her head and prepared to pedal on by, but the ruse failed. He had obviously recognised her through the driver's mirror and as she drew alongside he was already winding down the window.

'Hi there! Where have you been?'

Rachel braked to a halt and wiped her nose on the back of her glove, already reproaching herself for not taking the time to wash her hair before embarking on the expedition.

'Hello - I wasn't expecting to see you here. Shopping for food.' she said, pointing to the plastic bags dangling from the handles of the bike.'

'You look the picture of health - positively glowing. I've been trying to ring you all morning. Can I come in? I want to ask a favour. I think you might be able to help me. Let me carry those for you.' he added, grabbing the bags before she had time to reply. Rachel unpacked the food and went to tidy herself. When she came back he was in the kitchen making coffee. 'Here, warm you up. Didn't think you'd mind. What are you doing tomorrow, Rachel?'

'What I always do on Sundays. Laze around and curl up with the papers. Why?'

'Do you know much about computers?'

'A bit.' said Rachel, modestly.

'Apple Mac?'

She nodded.

'Good. I thought that's what you'd use at work.'

Rachel looked puzzled. 'Why?'

'The old man's trying to sort out my uncle's affairs. Everything seems to have been left in a fearful mess. Pa says the study is a nightmare. He's asked me to go round to Uncle Vinney's place in the morning, to check out the computer. He doesn't like the things, never had much to do with them - a bad case of technophobia. Leaves it all to his staff. The thing is,' he explained, 'I've not had much to do with Macs so I was trying to think of someone who might be able to help. I was wondering if you'd come with me, since you know your way around the system?'

'Well - I suppose I could.' Rachel tried not to sound too enthusiastic. 'But I don't think your parents would be very happy about some stranger poking into Dr Rush's private affairs.'

'On the contrary. Father told me to get it dealt. He'll pay you well for your time.'

'He will not.' said Rachel indignantly. 'If I help you, it will be because I want to. I don't want any payment. Why don't you ask Frank Newbolt or one of his other colleagues?'

Julian shook his head. 'That's exactly what they don't want. They prefer to get someone who doesn't have any connections with FINGERS. Anyway, they see Frank and Elizabeth socially. It's more discreet this way.'

Rachel laughed. 'Julian, how can you say that! You know where I work.'

'Yes, but they don't. I didn't tell them. Nor must you.'

'I'm hardly likely to bump into them.' she said, beginning to feed the cats.

'Oh, that's the other thing I forgot to mention. You're invited to Sunday lunch afterwards. At home. Say you'll come.'

He followed her through to the living room. 'Will you do it?'

Rachel sat down. 'What exactly have you told them about me?'

'Nothing much.' he said, sheepishly. 'Actually, I just told Mum about you - that I'd met someone I really liked and that you knew about computers. It was her idea that I brought you back for lunch. She get's pretty lonely. Simon's going to Chester to visit his fiancée's parents. I doubt that Father will around. He'll probably be at the golf club. That's where he usually spends Sundays. Are you cross?'

Rachel shook her head. 'No - how can I be cross with you? It's just - well, a bit quick. We hardly know each other. And what am I supposed to say if she asks where I work? I'm not prepared to lie about it.'

Julian shrugged. 'She won't ask. If she does, just say that you're doing media studies - she won't have a clue what you're talking about and she'll change the subject. Tell her you're interested in art and the theatre.'

'I am.' said Rachel.

'There you are, then. No lies and nothing to worry about.'

'All right.' She looked at the clock on the mantelpiece. 'Now, I do have some things to get on with - like my lunch.'

He stood up. 'Are you chucking me out?'

'Yes.'

'Fancy going to the cinema tonight?'

'No. You can't take over my entire weekend.'

'You're a hard woman, Rachel Mackenna. Shall I call for you around half past nine?'

'Julian, it's Sunday. Make it ten.'

'Do I get a kiss?'

'Don't push your luck.' she said, and then relented.

8
Sunday morning

Rachel turned to look back as they waited on the steps. Huge rhododendrons and azaleas formed thick hedges along the drive, so tall that she guessed they must have been planted in Victorian times. Beyond, large Corsican pines rose majestically from the gently sloping lawns. There was something reassuring about the place. The hall and grounds exuded an air of permanence. Something solid and indestructible, so comfortably settled that it had long since become a part of the surrounding landscape. As she watched, a trio of grey squirrels chased across the drive, up onto the high stone wall and into the trees beyond. Julian rapped the knocker again.

'Mrs Jackson is expecting us?'

He nodded. 'Yes, it's all arranged. Mum rang to see if it was convenient. I think she's coming now. I can hear footsteps.'

The door was opened by a new Susan Jackson, who had adorned her face and looked ten years younger. Gone was the middle aged drudge, apologetic and downtrodden, replaced by a self assured woman with high and hitherto unsuspected cheekbones, who stood upright, shoulders back, and appeared taller. The drab, lank hair had been lifted by fine blonde highlights and sharply restyled into a shining bob which danced as she moved. A thick fringe framed large blue eyes enhanced by grey blue smudges of colour along the eyelids and mascara thickened eyelashes. Pink lipstick, a shirt of creamy silk, well cut grey jacket and matching trousers completed the transformation. Even Rachel, who had only seen her once, had difficulty in concealing her surprise.

'Good morning Julian. Do come in.'

'Hello, Mrs Jackson. This is Rachel, a friend of mine. She knows a lot more about computers than I do. She's volunteered to help.'

Susan Jackson led them through the hall and dining room and down the passageway towards the back of the house. Pausing before the study door she turned to face Julian. 'I expect your father warned you about the state of the study. He asked me leave it as it was, so nothing has been touched.' She opened the door and ushered them inside. 'I'm afraid it's rather chilly. I opened the window this morning, just to freshen the room. It smelt so stale. I'll close it now that you're here.' She paused in the doorway. 'I've made a big pot of coffee, Julian. I'll just bring it through, then I'll leave you to get on.'

'I can't believe that's the same woman.' whispered Rachel, once the housekeeper was out of earshot.

'Just shows what you can achieve with a bit of time and some money well spent. It's good to see her making an effort to improve herself. Good luck to her. She's had a dog's life, from what Mum's told me. Did you know everything has been left in trust for her son?'

'I had heard rumours.' said Rachel. 'Not really any of my business.'

'Mum expected him to leave it all to Simon and me. Apart from her, we're his only blood relatives.'

'Aren't you angry?'

Julian shook his head. 'No. Simon's disappointed, but what's the point? You might as well be philosophical about it. I've seen what's happened to friends of mine who came into serious money when they were too young to deal with it. You soon begin to realise that it can cause more harm than good. It would certainly have changed things for us, but not necessarily for the better. Too many choices would have been taken away. I think it might have stopped me from trying so hard, if there was no need to strive. At least I'll always know that I've made my own way in the world - whatever that might be.'

She glanced at him. 'It really is a beautiful place, though.'

Julian looked round the study. 'You wouldn't think so from in here. Did you ever see such a mess. This room just about sums him up.' He crossed over to the desk and switched on the computer. There was an internal clunk, followed by the start-up sound. They listened in silence to the repetitive clicks as the system began to load and a moment later they were staring at a screen filled with a fluffy blue desktop and two icons - one for the wastebasket, which was empty, and one for the hard disk. All very neat and tidy.

He shook his head slowly. 'I mean, the incongruity of it. This fantastic piece of hardware that most people would kill for, stuck in the midst of all this filthy clutter and chaos. If you want to know about him, look no further. This room *is* Uncle Vinney.'

Rachel sat at the desk, opened up the hard disk and scrolled through the contents, checking each folder carefully. In addition to the standard system software which she had expected, the Applications folder contained two programmes which were unfamiliar. She loaded the first, a sophisticated spreadsheet and database with complex comparison tables. 'Julian, just check if there are any manuals on that book shelf. I don't recognise either of these. One seems to be designed for working with negatives, but there's nothing stored.'

'That will be for his DNA tables. There's nothing here. He probably helped himself to copies of FINGERS own software. It will have been written specifically for them. What we're doing now is probably industrial espionage.'

Rachel laughed. 'It might be if I could make head or tail of it. As it is, I think their secrets are quite safe.'

'Try the floppies.' suggested Julian, removing a small grey storage box from one of the desk drawers. He began to flip through the batch. There were around thirty standard diskettes, each labelled in Vincent Rush's illegible, spidery scrawl, some dating from the 1980s. Rachel glanced through and handed most of them back.

'These are no use. They're defunct - from an earlier system. If I try to open them on this machine it might delete anything stored on them. Find the more recent ones. He may have copied the earlier stuff across.'

Julian sorted through them carefully, setting aside the newer ones. There were only six. Rachel worked through, loading and checking each one. She shook her head, baffled.

'What is it?'

'There's nothing on them. They're all empty.'

'They can't be.' said Julian. 'Look, they've all been labelled. That's Uncle Vinney's writing - it's quite unmistakable. Not that it means anything to me, it's some sort of formula or coding.'

Rachel nodded. 'Yes, look here, the same codes come up on the icons when they're installed. He must have used them, otherwise it would just say 'Untitled'.'

'So why can't we read them?'

'Because they've been wiped.' said Rachel. All the data has either been erased, or dragged off the disks into the trash bin. I can't access any of it - not this morning, anyway.'

'How do you mean?'

'Well, there is a way of recovering the lost files. I might be able to borrow a retrieval programme. It checks through the computer's memory and can usually restore data that has recently been deleted. Even if the files aren't retrievable it searches the directory and produces a list of them. It also gives their size and the date on which they were last opened.'

'And the time?'

'I'm not sure. Maybe. Why?'

'Because if Uncle Vinney did it that night - before he went to the moss - well, the implications are obvious, aren't they?'

Rachel suppressed a sudden shiver. 'Perhaps it's better not to meddle. I mean, do you really want to know? It still wouldn't prove anything, and you might feel obliged to mention it. That's not something you'd want to come out. Is it?'

Julian shook his head. 'No. For Mum's sake. That aside, I'd still like you to try. I'm intrigued. I want to find out what he was up to.'

'What will you tell your father?'

'The truth - that we need some special software.' He looked at his watch. 'Oh dear, why do computers always make one lose track of time? I hadn't realised we'd been here so long. We'd better get going or Mum will be complaining that I've ruined her lunch.'

9
Looking Back

After they had taken their leave, Susan Jackson returned to the study to collect the coffee tray. Suddenly changing her mind as she reached the door, she retraced her steps and, setting the tray down again, moved some books and documents off a chair and positioned it before the desk. She sat down and for the first time ever leant back with her legs stretched right out, crossing them at the ankles in a way which made her feel deliciously insolent. Her eyes wandered around the forbidden room. Everything, apart from the now empty seat facing her from the opposite side of the the desk, was exactly the same as the first time that she and Brian had been summoned there. And the big computer. That was almost new.

She stared at the cables poking out from its rear end, remembering that day when she had hurried home at the end of her shift, bathed and washed her hair and then spent another hour trying to decide what to wear. Rummaging through her meagre wardrobe with growing discontent, most of the clothes had ended up rejected on the bed. Standing in front of the wardrobe mirror, surveying the hemline of that black skirt with a distinct lack of confidence, asking Brian if he thought she looked all right. He'd said yes, she looked fine, without bothering to turn round. It would just have to do, she said, tucking a frilly pink blouse inside the waistband. Then she had checked the shoulders of her checked jacket for stray hairs and wished her reflection good luck. Fourteen long years ago.

After all the rushing they had got there far too early. Brian parked the borrowed van up on the verge alongside the entrance to Medlar Hall, drumming against the curve of the steering wheel with the tips of his fingers.

'You look great, Susan. Calm down.'

'It's the waiting. I hate this waiting, I can't stand it. I want to get it over with.'

She scrutinised him carefully, trying to see him through the eyes of a prospective employer. He had agreed to have his hair cut and was now looking reasonably presentable in his brother's tie and jacket. Beyond the windscreen the lights of Medlar Hall twinkled across the field, below tall gables now silhouetted against the evening sky.

'What a pad!' Brian whistled, enviously. 'I never thought we'd get the chance to end up in a place like this.'

Susan picked at a finger nail. 'Don't count your chickens.' she warned primly and then, turning to him excitedly, 'Oh Brian, I do hope we get it. It would be the answer to all our problems. Look, have another of these.'

She popped a mint into his mouth and he grimaced.

'Go on - suck it slowly. I don't want him to smell beer.'

His dark brows knitted in irritation.

'Don't you start all that again. Do you know something? I can't stand women who hen peck. You're turning into a real nag, Sue.'

'No I'm not.' she replied, patiently. 'Why can't you understand? I just want to be sure that everything's right. That's the reason. Don't go spoiling it Brian, please. We'll never get another chance like this.'

Gazing across at Medlar Hall, she took hold of his hand. 'Do you really think we would be able to run a place like that? Just look at the size of it! It's terrifying. Mrs Whitehead said we would have to be responsible for everything. She told Mum that her brother has let everything get in a very bad way.'

Brian lit another cigarette.

'We'll just play it by ear, Sue. Like I told you, as long as we sound confident. The main thing is to get in here. We can start

to panic about it once we've got our feet under the table.'
Susan checked her watch.

'Oh, God, it's five to - I'm really nervous now. We'd better go and get it over.'

She crossed her fingers as Brian turned the old van into the drive way.

'Which door?'

'Not the front, that wouldn't be right. Mum said there's one round the side of the house.' She reached over and straightened his tie. He slicked a comb through his hair and kissed her.

'What's that for?'

She took a small mirror from her bag and applied more lipstick.

'For luck.' said Brian, climbing out of the van.

The door was opened by Dr Rush himself and they followed him in silence down the long, dark passage. He ushered them into a small, book lined room and motioned them to sit in the two chairs positioned before a large old desk. He took his place behind the desk and stared searchingly from one to the other, toying with the rim of his spectacles whilst they watched him, uncomfortably.

He cleared his throat. 'Right, Mr and Mrs Jackson - Brian and Susan, isn't it?'

They nodded in unison.

'Well, as you already know, my sister has suggested that you may be suitable for my requirements. I'm looking for a married couple to live in and run the house. Barbara - Mrs Whitehead, has explained your circumstances. I gather you need a decision rather urgently?'

Brian nodded again, whilst Susan sat rigidly on the edge of the chair, clutching her handbag. Rush was watching her intently. She was well built, fresh faced beneath the makeup. Aware of his silent appraisal, she fingered a tiny gold medallion around her neck. Quiet and respectable, thought Rush. He turned his attention to the husband. Small and stocky, with a swarthy complexion and darting brown eyes beneath heavy brows. Black hair worn a shade too long and despite his recent shave the dark shadow of beard was already beginning to show. He was off rougher stock than the girl and Rush, sensing a roosting potential for belligerence behind the cock-sure facade, did not like him.

He cleared his throat. 'First of all I will explain my requirements, then you will both know exactly what the job entails. You, Susan,' - here he paused and treated her to a rare smile, 'you would be responsible for all cleaning, shopping and some cooking, although I generally eat out. There is also the laundry. You would be in charge of the day to day running of the house, and it is a very large place, I warn you. Do you think you could cope with all that?'

He noted the skin stretching over her knuckles as her grip tightened on the handbag and when she spoke the voice was so quiet that he was forced to lean slightly forward to hear.

'I should think so, Dr Rush, once I'd - sort of got into the swing of it all.'

'Well,' he spoke quickly, coming to her rescue, 'if you're even half as efficient as your mother, Susan, I would be well pleased with you. My sister has spoken very highly of Lillian. You, Brian, would be in complete charge of the gardens, plus all outdoor maintenance, minor repairs, ensuring that the central heating boiler is serviced, that type of thing. How do you feel about that?'

Brian leant forward, eagerly. 'I can turn my hands to most things, sir. I'm really quite handy, aren't I, Susan?' He grinned pleasantly. 'Jack of all trades, that's me.'

'And you hold a clean driving license? I was thinking we could get some form of transport for you. I don't drive, myself, I would have to leave it to you to organise something suitable. Now, are there any questions you would like to ask?'

Neither of them spoke.

'Right. I do have one or two further queries. They are of a rather more personal nature, I'm afraid. As you can appreciate, if you are going to be living under my roof, I need to know a little more. How old are you, Susan?'

'I'll be thirty two in January, Dr Rush.'

'And how long have you been married?'

'Six years.'

'Are you both in good health? No problems of which I should be aware?'

The couple shook their heads vigorously. Rush rubbed his hands together, pleased with the way the interview was proceeding.

'Excellent. One more important question, and I expect you to answer honestly. Do you intend to start a family?'

There was a heavy silence, eventually broken by Brian.'There's no need for you to worry on that score, sir.'

'The thing is, Dr Rush, we can't.' Susan was horribly embarrassed. 'I mean, not very easily. We've had tests done and - well, you know.' she finished lamely, scarlet faced.

Nodding sympathetically, Rush decided that it was now safe to step out of line.

'Forgive me for asking, my dear, I did not intend to be impertinent. Now, one final matter. I require blood tests for both of you. It may sound rather a strange request, but, as you may know, I am involved in medical research. We do have to be extremely careful.'

The pair of them sat in silence. He looked from one to the other. 'I take it you have no objections? It really is nothing to be worried about.'

'We'll go to the doctor tomorrow.' said Susan, obligingly.

Opening one of the desk drawers, he smiled at her warmly.

'No need for that, Susan. I can run the tests myself.'

He placed a couple of disposable syringes on the desk top and stood up. 'If you could just roll up the sleeve of your jacket, my dear - no, maybe you'd better take your jacket off. There, that's better. It will only take a moment, nothing to get alarmed about.'

Susan obediently held out her arm whilst her searched for a vein and deftly inserted the needle. She watched, half sickened, half fascinated, as he drew off the puddle of blood. He handed her a small square of lint.

'There we are, just hold that in place for a minute or two.'

He turned to the husband, who had grown slightly pale. Susan held her breath, silently praying that Brian would not make a fuss, not refuse to comply with the request.

'Now, which arm is it to be?'

Brian shrugged and rolled up one of his shirt sleeves.

Rush carefully labelled the samples and dropped them into the desk drawer.

'There we are, all done. I'll have these checked out tomorrow and give you my decision before the end of the week. I know you are both very anxious to know.'

'Dr Rush, I was just wondering -'

'Yes Susan?' he interrupted, rather sharply.

'I was just wondering if we could perhaps take a look at our - I mean, see where we would be living. If we got the job, I mean.'

Rush looked surprised. 'Oh, yes, I see. Of course, how very remiss of me. In fact, I really ought to show you over the house. Come along.'

The enormous lounge was obviously little used. An attractive room, with large French windows opening out onto the garden. High beyond the intricate but extremely grubby chandelier she could just make out the rails of a small galleried landing in the gloom.

'Far too dark to see much outside.' he apologised. 'Still, that will be your department, Brian. I can see Susan is keen to look over the house.'

He led them to the dining room, which sported a vast,

chilly looking marble fireplace and a large dining table, thick with dust. Susan followed him down the long passage into the kitchen of her dreams.

'Oh, this is fabulous!' she exclaimed, forgetting her shyness as she gaped at the long run of units, track lit breakfast bar and the expensive Italian tiles. Tearing herself away reluctantly, she followed the men into the hall, where a wide and imposing staircase led to the gallery and the first floor.

'Now, I only ever use this end of the house. If you would like to go along that corridor it leads to the other wing. There are three good sized rooms and a bathroom, so, apart from the kitchen, you would be virtually self-contained. There is even a separate entrance, through the old stable block.'

Afterwards, he accompanied them back to the van.

'I will let you have my decision very quickly.' he promised. 'I'll contact you via my sister.' He held out his hand.

'How do you think it went?' asked Brian, as soon as they pulled out of the drive.

'All right. I think he's an odd sort. Horrible clammy hands.'

'Probably a bit cracked.' said Brian. 'They're all supposed to be weird, these scientist types. What a house, though! I can put up with him if it means living there.'

'I wonder what he wanted blood tests for? I've never heard of that before.'

Brian was already turning the van into a pub car park.

'Probably checking for that new plague that's started in America. They're all panicking about it. It was in the paper. Called aids or something like that. Don't worry about that, Sue. He can have a whole pint from me if it puts a roof like that over my head. Maybe he wants to see if there's any blood in my alcohol stream.'

He locked up the van. Susan giggled.

'Gosh, I do hope we get it. Imagine living in a house like that.

And fancy buying a car for you, Brian! I can hardly believe it. He must be very wealthy. Brian?'

She was hesitating, lingering in the doorway of the pub.

Brian turned back, impatiently. 'Come on, I've got a terrible thirst on. What is it? What's the matter now?'

'Brian, do you think there's a catch?'

'Catch?' repeated Brian, puzzled. 'What do you mean, catch? How could there be a catch? We've just dropped right for once, that's all. He needs a couple of nursemaids and we're available. It's a case of being in the right place at the right time. It's as simple as that. Why do you always have to look on the black side? Just thank your lucky stars.'

'I suppose so.' Susan followed him to the bar. 'It's just that - well, it just all seems too good to be true.'

But Brian was no longer listening. Relieved that the ordeal was over, he was more concerned with attracting the attention of the barmaid. When he finally caught her eye, he ordered doubles. As he told the barmaid in loud tones, it was high time he had something to celebrate.

Blood samples screened to Rush's satisfaction, the Jacksons had moved in to their quarters at Medlar Hall on a damp and misty Thursday towards the end of September. Delighted to be finally freed of any responsibility, Brian Jackson had walked out of their house without one backward glance. Susan paused to linger, shedding a predictable tear as she glanced round the now empty little room that had become the ashes of her dreams. At this point Brian returned and hustled her out to the van.

'Come on, better than that, Sue. You can't really be sorry to leave this box. It's just an old dump compared to what we're going to.'

'You don't understand.' she sniffed. 'You really don't understand, do you? This was my home. It was ours - or it would have been, eventually.'

He slammed the van door and started up the engine.

'Yeh - in another twenty-odd years. Let's get it right, Sue. It was a ruddy great ball and chain, that's all that place was. Having to stay in every night so we could keep up the payments. Look ahead, not back. Think where we're going to live now!'

Sticking his nose in the air in mock grandeur, he announced 'Mr and Mrs Jackson of Medlar Hall, at your service.'

His exaggeration of Dr Rush's well bred tones raised a faint smile and she made a great effort and stopped herself from looking back as they turned out of the avenue.

Vincent Rush had allowed them a couple of day's grace to settle in. Their shabby bits of furniture, which had taken just two trips in the van to transport, looked lost and extremely threadbare in the large, high ceilinged room which they had chosen as their new sitting room. On Saturday afternoon, Brian went off to get Lillian Bayliss, and Susan took her mother on a guided tour of the house. Lillian shook her head in dismay as they made their way from room to room. 'I can't get over the state of the place, Susan. I had no idea it was this bad. No one's touched it for years. You've got an awful lot of work here.'

She ran a hand down the banister rail, grimacing in mock horror at the grey layer of grime which transferred to her fingers. 'You'll just have to work your way slowly through, tackling one room at a time. I should warn Dr Rush that it will take quite a long time to get the place back in order.'

By this time she was inspecting the furniture with a keen eye, noting the good mahogany dining table and chairs and the ornately carved sideboard.

'Well, there's nothing here to compare with Mrs Whitehead's collection, but he has got one or two fine Victorian pieces.'

'I don't know how you can tell the difference, Mum.' said Susan, impressed.

Lillian stroked the sideboard, leaving a finger trail in the dust. 'You get to understand them, after caring for them week by week. I find myself wondering about the men who made them. Craftsmen, they were - real craftsmen. Now you just listen to what I'm telling you, Susan. This sideboard will come up a treat, but first you must wipe it down with a vinegar solution. Work fast, until you've removed this old finish. Just look how it's preventing that lovely grain from showing through.' She ran a finger nail against the surface. 'Somebody has used a modern spray on this!' she exclaimed indignantly. 'Beeswax, Susan. Always beeswax, then you can start to build up a good patina. Same with that long case clock out in the hall. The timber's starved. It's crying out for beeswax, poor thing. And as for that chandelier, it's an absolute disgrace. Just look at the poor thing, yellow with smoke and covered in fly muck, when it should be twinkling like a rainbow. That's a day's work in itself. It'll be worth the trouble, though, you'll see. And as to the state of those brasses, oh dear! You must see those are kept up properly, you know.'

Lillian raced through the house, bombarding her daughter with torrents of advice until Susan began to despair.
'I'll never cope with it.' she wailed. 'I can't manage all this.'
'Don't be so silly.' rebuked her mother. 'Of course you will. Little by little, just take your time about it. It's a wonderful challenge, a fine place like this. You must start to care for it, make it beautiful again. You'll find it a sight more rewarding than sitting at a checkout till all day. Now, do I have to get that cup of tea myself?'
She followed Susan to the kitchen. ''Well, well! Now, this really is something! I remember Mrs Whitehead telling me all about it, when Mrs Rush was having the plans drawn. She was very envious at the time. Mind you, she's planning to have her's refitted soon, and there'll be no half measures there, you can be sure of that.' She paused to light a cigarette. 'Well love, I hope you'll be very happy here. You're a very lucky girl, you know.' She opened a bag and produced a small parcel, neatly gift

wrapped. 'A little house warming present.'

'Oh. Mum! You shouldn't have.'

Susan tore open the wrappings. Inside was a small basket of dried flower heads, impregnated with perfumed oil. Tied to the handle by a narrow blue ribbon was a tiny Corn Dolly. Susan stared down at the gift.

'To bring you good fortune in your new home, Susan. You're a good girl and I do want things to work out for you here. The Corn Dolly is a lucky mascot. I just hope -' she stopped.

'What? What were you going to say, Mum?'

'Nothing.' said Lillian, sipping her tea.

'Go on. Say it. I can guess what you were going to say'

'Well - I just hope that Brian pulls his weight.' She sighed. 'I'm a bit uneasy about him, that's all. I stuck my neck out when I recommended him and I don't want him spoiling things.'

Following her mother's advice, Susan began to work her way through Medlar Hall, room by room. Day by day another section was gradually rescued from its layers of grime. Windows sparkled and woodwork began to gleam. One day the chandelier came back to life, flashing iridescent diamonds in the morning sunlight which now streamed back into the house on frosty mornings since Brian had dragged out long ladders from the sheds and clipped back the encroaching creeper.

Only Dr Rush's study remained neglected, for to this sanctuary he would allow her only limited access and insisted on staying in the room, guarding his drawers and papers with such nervous intensity that she was glad to content herself with what her mother always referred to as a 'lick and a promise'.

As if in gratitude for all the attention so suddenly lavished upon it, the house began to respond. Those long, empty years were suddenly replaced by the sounds of living. Music from a distant radio, kitchen noises and Susan humming softly to herself, for she was happier now, and a little in love with the place. Brian whistled cheerfully as he pottered around outside, but this did not last for very long. He soon announced that it really was the wrong time of the year to begin any major new undertaking outside and set up a cosy little base camp for himself in the old tack room at the back of the coaching sheds.

The Jacksons settled into their new way of life with surprising ease and the weeks passed quickly. Routines became established and of their employer they saw very little. He only ever had one visitor, an earnest looking woman who could certainly never be mistaken for a girlfriend. Susan took an instant dislike to Lydia Pendle and found herself going to considerable lengths to avoid the older woman.

'I can't understand why you let that queer old woman bother you so much.' remarked Brian, one day, when they were sitting in the kitchen and Dr Rush had just departed in Miss Pendle's car. 'She's harmless enough. Anyone would think that she came round here to interfere, the way you go on about her. Have you found out who she is, yet?'

Susan passed him a cup of tea.'I got Mum to ask Mrs Whitehead about her. It seems that she works on the local paper, been there for donkey's years. Mrs Whitehead said she's a bit of a bore when she gets talking. Always rattling on about ancient history - real ancient history, I mean, not water under the bridge. She's been seeing Dr Rush for a few months now. Before that he never went out at all. Spent all his time at work, or just cooped up in here. Miss Pendle seems to be the only friend he's got. I feel a bit sorry for him, really. He must get terribly lonely.' Brian laughed. 'I don't think he needs any of our sympathy, Sue. I shouldn't feel too sorry for him. You've got two weirdoes together there. They probably deserve each other. Stop letting them worry you. At least they leave us in peace. And she never stays the night. It would be a whole lot worse if he had some woman in tow who'd be trying to call the shots. Someone bossing you about every time she came round.'

November had been well advanced when Dr Rush first

appeared in the kitchen one Sunday morning. Susan looked up nervously as he entered.

'Good morning, Susan. Both settled in by now? Everything running smoothly?'

Susan dried her hands. 'Yes, thank you, Dr Rush. As long as you're happy with us?'

He seated himself at the breakfast bar and she offered eggs and bacon, which he accepted. When the food was ready, he motioned her to sit down.

'Well, my dear,' He paused to butter a piece of toast. 'I know I'm not here very much, but I can see that you've worked wonders with the place.'

She flushed with pleasure and stood tongue tied as he continued to eat in silence. When he had finished she removed his plate and plucked up courage.

'There was something I wanted to ask you.' she said at last. 'I was wondering about Christmas. Decorations and things like that. I thought I could send Brian for a tree - a really huge one, the lounge would take a tall one, it would be ....'

'Christmas?' interrupted Rush. 'When is Christmas?'

She shot him a curious look, uncertain as to whether she was being teased.

'Quite soon. We really ought to start preparing for it.'

'I never bother about holidays and that sort of thing.' he said, brusquely.

'Oh, but you should!' Susan spoke with uncharacteristic boldness. 'Here you are, with this lovely old house and it really ought to be dressed up for Christmas. I was going to ask Brian to order a big tree. You could have a lovely party - a good old fashioned Christmas party, and show it off to your friends, now that it's looking so nice.'

She began to run hot water into the sink. 'I can just see Medlar Hall full of people, all enjoying themselves, like you see in those old films.' she finished dreamily and turned round to find

Dr Rush shaking his head.

'There will never be anything like that here, Susan. I lead a quiet life. I don't have friends. I never entertain.'

'Oh, I see.' She began to scrub at the frying pan. 'I'm sorry.' she said, after a long silence. 'I didn't mean to speak out of turn. I thought it would have been nice to invite your sister and her husband. I just - well, I wanted to do it for them and you as a sort of thank you - for giving us the job.'

He rose to leave, turning as he reached the door. 'You don't need to thank my sister for anything. You are here because that is what I wanted.'

A moment later he was gone, leaving her staring at the empty doorway. The remark had made her uneasy. She returned to her work, trying to shrug off the feeling, but it had lingered for a long time.

**

Susan got up and returned the chair to its former position, putting the books and papers back on the seat. Picking up the tray again, she closed the study door behind her and took the coffee things back to the kitchen. Then she made her way upstairs, and opened the big blanket chest which stood on the landing outside her bedroom. Lifting the contents to one side she removed the building society book from its hiding place and took it into the bedroom. Sitting on the edge of the bed she opened the pages, running her fore finger down the entries. Interest added. Interest added. Interest added. Page after page. Left untouched year after year, it had compounded and accumulated. She stared down at the final total, trying to translate it into hard, tangible cash, wondering what so much money actually looked like. She had intended it for her son, to give him a good start in life. Now that Dr Rush had assured his future it seemed that Ben would have no need of her help. The solicitor she had consulted had been quite confident about that. The last entry was a small withdrawal, the first in the entire book, which she had made last Monday lunchtime.

Passing the dressing table she caught sight of herself in the mirror and was surprised to find herself smiling. The reflection beamed back and then broke into a broad grin. For the first time in her life Susan liked what she saw. Everything, every horrid shred of the miserable past had vanished. Lost, wiped away.

She started to giggle. A moment later it turned to uncontrollable laughter. Soon she was convulsed. The sound filled the room until the room could no longer contain it and it spilled out into the corridor and cascaded down the stairs, bouncing off the walls. It was the first time in many long years that Medlar Hall had resounded with laughter. It was also the one truly happy moment that Susan Jackson had ever experienced. Just once, in all her forty seven years. Rare and precious laughter, suddenly caught up in a head-on collision with time. Laughter which made no apologies and won the day unscathed.

10
Sunday Lunch

Barbara popped little skewered rolls of bacon around the edges of the roasting tin, basted the pheasants on their beds of toast, and returned them to the oven. With everything else under control, she was free to attend to the finishing touches.

Choosing the smallest of her Moorcroft vases, (she had recently joined their Collectors Club and was prey to the special limited editions) low and broad based, with full blown anemones slip trailed over a deep midnight blue glaze, she carefully arranged the real thing, two bunches of dark red and purple anemones purchased specially for today. She carried them through to the dining room and placed them carefully in the centre of the table, which was already laid for three. Lifting the long stemmed crystal glasses towards the light, she gave them a final polish, checking carefully for smears. Finally satisfied that the luncheon setting met with her approval, she placed another couple of enormous logs into the already roaring fire and then, with an enjoyable, spite driven stab, drew the cork on one of Charlie's finest clarets and left it on the mantle shelf to breathe. Retiring to the the window seat in the morning room, which overlooked the front drive, she waited for Julian to arrive with his guest.

Leafing through one of the Sunday supplements she paused over a feature on British families living overseas and found herself thinking about Lillian. Since Jennifer and her husband had emigrated to Australia, Lillian had had to be content with letters and the occasional telephone call, which always left her close to tears. The grandchildren existed in a series of photographs, which she would proudly bring to show

Mrs Whitehead before placing them in the treasured album, the most recent picture taking pride of place, in a gilt frame, on top of the television set. 'They call me Granny Bayliss.' she had once told Barbara, importantly. 'And Peter's mother is Granny Gibson, so they don't get us mixed up.'

A thin, tired looking woman, who loved to buff newly waxed old oak until it shone like glass, Lillian always talked to the piece of furniture as she worked.

'Come along, my lovely, gleam for Lillian. Plenty of elbow grease, that's what we like, isn't it?' Sweating with her exertions, she continued to coax out the sheen until the old settle began to shimmer in the morning sunlight, as if the wood spirit herself was dancing along the surface of the timbers. How many times had she, Barbara, hesitated in the doorway, eavesdropping, reluctant to interrupt the chant?

Honest and conscientious, Lillian took a very particular pride in the gleaming patina that her years of toil had wrought upon the Whitehead's increasingly valuable collection of early English oak. Some might have felt a twinge of envy, even resentment, having spent so many years cleaning for the well-to-do. Lillian, however, who considered her position a status symbol, was proud to be trusted with the back door keys to the Whitehead residence.

Reared in abject poverty in the overcrowded back to back housing which had been thrown up during the nineteenth century to accommodate the burgeoning population of factory workers then flooding into Manchester from the surrounding countryside, Lillian was eternally grateful for her present lot. During the 1960s, the depressing, sub-standard 'rows' of her childhood had been bulldozed, and the inhabitants dispersed to sprawling new estates beyond the city. Even Wilmslow had been commandeered into accommodating its quota of the 'overspill' and Lillian had been pleased to return to the more rural environment of her forefathers. Once settled into a nice new council house, she had kept herself to herself, remaining aloof from most of the neighbours.

Over the years, Barbara Whitehead had grown fond of the practical little woman with her work-worn hands, Manchester accent and no-nonsense approach to life. Lillian gradually became an integral part of the daily routine and, despite their widely differing backgrounds, the long standing domesticity of their relationship had created a bond. Between them there had developed a certain warmth which neither woman found within her own circle.

From time to time, the elegant Barbara experienced a flicker of guilt as the older woman toiled. It came when she was arranging the flowers or making telephone calls to her friends, deliberately busying herself to keep the emptiness at bay. With the two boys away at boarding school and a husband with an ever increasing work load to detain him at his Manchester offices - was it really work? - she sometimes wondered, pushing the thought away as swiftly as it flitted into her mind, Barbara had reached that stage in a woman's life when she begins to feel slightly redundant.

She suddenly found herself recalling that long ago morning when the problem of Susan had first cropped up. By then Lillian Bayliss, widowed early, had been 'doing' for the Whiteheads for ten years.

**

'Coffee's out.' she called, 'Come now Lillian, whilst it's hot.' Lillian had replaced the lid on her huge tin of beeswax and scurried into the enormous kitchen. Barbara was already seated at the vast pine table.

'Sit down, Lillian. Time you had a break.'

Lillian extracted a packet of cheap cigarettes from the pocket of her overall.

'Here, take one of these.'

Barbara rolled a fatter, longer and more expensive stick across the table top, flicked open her slim gold lighter and held it for Lillian, who inhaled the smoke and broke into a fit of coughing. She put her hand over her mouth, excusing herself.

'Lousy habit.' she said, when the coughing had subsided.

'We've all got to have some little pleasures.' replied Barbara, daintily tapping her ash into a heavy crystal ash tray.

Lillian cradled the mug of coffee. 'Truth is that I've been hammering them a bit, just lately.'

'Is something worrying you?' asked Barbara, genuinely interested. 'You haven't said anything.'

'To tell you the truth, Mrs W, I'm worried sick about our Susan. She's tried that hard but she can't make ends meet. Even though she's gone back onto full time at the supermarket, she's just not bringing enough in. And he can't find anything permanent. I knew he'd never hold down that job at the airport. They should never have saddled themselves up with a mortgage. They're in a right mess now.' She bit her lip. 'I'm sorry, I know I shouldn't be going on about my problems like this.' Lillian sighed and fiddled with her hair.

'Don't be silly, Lillian. A trouble shared, as they say.'

In those days Barbara had thoroughly enjoyed those glimpses of the son-in-law's precarious lifestyle which Lillian occasionally provided. 'They're still together, aren't they? Every marriage has its rough patches. Life is full of ups and downs.'

'I don't know what our Susan sees in him!' Lillian burst out with unusual vehemence. 'She could have done a lot better for herself than that. He's too fond of the beer, you know. I told her often enough - never marry a man with a liking for the drink, I said, you'll never have a penny in your purse. Of course, she thought she knew best, like they all do. Didn't listen to me when she should have. I've seen what drink can do to families.' Her eyes welled with tears and she blew her nose loudly.

'He's probably under a lot of stress, Lillian. It can't be very nice, being unemployed. Something's bound to turn up. Surely things can't be that bad?'

'But they are, Mrs W. Just between you and me, I wouldn't like it to go any further, but the building society's going to take that nice little house off them. They're going to lose everything our Susan's worked so hard for. All those fancy ideas she had. The way things have turned out, it's just a blessing that they didn't start a family. They'll be back on the council estate next - in one of the flats, at that. And there's one or two that will enjoy seeing them come back down with a bump. I know what they're like on that estate. Brian wouldn't know stress if it bit him on the backside. He doesn't give a damn about anything, that one.'

Over the years, Lillian's endless string of family problems and mishaps had become Barbara's own private soap opera and she found herself looking forward to the next instalment with a certain degree of relish. Now, as she gathered up the empty coffee mugs, she said, comfortingly, 'Well, I certainly shouldn't go worrying yourself about what other people think. I stopped bothering about that sort of thing years ago. I expect they've all got one or two skeletons in the cupboard.'

Lillian, tempted to point out that it was all right for Mrs Whitehead, held her tongue. It would never do to overstep the mark. 'Shall I carry on with the hall, or would you like me to make a start upstairs?' she asked instead, thus bringing the morning's episode to its conclusion.

**

The sound of a car door interrupted Barbara's train of thought. and a moment later she heard the front door open.

'Mum, where are you? I've brought Rachel.'

'I'm here - in the morning room.'

Julian appeared in the doorway with a young girl, enviably slim, smiling shyly.

'Let me introduce Rachel. I hope we're not late. Something smells good.'

'No - perfect timing. I was just having five minutes in here whilst I was waiting.' Barbara stood up and held out her hand. She was an elegant woman, tall and still in good shape, her fine, strawberry blonde hair worn short and sleekly capped into the nape of her neck. Beneath the crisp white apron she was simply but expensively dressed in a pleated checked skirt, a plain navy jumper adorned with a discreet string of small pearls and flat heeled navy deck shoes.

'Hello, Rachel. I'm so glad you could come. Lunch is almost ready. Why don't you both come along to the kitchen, then we can chat whilst I carve.'

Julian drew out a chair for Rachel at the kitchen table and Barbara lifted the enormous roasting tin from oven, removed the pheasants to a carving dish and began to make gravy.

'Can I do anything to help, Mrs Whitehead?'

'Call me Barbara. No, it's all under control - unless you'd like to pour us a sherry - it's on the dresser, You'll find the glasses on the shelf above.

'Not for me.' said Julian.

'We weren't asking you.' said Barbara.

'Where's Dad? Isn't he joining us?'

'Need you ask?' She turned to Rachel with a sigh. 'I'm a golf widow, one of thousands.'

Not sure what to say, Rachel smiled politely as Julian passed his mother a glass of sherry and they watched in silence as Barbara deftly carved the birds, transferred the slices carefully to the plates, garnished them with watercress. and added generous servings of game chips. She opened the serving hatch, removed two vegetable tureens from the warming oven and handed Julian a pair of oven gloves. 'If you could go though to the dining room, darling, Rachel and I will pass things through to you.'

Lunch was accompanied by polite conversation. When Julian was clearing away the plates, Barbara topped up the wine glasses and lit a cigarette.

'So, how did you get on at Medlar Hall?'

'Not very well. I'm afraid I didn't have much luck with the computer.'

'But Rachel thinks she may be able to sort it.' said Julian, returning to the table. 'We need to go back again.' He began to explain, but after a moment Barbara held up her hand.

'It's no use, darling. I don't understand the first thing about computers - after my time. I'm sure Rachel knows what she's doing. Anyway, how was Susan?'

'I hardly recognised her.'

As Julian attempted to describe the sudden transformation Barbara turned to Rachel.

'So she's started to tart herself up?'

'Well, no, I wouldn't say that.' said Rachel, rather taken aback. 'She looked really nice. Smart, but in quite a discreet sort of way. I mean, I don't know her, or the way she used to look, but she'd obviously been to the hairdressers recently. She was wearing a very nice trouser suit. Light grey. It looked quite expensive.'

'Charlie said she was really down at heel when he went to see her the other Saturday. It looks as though she's already started spending it. Bit of a cheek.'

'Mum, don't be so hard on her. She's trying to make an effort.'

'Getting dolled up to visit the solicitor, I expect.' Barbara emptied the remainder of the claret into her glass.

Julian gave her warning look. 'Now, Mum, don't start.'

Unsure as to whether he was referring to the conversation or the intake, Rachel tactfully changed the subject. 'You've got some beautiful furniture, Barbara. The carving on that corner cupboard is magnificent. Is it Jacobean?'

'Yes. A fine example. Are you interested in antiques?'

'Well yes, although I'm not terribly knowledgeable. But anyone can see that you've got some wonderful pieces here. Oak is my

114

great favourite. There's something so English and solid and dependable about it.'

Barbara laughed. 'I'll take you through the house after lunch, if you'd like to see the rest. The credit really belongs to Lillian. Our collection is her pride and joy. It's taken her years to achieve this degree of patina.'

Later, when Rachel was helping in the kitchen, Barbara grew more talkative.

'Lillian's offered to leave - because of the will and all the potential trouble. Charlie wants her to go. Barbara wants her to stay.' Barbara suddenly sat down. 'Been with me for years. She doesn't come in every day, like she used to, she's not in very good health. I mean, she's turned seventy now, but I couldn't let her go. I couldn't bear the thought of even trying to find someone else to take over from her. They just don't take the pride, these days. Old Lillian is quite irreplaceable. I can't possibly keep this place up to scratch without her.'

'And that was Lillian's daughter I met today?'

Barbara nodded, pursing her lips.

'I was the one who arranged for Susan and her husband to live in at Medlar Hall. I mean, I couldn't be expected to go round every weekend to clean up the chaos. And there was never any food in the house. Vinney was hopeless. You're not going to believe this, but I actually ended up taking boxes of groceries round there. I was becoming extremely concerned about him. It just wasn't on. Getting the Jackson's in solved everybody's problems - or so we thought at the time. Of course, nobody had bargained for the child.' She fell silent as Rachel continued to load the dishwasher.

**

It was July and Lillian was singing. Hardly aware of the half remembered melodies, she trilled away quite unselfconsciously as she worked. It had started out as a bit of a hum while she dusted round in the morning room and gathered strength as she

115

set the sitting room fire, just in case Mrs Whitehead wanted it lit for the evening. By the time she had got to brushing down the stairs, she was carolling away to her heart's content.

Seated at her dressing table, Barbara smiled to herself, trying to remember when she had last heard anyone singing aloud for the sheer joy of it. No, she couldn't think of anyone at all, let alone Lillian, of all people! Lillian, who carted the world and its woes along with her, every step of the way.

Lillian was thrilled to bits - really made up about it, she told Mrs Whitehead, excitedly. True, Susan's baby was going to be her third grandchild, but in a way, it was like her first. They were a fine pair, those never seen little Australian kids, with their sun bleached hair and golden tans. Joanne with a nose full of freckles and a bright green ribbon in her long hair, her younger brother at her side, grinning wickedly to reveal a large gap where his front teeth had recently been.

'Promise a new photo as soon as second teeth have arrived!', Jennifer had scrawled on the reverse, and the message had upset Lillian, accentuating the fact that she would never see their growing.

'Coffee's ready, Lillian!'

'Coming, Mrs Whitehead.'

'Well, I've never heard you sound so happy.' Barbara greeted her as she came through to the kitchen.

The older woman could not stop talking. 'Like I said, it's ever so good of Dr Rush. Our Susan says he's been really smashing about it and they can all stay on, even after Baby arrives. You know what he told her? He said every other mother manages to run a house as well as a baby and there's no reason why she should be any different. He must think a lot about her, deep down. 'All shoulders to the wheel, Susan.' That's what he said. That Brian's going to have to buck his ideas up and help her a bit more. Maybe it will be the making of him, having some real responsibilities.'

Barbara poured more coffee. 'Here, have another cup, since this is such a special day. I must say I'm very surprised, Lillian. Vincent can't stand children, you know. Never could. I suspect that's why that he and Ursula never started a family. And he never showed the slightest interest in my boys when they were small - or now, come to that. He must be mellowing in his old age.' She passed Lillian a cigarette.

'Even that strange Miss Pendle has been ever so kind to our Susan recently.' Lillian inhaled on the cigarette. 'Do you know her, Mrs Whitehead?'

'Sort of.' replied Barbara, in a tone that implied dark secrets best left untold. 'Got designs on our Vincent, has she?'

Lillian flushed. 'I wouldn't know about anything like that.' she said hastily. 'I do hope I haven't spoken out of turn.'

Barbara shook her head. 'I was only joking. I've got her down as a confirmed spinster. No, what Vincent gets up to is his own affair.' She leant forward confidingly. 'Always such a loner, Lillian, even when he was a child. No one could ever tell how he really felt about anything. There was a time when I thought he was suffering from depression. Later I came to realise that he's perfectly happy in his own little world. Anyway, enough about Vincent. This is splendid news about Susan, especially after all those disappointments in the past. There must be something in the water at Medlar Hall! Do be sure to give her our congratulations, Lillian. As a matter of fact I'm really pleased that he's got some people around him at long last. I wasn't at all happy when he was there alone in that house. It wasn't natural. Go on, have another biscuit.'

11
August 1983

Having worked on late into the night, Vincent Rush had awakened later than usual that particular Sunday morning. Drawing back the bedroom curtains he blinked short sightedly as a bright stream of sunlight entered the room. He pushed his feet into a pair of elderly slippers, rummaged amongst the clutter on the bedside table for his spectacles and shuffled downstairs.

Waiting for the kettle to boil, he went to check his current project, dragging a large fermentation bin from the recesses of the larder. Kneeling down beside it, he removed the lid and began to prise out the flat wooden board, which had absorbed moisture and expanded. Now tightly wedged, several minutes elapsed before he finally managed to remove it. Freed from the constraining board, the thing inside bobbed up, turning slightly as it broke surface. He examined it gingerly and smiled. Excellent. No tightening, no indication of shrinkage.

He was just adding a carefully measured amount of polyethylene glycerol to distilled water when the shrill sound of the doorbell startled him. Peering through the creeper covered kitchen window he recognised his sister's red Volvo. Hastily replacing the board and cover, he mauled the heavy bin back into the larder, before opening the side door to the sound of church bells, drifting across the fields.

'There you are!'

Barbara stood on the step, holding a large box of assorted groceries. She was dressed in what she considered to be sensible 'working' clothes - a sage green track suit complete with the designer's motif, to show that it was not intended for

118

jogging, and red gold curls under the control of a silk Hermes scarf, tied gypsy fashion.

'Don't tell me I've woken you up, Vinny. You kept me standing around for ages.' she grumbled, 'Here, take these through to the kitchen.'

She thrust the box into his arms and pushing him aside strode purposefully towards the kitchen. He followed her and stood rigidly as she came forward to kiss him. She felt him stiffen and withdraw fractionally from the contact. Not surprised, since in the case of her brother the normal rules of behaviour did not apply, Barbara was nevertheless a little hurt by Vincent's rebuffs. He had always been the same, not changed since childhood. She stood her ground, casting a critical eye.

'Well, I have to say that you look a bit seedy, Vinny. And not even dressed yet!' She shook her head in mock despair.

'Bossy old Babs.' he said, without enthusiasm. 'Still playing big sister.'

'Not before time, either.' replied Barbara, glaring round the kitchen. 'Honestly, Vincent, just look at the state of this place. How can you live like this?'

Donning a frilly apron, she began to scoop up dishes, loading them into the dishwasher. 'When did you last run this machine? It still works, doesn't it?'

Vincent shrugged. 'As far as I know.'

'It's a good thing I have come round!' she exclaimed, throwing open one empty cupboard after another. 'You'll starve yourself to death at this rate. Have you had anything to eat?'

He shook his head.

She began to unpack the groceries. 'Right, full English breakfast for you. You can have it out in the garden. Get some fresh air. I'll bring it out when it's ready. Go on, get out of the way. I'm going to tidy you up.' Silencing his protests, she shoo'ed him out into the walled garden at the side of the house. 'I don't want you poking around, disturbing my things, Barbara.

I want them left as they are. I know it's turned into a bit of a shambles since Ursula left, but ....'

He stopped in mid sentence. It was the first time she had heard him mention her name.

'Do you miss her a lot?' she asked, more gently.

He sat down on a garden bench, studying his bare feet intently. 'Not a lot.' he said, eventually. 'Just sometimes. The house has got a bit untidy.'

That was an understatement. There was a stale, dead smell hovering around the place. Barbara worked her way through the rooms, flinging windows open and brushing up the black corpses of flies which littered every window sill. The study was worst of all, giving off a particularly unpleasant odour. She finally tracked down the source - the remains of a Chinese takeaway, still in foil containers, mouldered beneath his leather armchair. Given that she was not addicted to physical toil, Barbara made a sterling effort that Sunday morning, restoring some superficial semblance of order. Vincent kept out of her way and when she had finished she carried a tray of tea out to the garden.

'Now, Vinney, not one word. Just sit still and listen. There is absolutely no way that I'm going to continue coming round here to clean up your messes.'

'I never asked you to.' he protested.

Barbara glowered. 'Shut up. It's patently obvious that you're not even fit to look after yourself, let alone capable.'

Vincent raised his eyes skywards.

'It's no use looking like that! Listen to me.' she snapped. 'I'm telling you quite seriously. Either sell up and get yourself into one of those smart new flats, where the service is all included, or get a housekeeper. Better still, take on a live-in couple, and then the man could attend to the gardens. It's such a shame - they're an absolute disgrace. Ursula would have a fit. She really loved this garden.'

He sighed, genuinely weary of the tirade.

'Well, she couldn't have loved it that much. She's the one who decided to walk out. I didn't ask her to leave, Barbara. I know you mean well, but I'm all right, really I am. We've already been through all this. I like living here and I have no intention of selling up.'

She handed him a cup of tea. 'Then get some live-in help. You can afford it. Stop being so penny-pinching.'

He shook his head. 'Money's got nothing to do with it. I like my privacy, Babs. I don't want people around, getting in my way. No.'

'But it wouldn't be like that.' she persisted. 'You could easily open up that wing over the stables. There's even a spare bathroom. And from what I've seen you don't appear to have been anywhere near that part of the house for a long time anyway, so I can't think that it would make any difference to you. You'd hardly know they were around.'

She gazed up the mellow brickwork, her eyes travelling along the row of gables, and sighed. 'This was - still is - a lovely old place, Vincent. If you insist on remaining here, you have a responsibility towards it. You can't just go on ignoring it, leaving it to deteriorate. You wouldn't have to pay a lot, you know. Not if you were providing the accommodation.'

'I don't want anyone else living here.' he repeated, stubbornly. Shaking her head Barbara stood up. 'In that case, you'll just have to stew. I must go now.' She leant down and kissed him on the cheek. For once he did not pull away.

'There, that's better. Didn't hurt, did it? You always were a stubborn little blighter.' she said, affectionately. 'Just promise me that you'll think about what I've said.'

During the following week he had worked ceaselessly in the lab, preparing scores of slides from tissue samples. By the time he had finally completed the last set of smears, Friday evening was well advanced. Oblivious to the lateness of the hour, he began to study the penultimate slide under the high intensity scanner and his fatigue suddenly vanished. He stared down at the screen and slowly increased the magnification. He polished his spectacles carefully and turned his attention back to the image on the screen. Amongst the cluster before him, clearly visible to the trained eye lay one, just one, perfect cell, with the nucleus apparently still intact. He forced the wave of euphoria aside.

It was almost inevitable, having spent the greater part of his career in perfecting complex techniques of genetic surgery, that Rush should have long since abandoned any sort of moral posturing which might pose an ethical dilemma. Over the past decade he had reorganised the inherited characteristics of a wide range of living things. Graduating from simple yeast moulds he had clambered, via the fruit fly and the poor ubiquitous guinea pig, ever onwards up the evolutionary ladder. At this moment in time he had the ability and the means at his disposal to add or subtract, to enhance or counteract. To follow, in fact, any direction that his curiosity chose to pursue. He would reconstruct in order to experiment. Eliminate this, eradicate that, an enhancement here, a minor alteration there. Quite without qualm, he would frequently rip apart some genetic blueprint like a broken string of beads. Having done so, he then rethreaded the components in any combination he wished. Then watched dispassionately as the results of his experimentations began to develop and grow. During his time at FINGERS, Vincent Rush had created some terrible things. The majority of them had ended up in the incinerator.

Glancing at the clock on the laboratory wall, he suddenly realised with some irritation that the chauffeur would once again be cooling his heels outside the main entrance. With great reluctance he extracted the precious slide from the scanner and placed it into storage.

On Monday, he would move on to the second stage.

Lifting the DNA sequences from that cell nucleus would be child's play. Straightforward engineering. By Monday night they would be inserted into plasmids, ready for introduction to their host bacteria. He smiled to himself. No micro manipulation this time. This was one sample with which he had no intention of meddling. The replication would be exact. He hung up his lab coat and inserted the card key into the door. He was still smiling as it closed to behind him.

12
September 1983

Opening his post that Tuesday morning, the manager of the local branch office of a large building society was relieved to find that an authorisation, already several weeks overdue, had finally been processed. He immediately issued instructions that a notice to quit be served immediately upon the occupants of a small, semi-detached house on the edge of town.

Her left shoe had been rubbing all day and now there was a large blister on her heel, which grew increasingly painful as she limped home from work. 1983 had been a pretty miserable year so far. It was about to get even worse.

Things were out of control now, as the fates conspired, gathering to create some dreadful impact on her hitherto totally predictable little life.

As she turned into the avenue she immediately noticed, with a familiar sinking feeling, a decent car parked outside her house. Too new. Still shiny. Certain that had nothing to do with to any of the neighbours, her fears were confirmed as she reached the gate, when an anonymous little man in a fawn suit climbed out and approached her.
'Mrs Jackson?'

The smile congealed on her face as he silently thrust an envelope into her hand and returned quickly to his car. She tore open the letter as he drove off and her expression darkened still further as she slowly read the contents. Across the road, a lace curtain moved.
'Nosy old cow!' she mouthed, raising two fingers in a defiant gesture before letting herself into the house.

She kicked off the crippling shoes and reread the letter

whilst the kettle boiled. Changing into a pair of old jeans and some backless sandals, five minutes later she left the house and walked round to see her mother.

'Well, it was only a matter of time, Susan.' said Lillian, waving the letter. 'We knew it was going to happen.'

Susan snatched back the correspondence and stuffed it back in the envelope.

'It was still a nasty shock. That slimy little toad sat outside, waiting for me to get home. And that evil old busy body over the road, clocking it all.'

Lillian lit a cigarette. 'You shouldn't have to be dealing with this sort of thing.' she said, beginning to feel annoyed. 'Where was Brian? I know, don't tell me. Down the Pool Hall with his mates, while you're stuck in that bloody supermarket. It's never right, Susan. What sort of a man does he call himself? It's high time he grew up.'

'Now, Mum, that's not very fair.' said Susan defensively.

Lillian sniffed. 'Don't tell me about fair. The truth was ever painful. You can't say I didn't warn you. Your poor Dad, it's a good job he's not around to see this. He'd be turning in his grave if he knew the way you've been dragged down by that good-for-nothing layabout. Well, he'd better stick his idle backside into gear now and get on down to that housing department. Fast. There's not enough room here. Not for both of you.'

When Susan started to cry, Lillian softened and put an arm around her daughter's shaking shoulders.

'Poor love. There, don't take on so. It'll sort.'

Susan blew her nose.

'If he could just find some work, Mum. Can't you ask Mrs Whitehead? She might give him a few hours. He could do some gardening.'

'She's already got Tom Davenport. He's been doing it for a long time now.' Lillian stared helplessly at her daughter's miserable face. 'All right, I'll ask her anyway, but only because of you. I wouldn't like to recommend that Brian to anybody. He's not reliable, Susan. I warned you about him years ago.'

Susan stood up. 'I'd better be getting back. He'll be waiting for his tea.'

'And that's another thing.' Lillian followed her to the door. 'He should be there, getting the meal for you, after you've done a hard day's work.'

Susan stuffed the letter into her pocket. 'Don't keep going on about him, Mum. It isn't going to solve anything.'

Lillian shook her head, sadly. 'You'd have been much better off with Alan, Susan. He was really keen on you, you know. He's done really well for himself.'

'I didn't love him.'

'It would have come, given time. You deserve better than this. I hate to see you so unhappy.'

When she arrived home, Brian was stretched out on the settee, watching children's television.

'You're late.' he said, without taking his eyes from the screen.

Susan threw the letter at him. 'You'd better read that.'

'Not now, I'm watching this. I'll look at it later.' He tossed it to the floor.

'Now! Look at it now!' she screamed and switched off the television set.

'What did you do that for?' he grumbled, sitting up. 'Had a bad day? What's got into you? Wrong time of the month?'

'You can say that again!' she raged. 'Just read that sodding letter. I told you they would. You'd better start to take things seriously for a change.'

Her eyes again filled with tears as she sat down heavily in the chair. 'We've got nothing left. Everything's shabby. I can't even afford a new dress. No home, no savings. Some sodding awful council flat if we're lucky. And me - what have I got to look forward to? Years and years stuck on that bloody checkout, bored rotten. Just take a look at yourself, Brian. A string of odd jobs, a bit here and a bit there. You've never buckled down, never made anything of yourself and it just isn't fair. I've tried so hard and now you've dragged us down into the gutter. We don't have any future at all.'

He put his hands over his ears and roared at her to stop. She shrank back.

'Will you bloody well pack it in, Susan? I can't stand any more of it. I'm trying, aren't I?'

She flounced out of the room. After a few minutes he appeared in the kitchen doorway. 'Don't keep blaming me for everything, angel. Why is everything always my fault?' The anger had been replaced by a wheedling tone.

'I do blame you - and so does Mum.'

A sharp, sarcastic look darkened his face. 'Ah, so that's it. That's where you've been. I get it, now. I might have known. Can't you see what her game is? She's just poisoning you against me, Sue, and you're daft enough to let her. She wants to split us up. She never did like me. Not good enough for her little girl, am I?'

Susan poured hot water over the teabag and puddled it around in the mug with a spoon, staring down into the liquid, watching it grow darker.

'It isn't Mum's fault that you lost your job at the airport.' she said at last, without looking at him. 'You blew it, Brian. If you'd kept your nose clean we wouldn't be in this mess. You're the one that's ruined everything.'

He came over and put an arm around her. She stiffened, but did not pull away.

'Come on, Sue, this isn't like you. I've told you about that a hundred times over. You know what happened. They were all at it. I was just the poor sod that got caught. The scapegoat. At least they didn't prosecute.'

'No.' sniffed Susan, 'At least they didn't do that.'

'Let's go out for a drink. Cheer you up.'

'We can't afford it.'

'That's all the more reason to go. The price of a couple of drinks ain't going to make any difference now. You need cheering up. Get your jacket.'

She took the tea through to the living room and sat down, looking around at the pretty pink curtains and matching cushions that she had sewn, the silk flower arrangement and the glass fronted cabinet they had bought last Christmas. There was the new grey rug, chosen from a friend's catalogue. She still hadn't finished all the payments on that. The rest of their furnishings remained an ill-assorted collection of castoffs and hand-me-downs, donated by various members of the family.

'Come on, hurry up and finish your tea. We'll pop round to the Bull. It'll take our minds off things.'

Wearily, Susan picked up her handbag. They walked down the avenue in silence. Once they were seated at a small copper topped table in the lounge bar, she began again.

'Mum's going to ask Mrs Whitehead if she needs any gardening work. If you could get one or two regular days at some of the big houses, you could build up a proper little business. Garden Maintenance Services.' A note of enthusiasm had crept into her voice. 'One of the girls at work was telling me about it. Her dad started like that after he got made redundant about three years ago and he's got more work than he can cope with. Maybe he'd take you on to help out. Shall I ask her?'

Brian drained his glass. 'I will try something, Sue, honestly. Stop going on at me. It's getting very boring.' He took hold of her hand and began to stroke it. After a few minutes he could feel her beginning to relax a little.

'I do want to work, you know.' he continued, 'I'll do anything to make you happy. You're all I care about, Sue. I really do love you.'

To his relief she smiled for the first time.

'There, that's more like it.' He squeezed her hand a little too hard and she pulled it away.

'You look really lovely when you smile. Look, give us a couple of quid and I'll get some more drinks in.'

Susan opened her handbag. 'I've only got a note.'

'That'll do.' he said, deftly extracting it from her purse. 'I'll need some change for the fag machine anyway.'

When they got home he took her off to bed. Afterwards she felt better, closer to him again. Maybe everything would be all right. For the time being she had stopped thinking about the slimy little man and the humiliation of the dreadful letter and the fate of her last five pound note.

**

Charles Whitehead placed his hand over the mouthpiece and called his wife. 'It's Vincent. For you.'

'Is something the matter?'

Charlie shrugged. 'Who knows, with Vincent? Sounds his usual self, but he's most insistent that he speak to you. Don't stay talking dear, I don't want to be left stranded with the Newbolts.'

'Give them another drink.' said Barbara, softly. 'I won't be long. Hello? Vinney? This is a surprise! What are you doing, ringing up on a Friday night? Is everything all right? I was intending to speak to you tomorrow. We were wondering if you would like to come to lunch on Sunday?'

'I can't, Babs, thanks. Too much to do. I'm just ringing to say that I've been giving some thought to what you were saying last week. You were right. I do have a responsibility towards the house and maybe it would be quite a good thing to have a live-in couple here. As long as they were suitable. I don't suppose you know of anyone but I'm really calling to see if you would like to organise it for me. Maybe place an ad in the local paper? I need a married couple. Not too old - and no kids in tow. Definitely not a family.'

Barbara beamed at the telephone. 'It's really funny that you should say that. I'm so glad you're starting to see reason, Vinney. We do worry about you, you know. Listen, I can't chat now, we've got Frank and Elizabeth here for dinner. Leave it with me. I'll get back to you in a day or two. You take care now, Vinny. Bye.'

The following Saturday found Vincent Rush looking distinctly ill at ease, pushing a wire trolley up and down the aisles of the local supermarket. From time to time he stopped to grab something at random from the shelves and dropped it into the trolley, his eyes raking the long line of checkout counters.

He finally found her at the far end of the store, her name displayed on a plastic identity badge pinned to her striped overall. He hovered around a high display of own-brand cereals, studying her intently.

She was so ordinary. A plain, homely sort of face, hardly the type anyone would subject to close scrutiny. One or two female shoppers were beginning to notice him. He grabbed a packet of cornflakes and joined the queue.

Mousy brown hair, short and straight, face devoid of makeup. Nice blue eyes, spoilt by a harassed expression. An an air of resignation in the set of her shoulders, a passive acceptance of her lot. Someone you could manipulate, he thought, watching as she endlessly keyed in the prices and rang up the totals. Not smiling, just taking the money and handing back the change. She never gave the customers a second glance, rarely looking up from her work. Even so - he extricated himself from the waiting line of people and pushed his trolley down to the express checkout by the main entrance.

13
Medlars

Rachel looked up as the office door opened.

'So?' Sophie, deposited a very wet umbrella in the corner beside her desk. 'How did you get on? I've been dying to find out. I nearly rang you, but I didn't get a minute. I went to London for the day, Christmas shopping. Got a lift down with Steve.'

'I know.' said Rachel. 'Trevor told me you wouldn't be in. How was the ball?'

'Terrific - now stop trying to change the subject. What happened with Jules? Will you be seeing him again?'

'I might.' Rachel said, demurely. 'Sophie, leave it until lunch time. I'm really busy at the moment.'

She turned her attention back to the compilation of the Coming Events column. A boring task at the best of times, this week, in the run up to Christmas, it had blossomed to almost unmanageable proportions. She continued to wade through the dockets, formatting each one neatly into sequence of date, place and time. She picked up the next slip and began to type it in.

Larch Green Nursing Home: Carol Service Sunday 14 December. 2.30pm. With the Children's Choir of St Bees Middle School. All welcome.

Rachel rummaged in the drawer of her desk and eventually found the note that Dorothy had left for her. *Lydia Pendle is in Larch Green Nursing Home.*

She remembered something that Julian had told her. He had been talking about the analysis of case histories.'When trying to establish a connection one should look for a common factor.'

'What does that mean, exactly?'

'Could be anything. Some link. There's usually something

131

which keeps cropping up again and again. A pattern or a person. It can be something so trivial that it is easily overlooked. It's an interesting theory.'

She took the piece of paper across to Trevor's desk. 'Have you got a minute, Trev?'

He looked up from his work. 'Sit yourself down. What is it?'

'A couple of things.' Rachel passed him the note from Dorothy. Trevor leant back in his chair. 'Poor old Lydia. I never thought she'd end up in one of those places. I ought to go and visit.'

'They're holding a carol service next Sunday. They've sent us a notification to go in Coming Events. I was just wondering - well, if you'd like me to go, I could do a little write-up.'

'You want to give up your Sunday to go to some geriatrics' carol service?'

'I honestly don't mind. I thought it might be a good opportunity to see Lydia Pendle. I keep hearing about her and I'd like to meet her. I could take her a Christmas card from the office.'

'Well, of course you can go. If that's what you want, who am I to stop you? I tell you what, get Sophie to organise a whip round and we'll send her a decent present. I'll choose it myself. Remind me on Friday.'

'Thanks.' said Rachel. 'That's a really nice idea.'

'Next?'

Rachel looked puzzled.

'You said you wanted to ask me a couple of things.'

'Oh, of course. It's a personal favour. I was wondering if I might borrow the file retrieval software over the weekend? A friend of mine has accidentally deleted some files and asked if I could have a go at trying to recover them.'

He nodded. 'No reason why not, as long as you don't forget to bring it back on Monday morning. You are planning a fun packed weekend, Rachel.'

She grinned. 'You never know, I might enjoy it.'

'I wouldn't hold your breath.' said Trevor, dryly. 'And don't forget to jog me about Lydia's present.'

'What are you going to get for her?'

He shrugged. 'I'm not sure yet. I think I know the type of thing that would appeal. I'll know it when I see it.'

**

There was no one at home when Rachel and Julian returned to Medlar Hall the following Saturday. Julian peered through the garage window. 'Susan's car is gone.'

'Does she know we're coming?'

'Oh yes, Mum spoke to her. Susan said she'd expect us at eleven.'

Rachel checked her wristwatch. 'It's after that now. Shall we come back later?'

'We may as well hang on here for a while and see if she turns up. It's a bit cold to be standing around though. Do you fancy a walk around the grounds?'

They made their way towards the rear of the property and climbed over a small stile which led into the paddock.

'It's such a strange name, Medlar Hall.'

'Yes, it used to be Medlar Farm. The original building dates back to the 16th century, maybe even earlier. What's left of it is buried somewhere in the middle - the area around the dining room and study, at a guess. Anyway, some time during the early 1880s the farm and land were bought up by a wealthy cotton manufacturer from Manchester, who quite literally raised the roof and added the various wings. You can see the influences of the Arts and Crafts movement right through the house. He must have just gone out shopping for the best that money could buy. Everything was obviously done to the highest standards with no expense spared. I'd love to have seen the original farmhouse, before it was extended.'

'And the name? What does Medlar mean? Do you know?'

He nodded. 'You're right, it is strange. The medlar is a fruit tree. One of the most ancient fruit trees. I once looked it up in an old

Victorian gardening book. It produces tiny brown apples. And this is the strange bit. They're not fit to eat until they've bletted.'

'What's bletted?'

'Gone rotten. In other words, you have to wait until they've fallen and decayed on the ground. They were left to rot at the base of the tree until the end of October. A Halloween treat - remember that old bobbing the apple game? The medlar has long since fallen out of favour, just like the crab apple and the quince. I suppose if you got right out into the countryside there will still be some elderly farmer's wives who turn them into jams and jellies. Medlars have a very peculiar taste and texture.'

'How do you know that?'

He grinned. 'Let's see if we can find one for you. The orchard would have been full of them originally, but they were all taken out and replaced with more popular varieties when the old place was extended. But they left one. The token medlar, I suppose. It's all gnarled and twisted. It must have been there for centuries. We used to collect the fallen fruit when we were kids. For the horses. I can remember trying one. Once was enough! Come on, I'll show you.'

She followed him through long grass towards the orchard, where Julian made his way straight to the old tree, which was just as gnarled as he had described. He bent down, feeling around in the grass. 'Ah - here we are. That's a medlar. In an advanced state of bletting, I'm afraid. It's gone over. It would have been at its best last month. Taste it.'

Rachel took the little fruit from his outstretched hand and studied it dubiously. The brown skin was covered in minute bright powdery blue scabs.

'Go on, be brave.'

Rachel pulled a face. 'You've got to be joking. It's completely mouldy. Look, it's growing cultures.'

'For a dare?'

She bit into the squashy brown flesh and pulled a face. 'Ugh - it's awful. I shouldn't have asked. Excuse me.' She spat it back into the grass and they began to retrace their steps.

'When we were small there were two fat little ponies in this paddock. Simon and I used to come at the weekends with Mum. She and Ursula would lead us round the lanes.'

'Was she nice?'

'Ursula? Yes, as far as I can remember. She always made a big fuss of us. Not like Uncle Vinney - we hardly ever saw him. We stopped coming after she left. I don't know what became of the horses.'

'Do you know why she went?'

'Not really. It was years ago. I must have been about ten at the time. From what I've gleaned since I don't think it was much of a marriage. And there were no children. I suppose she got pretty fed up, left on her own all the time. I've often wondered how she ever came to marry Uncle Vinney in the first place. Mum says she was encouraged to leave him, by well meaning friends. You can imagine the sort of thing. 'Before it's too late, while you've still got you're looks.' And she was a stunner. Perhaps it was a mid-life crisis - whatever that's supposed to mean. Middle age was beginning to loom.'

'Had she found someone else?'

Julian shook his head. 'Not according to Mum. Ursula just suddenly took off - fled from marriage. And he didn't try to stop her. Maybe she would have stayed if he had done. Started out as a shock tactic, a bid for attention and she'd over estimated her power over him.'

He looked across towards the hall. 'I mean, not many women would relinquish a place like this for no apparent reason. After she'd gone Mum said he became worse than ever. Turned into a scruffy celibate, just immersing himself even deeper into his work. She used to get really annoyed about the way he neglected this place.'

'Where did Ursula go?'

'Harrogate, I think. Somewhere in Yorkshire, anyway. She eventually landed a job that she liked, with one of the large hotel chains and she must have decided to make a career of it. She's done quite well for herself. You've got to admire her. She never demanded any maintenance, or much in the way of a financial settlement. I think she was quite proud - wanting to prove that she could stand on her own two feet. We were rather surprised when she started talking about contesting the will. Seemed a bit out of character. I suspect somebody was trying to encourage her. She must have been fairly half hearted about it, because she dropped the idea as soon as Dad came up with the right man for the job.'

He was interrupted by the sound of an approaching car and they made their way back to the drive, arriving as Susan's dark green Escort drew to a halt. She got out, flushed and full of apologies.

'I'm really sorry. Have you been waiting long? I expected to be back before you got here. We've been to pick Ben up from the station and the train was late.'

Lillian Bayliss emerged slowly from the passenger door. 'Hello, Julian.' she said, glancing at Rachel.

'Good morning, Lillian. This is a friend of mine.'

'Hello dear, you must be the young lady who understands all about that computer. Julian's mother was telling me about you.'

Julian leaned into the car. 'Hi, Ben, how's school? Back home for the Christmas holidays?'

Ben nodded but did not speak. Julian turned back to Susan. 'Would you like us to come back later, Mrs Jackson? Give you time to settle Ben in?'

'No, it's quite all right. Leave that case Mum, you're not to lift it. Ben will bring it. Come in Julian, and you can make a start. You don't mind using the tradesman's entrance, do you?' Susan unlocked the side door.

Rachel followed, turning to look back as she reached the house. Trailing after them, several paces behind his grandmother, was Ben Jackson, heaving a large suitcase. Small for his age, with a thatch of kestrel-coloured hair, a sullen expression and dark eyes. Her smile was not returned and as he turned away Rachel experienced an unpleasant prickling sensation around the nape of her neck. She followed Susan and Julian into the study.

'It's always so chilly in here. Shall I put the electric fire on?'

'Don't worry, Susan. We'll see to it.'

'I'll leave you to get on then. I'd better sort Ben out - and then I have to take Mum home.

'We can give her a lift when we've finished, if that's any help.'

'Thanks, but I need to go with her. She's expecting a call from Australia - my sister, you know, and I'd like to be there when she rings. How long do you think you'll be staying today?'

'I'm not exactly sure. As long as it takes, I suppose. Certainly an hour, maybe longer. Are we going to be in the way?'

'No, not at all. It's just - well, I was wondering about Ben. He doesn't want to come with us, but I don't want to leave him here on his own.'

'We can hang on until you get back, can't we, Rachel? He can come to the study and watch. He might enjoy that.'

Susan smiled. 'That's very kind, Julian. I'll probably be back before you're finished. I'll tell Ben, but I think he'll prefer to play outside. He'll be perfectly all right. You don't need to keep an eye on him or anything, it's just that I feel happier knowing that there's someone around.' She turned to Rachel. 'He's rather shy, you know. Not a good mixer. Lives in his own little world.'

'Just like your Uncle Vinney.' said Rachel, as Susan closed the study door behind her.

Still in his school uniform, minus tie, Ben Jackson sat on the low wall which bordered the garden, separating it from the paved area outside the study. Listening intently, he heard the fading sounds of his mother's car as it turned into the lane at the end of the drive, followed by silence. He continued to stare at the windows of the study, only a few feet away, swinging his legs, bashing the heels of his shoes against the brickwork.

Last Easter seemed a long time ago now. Just after his twelfth birthday. That was when Doctor Cleverdick had started those horrible sessions. Making him sit in the leather chair in his disgusting stinky study for hours on end. Hypnotising, poking around inside his mind, trying to find out stuff. Droning on and on about race memories and lost instincts and past life experiences. Anything would do, anything at all.

He'd made him sweat for it, kept him dangling for a long time. Then in the end he gave him what he wanted, gave it him good and proper. Served the nosy old creep right. He was really glad he hadn't told her anything about what went on in that study.

'I can't go back. No one can ever go back. It's gone, Dr Rush.' 'No, Ben, it's there, waiting.' Rush had studied him as dispassionately as everything else which fell beneath his microscope, but no amount of questioning would coax anything from the boy. It was cold down there, amongst the cobwebs. Cold and dark. A strange place where things waited. All there, still intact, things which wanted to be left in peace. Tempted by the disturbance they began to jostle, begging to be hooked. Ready to stage a comeback. Waiting for the box to open so that all that old stuff could burst from the chamber and fly into today. Up through the chink, the musty smell still clinging to its wake.

Rush had become increasingly ruthless. Paying scant regard to the effect upon his subject, he continued his psychological dig with mounting fervour, seemingly unable to stop. Right through the Easter holidays Ben had resisted, fighting against it. Until one day, frozen in that hated inquisition chair, there had been a subtle shift of power.

The session began as usual and then Ben had suddenly rebelled. He began transmitting the voice prints. More than ready by this time, they hadn't needed much coaxing. Soon they were coming through in mocking waves. Taunting Dr Cleverdick, egging him on. They forced their impatient way out of those revolving doors of consciousness the moment that they slowed down for long enough. Time to gatecrash the party, time to turn dreams into nightmares.

Tap it. Dig and scrape, teaspoon in one hand, sable brush in the other. Follow the convolutions, remember the way they look. Ever deeper, into the greyness. Disturb the ganglia. Activate the neurons. Root down the stem and suck out all the old stuff; all that precious old stuff. Come on, Dr Rush, vacuum it up, scoop it from its hidey hole. Poke it, prod it, torment it awake, then grab it when it bolts for the tunnel. Get it by the scruff and drag it out into the daylight. Give it an airing, take a good look. Sorry but it doesn't work like that, Dr Rush. *You have to come to us.*

It's time, Cleverdick. Time to satisfy the curiosity. Are you really ready? Ready to see where your meddling is going to lead? Come along then, come on down. Just drop in through that hole you've been digging. Slide down the greasy pole, sir, straight into the under mind and we'll give you a conducted tour. That is what you want isn't it, Cleverdick? We'll start off very gently to give you time to get used to the new dimension.

Ben remembered watching in fascination as Dr Rush began to gag and retch. His face had taken on an unhealthy, purplish tinge just before he collapsed across the desk, scattering his notes to the floor.

Ben suddenly began to feel better. Better than he could ever remember. Getting out of the chair and leaving the study had been like walking on springs. He had danced a silly little polka down the corridor to the kitchen, where he had made a pot of tea. While it was brewing he realised how hungry he felt and helped himself to a packet of biscuits from the tin. Then he poured the tea into a mug and carried it to the study.

'Drink this.' he said shortly, setting the cup down on the desk.

Vincent Rush had done exactly as he was told.

The today noise of Rachel giggling suddenly startled Ben from his reverie. Julian passed some remark, then came the familiar orchestral blast heralding startup, followed by a series of regular ticks as the system loaded. Silence returned, fractured after a few moments by two excited voices. Ben scowled at the study window.

'Any luck?'

I think so - look, it's starting to list them. There are dozens.'

She began to scroll down. Julian leant over her shoulder.

'They were all modified on the same date.' said Rachel

'So I see. And all within twenty minutes of each other, between 2.15 am and 2.35 am on Saturday November 1.' He bit his lip.

'It's not looking very good, is it?'

'Do you want me to carry on?'

Julian sighed. 'I'm not sure. I suppose so. That's why we're here.'

'It gives the chances of recovery as good. Shall I go for it?'

He nodded. 'Yes. It just seems a bit - I don't know. For the first time I feel as if Uncle Vinney really is dead.'

'It's giving me the shivers. Seems like a really creepy thing to be doing.'

Ben concentrated, directing the forces.

Rachel stared at the screen, watching as the programme began to convert the first of the lost files. As the progression line reached the 100% mark a document suddenly filled the screen.

Julian's voice. 'What the hell is that? It looks like hieroglyphics.'

Tiny droplets of moisture beaded Ben's forehead.

'I think I know.' said Rachel. 'It's converted into some

140

crazy symbol font, presumably to stop anyone reading it.'

'So after all that we're none the wiser.'

'We will be in a minute.' Rachel was beginning to enjoy herself. 'Watch this.' She went to Select All and the text became highlighted in bright blue. 'Now, I'm just going to change it back to a standard font and bobs your -'

Ben raised his head and began to concentrate, trying to gain control of the universal flow and make it spin. In his hands he cradled his little chunk of rock, willing it to take him towards the centre of the network.

Three million years in its formation, the bright faces of the surface crystals danced into the daylight as he slowly raised it high. His eyes grew fierce, penetrating the stonework, entering the study, homing in on the hard drive.

A strong smell of electrical burn pervaded the room.

' - something's wrong.' There was a note of panic in Rachel's voice. Julian averted his eyes as the screen began to dance and flicker. A static flash erupted from the monitor. Rachel leapt backwards, her chair crashing to the floor as the computer died.

Ben Jackson wiped his damp forehead on the sleeve of his blazer and made his way slowly towards the coaching sheds.

14
Christmas Carols

The night staff always awakened her too early. During their final rounds, before handing over to the morning shift at six o'clock, part of the routine included pulling back the curtains, leaving her to contemplate the wintry night sky. After they had departed she closed her eyes again and returned to something resembling sleep.

Since entering the nursing home Lydia had been plagued by two recurrent dreams caused, she had decided, by the injections. Usually it was the dog bite dream. Unpleasant, but at least she could cope with that one. The other was of a different quality. A thing she had set aside. Something from a lifetime ago. Whenever it visited itself upon her it never varied. A paralysing, petrifying, sweat soaking nightmare which filled her with terror, leaving a certain foulness lingering in its wake. Desperately trying to rationalise everything, she concluded that the bitter taste was probably caused by an excess of adrenalin. An adrenal hangover.

Snared. Cornered. Trapped. Too late to turn back. Ascending towards something from which there was no escape. Slowly rising to meet her fate, accompanied by a dreadful inevitability, knowing what was about to happen. When she finally saw his eyes they were wild, filled with torment, and something else. Something which she had never before encountered but immediately recognised. It was as if she already knew him and understood the terrible ingredients that had gone into his making. The desperate struggle for survival. Herded aboard some transport ship with the rest of the poor, starved refugees. Housed by the well meaning authorities in yet

142

another camp. An English one this time. A new beginning in an old POW camp which had suddenly become a rehabilitation centre. Left to get on as best they could, some of them even managed to rebuild their shattered lives, but he spent the empty, endless days they had given to him wandering aimlessly in the desolation of the hills. Camouflaged inside an old army greatcoat, the same drab colour as the over-wintered heather, trying to find some half remembered peace. It remained lost, forever eluding him.

Her half formed greeting dried on the wind as he produced the knife. Old and rusty, the broken blade always moving out of the line of her terrified vision as he thrust the jagged edge against her throat. Horribly aware of the smell. That reek of fear, did it come from him, or was it her own? The sallow, unshaven face lurched towards her and then hills were ricocheting and swirling around her for an instant before she hit the ground. Struggling and screaming, choking and bruising while he robbed her of herself. Left with a throat so hoarse that it was hard to swallow and an awful substance mingling with her own blood. Growing colder, ever colder, until it set. Lying quite still afterwards, alone and not yet fully aware of what he had bestowed in exchange. Easing his own torments for a few brief moments, passing them over to Lydia for a lifetime.

Left with this terrible gift, she sobbed scalding tears into the rough heather. This was to be the last time she ever cried. When she finally dared to look he had vanished.

She must have driven herself back down to the town. She remembered finding her way to the public lavatories to the rear of the deserted bus station, her footsteps echoing as she crossed the damp floor to one of those wretched, smelly cubicles. A broken door lock so that she had to keep one foot against it to hold it shut. The other resting on the lavatory seat she cleaned herself as best she could, slowly and painfully, with the sadistic sheets of hard shiny toilet paper provided.

The following weeks had been passed in a swamp of anguish, waiting for the shock-delayed sign which would put her out of her misery. Fully aware of the leaden weights of that repressive and mean-minded society - something to do with their horrid green ration books? -which were lying in wait, poised to crush her, she had offered silent, heartfelt thanks to all the gods of infertility when the long overdue period finally arrived.

She lay now, recovering. Forcing her arm slowly from the covers, on that long voyage towards the bedside table, she turned on her clock radio, letting the early morning Sunday programme bring her back towards reality. Beyond the narrow rectangle of her window dawn was beginning to break. At five minutes to eight the weather forecast brought a welcome digression. Her journey for the day. Head on pillow, unseeing eyes fixed upon the distant outline of the trees, she allowed herself to be transported.

The panorama of the island unfolded as she travelled with the wind at dizzying, breakneck speeds. The brilliant green of the south downs rushed beneath her, replaced by the distant froth of the Welsh coastline. Moments later she began her approach, skirting the mountain ridges as she whirled up the spine of the Pennine chain, en route for the Borders and beyond. Below lay the rises and contours of the Cairngorms and glittering in the far distance, shining waters. She hovered over the islands, whizzed across the Irish sea and levitated for a moment above the Giant's Causeway, sniffing the sharp salt air for a precious second. By the time the Greenwich time signal announced eight o'clock she was back in bed, back in the nursing home.

The young orderly knocked and entered without waiting for a reply.

'Hello Lydia, how are we today? Did we have a good night?'

'No we did not.' said the patient. 'And it's Miss Pendle as far as you're concerned.'

'Now what are we doing still lying in bed? Shall we get you into the chair? Why don't you come and sit by the window. The forecast's quite promising. We might get a bit of sun later.' She checked the old woman's pulse. 'A bit fast this morning. Do you need some painkillers? Doctor will be round later.'

'Good old Doc. I expect he will.'

'When did we last move our bowels?'

'Just fuck off and mind your own business.' said Lydia with such vehemence that the girl fled to tell Sister.

Sister Renshaw knocked on Matron's door and entered.

Matron looked up.'Is everything organised? Have you started getting them into the hall?'

'Not yet. They've had their lunches and the girls are doing the rounds, making sure they're all respectable. Everyone seems to be looking forward to it, apart from Lydia Pendle. She really is a stroppy old so and so.'

'Oh dear. Is she in pain?'

'I don't think so, she seems comfortable enough. She's just refusing to attend the Carol Service. Doesn't want anything to do with Christmas. She won't join in, says its against her religion.'

Matron began to tut. 'Oh dear. Isn't she a Christian? I had no idea. I'm sure it doesn't make any mention of that in her admission notes.'

Jane Renshaw shook her head. 'Try Druid, she said dryly. 'Druid witch. Gives me the shivers.'

Matron pursed her lips. 'Oh dear,' she said again, with a long sigh. 'Well, we can't force her to participate. Perhaps you could put some mistletoe in her room?'

Larch Green was a rambling Victorian mansion and had long outlived the distressed gentility it had once housed so graciously, together with the string of servants needed to run the place. The elegantly landscaped gardens had survived more or less intact and were reasonably well tended, but the building itself, adapted to conform to the health and safety regulations and the dictates of the local fire prevention officer, had gone the way of many such properties. The once elegant rooms, with their moulded cornices, velvet plush and bell-pulls, were now cunningly partitioned to accommodate the maximum number of long stay patients. Along with its current inhabitants, Larch Green had fallen prey to a weary, institutionalised atmosphere

Today the smell of Woodland Glade air freshener dominated the hall. On Matron's instructions it had been sprayed with a heavy hand in a last ditch attempt to override the lingering sub-scents of senescence and Sunday's over-boiled greens, just moments before the Vicar arrived.

At the end of the carol service Rachel inquired about Lydia Pendle and was directed to Jane Renshaw's tiny office.

'Hello, I'm Rachel Mackenna, from the local paper. We're going to write a little piece about the carol service and I was looking for Miss Pendle. She is here, isn't she?'

'Miss Pendle stayed in her room.'

'I've brought something for her. She used to work for the Gazette.'

'Well, I don't know whether she'll agree to see you. She can be very difficult.' She leaned closer and whispered, confidentially, 'I'd better warn you, dear. She can be very foul mouthed sometimes. Does she know you?'

Rachel shook her head. 'No, but I've brought cards from some of her old colleagues, and a Christmas present from the editorial office. We thought she might enjoy a visit. Since I'm already here this would be a good opportunity to meet her. Is she very poorly?'

'Well, some days are better than others. We keep her comfortable but she's very difficult. She hasn't settled in very well. Flatly refuses to mix.' Jane Renshaw sighed and shook her head. 'Lydia tends to - well, ramble. She's not very approachable, I'm afraid. If you'd like to take a seat in the entrance hall I'll go and ask her.'

Rachel sat on a wooden settle in the reception area, watching the depressing sight of wheelchairs, rugs and walking frames as the elderly inhabitants were escorted slowly back to their rooms, their young, uniformed attendants talking to them as though they were young children. So much for that myth about the wisdom of old age, thought Rachel, experiencing a sudden rush of sympathy for the unfortunate Miss Pendle.

Out on the front steps the Vicar was making his seasonal farewells to a small, nodding group of more mobile residents. 'Onwards and upwards.' he concluded with a jovial smile and what Rachel considered to be a distinct lack of tact, which appeared to pass unnoticed. Beyond the main entrance the choir whooped around on the tarmac, having undergone a rapid metamorphosis from mode cherubic to kids from hell. One lone and ineffective music teacher made frantic efforts to round them up and a few minutes later they began to board the school minibus in a disorderly manner. Rachel stood up as Jane Renshaw suddenly reappeared.

'Well, you're highly honoured, Miss Mackenna. They do get so confused - Lydia says that she's been expecting you! If you'd like to come this way.'

The winter sunset rinsed the far wall with a wash of diluted crimson as Rachel entered the room. Thin as a rail, Lydia Pendle was out of bed, sitting in a chair beside the window, wearing a brown woollen dressing gown and thick socks. The boyishly cropped hair, white and wiry, contrasted strangely with her gaunt face. She turned with obvious difficulty as the door opened and stared searchingly at her visitor, sharp, bright blue eyes missing nothing. After a moment she said 'I knew you'd come.'

Sister Renshaw gave Rachel a quick glance which said 'I told you so' and departed.

The silent exchange had not gone unnoticed.

'I suppose she's told you that I ramble.'

Embarrassed, Rachel held out her hand politely.

'Hello, Miss Pendle. I'm Rachel - Rachel Mackenna. Thank you for seeing me.'

'Call me Lydia. What they don't understand they put down to dementia - it's the easy way out for them. None of them are over endowed in the brains' department.' She gestured towards a second chair. 'Sit yourself down.'

The room was surprisingly pleasant. Residents were encouraged to bring their favourite bits - small things of sentimental value and family photographs. Lydia appeared to have rebelled. Her favourite bits consisted of a peculiar, crudely carved stone head which had thick, unsmiling lips on each of its three faces, a small bronze replica of Stonehenge (limited edition purchased during a visit to a trade fair on British Tourism), a very large silver framed photograph of a pair of spotted tabby cats and books. Lots of books. Alongside the bed stood a small bookcase, absolutely crammed with rare volumes, mostly still in their original bindings. Rachel could smell them.

Jostling against each other. Calf skin. Vellum and morocco. Moroccan leather. Having stumbled upon it by pure chance during a holiday with a group of college friends, Rachel knew precisely where it had originated. For a moment she was cast back, passing through the ancient arches of Bab Guissa into the vast warren that is Fes el Bali, an eighth century time warp where the tourist remains of minor significance. Separated from the others she had become lost within the perplexing labyrinths of the great medina, where the streets are so narrow that not even a cart can pass. Suddenly she had stopped in her tracks. Sickened to the pit of her stomach, watching in impotent anguish as a small donkey teetered beneath the weight of two dozen gas bottles. The donkey was followed by a cruelly

148

overburdened mule train. Crates and boxes slipped and slid at crazy angles, banging against the poor beasts at every tortured step. A whip hissed. Prematurely aged horses, untreated leg wounds plagued by flies, struggled with massive wooden beams, building materials and long and unwieldy rolls of beautiful, hand knotted carpets. The medina was alive with these gaunt and ribby shadows, fallen, cursed and beaten back to their feet, bulging panniers scraping the walls as the crowds took refuge from the driver's wielding stick, pressing back into the narrow doorways, out of harm's way. Moving deeper into the medina she had quickly realised that these poor beasts had been the fortunate ones. Most wretched of all were the small mules and donkeys condemned to work at the dying and tanning pits, slithering on a perpetual treadmill up and down the steep, slimy alleyways which led to the river. Wandering though the souks and fondouks she had come to the small stone bridge which crosses the River Fes. Along the edges of the river banks were thousands of skins, laid out on the flat rooftops to dry in the dazzling North African sunlight. The scene in the foreground was mediaeval. A reeking stench rose from the untreated skins, which were all around, stacked on the ground and heaped against the walls, waiting to be scraped. A string of donkeys stood in abject misery, waiting alongside a hideous pile of decapitated heads, ivory horns jutting from the nauseous heap.

To one side lay the brine pits. Crudely sculpted from some greyish daub, they had been in constant use since the day of their creation. Thigh deep in the greasy slurry, thin stick-men ceaselessly pummelled and trampled the sodden hides. Rachel had gazed down into this hell hole from a narrow stone platform. In the series of dark caves which surrounded the tanning basins, treated skins were undergoing some manual softening process. The poor remains received far more attention than they ever had when alive. Naked chests heaving as they rasped for breath, the workers toiled, strenuously beating the hides with some primitive tool which resembled a loofah.

A short distance upstream lay the Street of the Dyers, stained, awash with strange fluids of every hue. Of similar construction to the brine pits, the dying vats offered a dazzling spectrum. As the dyers turned the skins, the dye waters slopped over the sides, collecting on the hot stones in colourful, smelly puddles of poppy, saffron, and mint, whilst the donkeys staggered and swayed beneath the burden of dripping hides, in terror of losing their footing as they were driven at an impatient pace back up the stepped alleys.

Rachel had been trying to forget about it ever since. And suddenly here it was again, gracing this book shelf. Encasing the precious manuscripts. Bound around thoughts and ideas that had become sought after items for the collectors. Those which the shelves could not accommodate had been stacked against the neighbouring wall.

Amongst these treasures a surreptitious glance revealed: all three volumes of Ormerod's 'History of Cheshire', Leycester's 'Historical Antiquities Concerning Cheshire' 1673, 'Folklore: Customs and Tales of my Neighbours' by Fletcher Moss - one of only 200 copies, published in 1896, and the unabridged first edition of Fraser's 'Golden Bough', which had been custom bound in dark brown leather. The next shelf contained a long run of The Antiquary, some Gentleman's Magazine Annuals and more esoteric items, which included Reginald Scot's 'Discoverie of Witchcraft' and a Folio edition of the 'Hammer of Witchcraft' - Malleus Malificarum. Lydia appeared to have brought her entire library. Rachel was not to know that this was only a fraction of the collection painstakingly amassed by Lydia. The major part had already been donated to the Institute of Celtic Studies.

Reluctantly, she turned her back on this unexpected bonanza and treated Lydia Pendle to a bright smile.

'Something has just disturbed you. Something about my bookshelf. What is it?'

'Nothing.' said Rachel, taken aback. 'Really, nothing at all.'

Lydia stared at her intently. 'I felt it. Was it one of the books? Which one?'

'No, of course not. You're mistaken. Now, Trevor and Andy asked to be remembered, and Dorothy Platt sends her regards. They've sent gifts for you. And Trevor asked me to give you this.'

'I'm never mistaken.' Lydia insisted. Ignoring the cards and the flowers and the pot plant she began to tear the wrapping from the parcel with shaky hands, struggling impatiently and refusing Rachel's offer of help. Finally a hefty, recently published tome on Jungian psychoanalysis was revealed. Brightening visibly, she skimmed down the fly leaf before turning to the index. Ignored and forgotten, Rachel sat in silence, wondering how to regain Lydia's attention.

'This is very interesting. It was reviewed in one of the literary supplements a couple of weeks ago. Clever Trevor. I'll try to drop him a line.' She looked up and scrutinised her visitor closely. Rachel waited, wondering what was coming next.

'Is that Andy Thrower still backing losers?'

Rachel heaved a silent sigh of relief and smiled. 'Afraid so.' She picked up the photograph. 'What beautiful cats. Yours? Are they Egyptian Maus?' she asked.

'That's a bit clever. Has that bloody Trevor being briefing you?' Rachel replaced the photograph and looked at Lydia severely.

'You're being very defensive, Lydia. Of course not. Why on earth would he want to do that? As a matter of fact I happen to know quite a lot about pedigree cats. My mother used to breed them.

Lydia glanced up from the book. 'What sort?'

'Korats. I don't expect you will have heard of them. Most people haven't. They're quite rare.'

'I know.' said Lydia, dreamily. 'The native cat of Thailand, originating from the Korat plateau. Cats of ancient lineage, reputed to have been the guardians of the ancient temple of Angkor Wat. One of the last remaining pure breeds, as I recall, with a coat the colour of the clouds and eyes as green as the young rice crop. Bearers of fortune, bringers of rain - and the promise of a good harvest for the village. I remember when they were first introduced here. As a matter of fact, I freelanced an article to one of the cat magazines. I had interviewed a cat breeder who possessed one of the original imports. How many have you got?'

'Two. Now tell me about yours.'

Lydia struggled to pick up the photo frame and failed. Rachel passed it to her.

'Pharaoh and Osiris were with me for fifteen wonderful years. Had them put down last April, when my condition was diagnosed. One of the hardest things I ever had to do.' she said, in very matter of fact voice, stroking the glass. 'Here, put it back. I need to lie down now - could you help me back into bed? Save calling the bloody nurse.'

Rachel got up. Shocked at the weightlessness, she helped Lydia to the edge of the bed. She was no heavier than a child.

'You'll have to bring my legs up. They don't work anymore.'

As she lifted Lydia's thin, useless legs onto the mattress she noticed two jagged white scars running down the outside of the left calf.

'Dog bites.' said Lydia, ruefully. 'Old battle scars. Long time ago.'

'There's something down there on the floor. Hang on, I'll get it.' She knelt down, feeling around in the shadows under the edge of the bed until her fingers encountered a tiny terracotta tablet. She drew it out and held it out to Lydia.

'Oh, so that's where it was. I knew one was missing yesterday.'

'What is it?' asked Rachel. curiously.

Lydia glanced up. 'Don't you know? I thought you would. It's a rune. I must have dropped it when I was trying to get them back in their pouch. Thanks.'

Still she did not take it from the outstretched hand, so Rachel put it down on the blanket.

'Now turn it over.' said Lydia.

Rachel did as she was told.

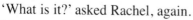

Lydia studied the engraved symbol in silence and then stared hard at Rachel, shaking her head slowly.

'What is it?' asked Rachel, again.

'A reversed Peorth.'

'I don't know anything about them. What does that mean? How do they work?'

'Divination - the runes can access natural energy fields. They are made of natural materials, you see. The earth, or stone or clay or wood. Bone too, in the old days. So they can resonate. They tap us into the forces, linking our own vibrations into those of the planet - and the universe. Quite uncanny, once you become attuned to them. They are never wrong, even when you think they can't possibly be correct.'

'Oh, I see. And do you read the Tarot cards as well?'

'Not very often. They don't resonate nearly as well as the runes - not for me at any rate.'

'Oh, I see.' said Rachel again, although she didn't, not really. 'So what does that one mean? What was it?'

'Peorth. It represents something unresolved, something hidden. This time it has appeared reversed. That signifies unpleasant revelations. Uncomfortable disclosures. The exposure of dark secrets. It's all right, my dear. No need to look so alarmed. It's for me, not you. You can choose yours in a minute. Now, are you going to tell me why you're really here, or would you like me to tell you?'

Rachel flushed. 'I understand that you knew Vincent Rush.'

'He's dead.' said Lydia

'I know that. I was sent to cover the funeral.'

'Came here the day before he died. I knew it was Vincent. Someone in a chauffeur driven car, they said. Of course, I refused to see him. Not after all those years. I watched him from the window though. He turned round and saw me as he was getting back into the car. That's when I knew what was happening. Looked bloody terrible.'

'What do you mean? How could you know? What was happening?'

Lydia laughed. 'The forces, of course. They had finally caught up with him. And serve him bloody well right. Nothing anyone could do about it. No point in trying to stop the inevitable. I'm glad I didn't let him get near me.'

'Why would he take the housekeeper's car and drive to Lindow Moss? He never drove himself.'

'I know.' said Lydia, with a strange half smile. 'And he never would.'

Rachel leant closer, over the bed. 'You mean someone else took him there? Who was it? If you know, Lydia, you must say. It's important.'

Lydia turned her head on the pillow and stared hard into Rachel's eyes. 'You really want to know?'

Rachel nodded expectantly. From somewhere down the corridor came the sound of a young baby crying.

'It's Sunday.' said Lydia. 'Somebody's great grandchild.' She looked at Rachel and shook her head slowly. 'It's crying for us. Crying on our behalf, because it hasn't discovered how to weep yet. Either that or it needs its nappy changing.'

The crying continued.

The old woman closed her eyes. Words had developed a habit of strangling themselves somewhere at the back of her throat. Just like the day when she had bent over the pram. Seeing him lying there. Unable to bypass the aura of reverence which had rendered her incapable of achieving the correct note when she tried to offer her congratulations to the proud mother. Choked by feelings of embarrassment as her shadow fell across the newborn child. Babies had always made her feel that way, but knowing the history of that particular child had made it even more difficult to sound natural.

She had bent closer. Stuck her head right inside the hood. Smelt the warm and milky waft of him beneath the blanket. Seen perfect innocence. It was always there, in the newborn. So helpless and vulnerable that the trust was almost heartbreaking. Something possessed only once, fleetingly, by the young and innocent, animal or human. It endured throughout their suckling time. Nature's clever way of ensuring that the nurturing instinct was aroused. Later it gradually vanished as something else took over and stamped its mark. Something like cunning or self interest - no, self preservation. That was it. Self preservation changes the way that they look up at you, altering the eyes in some indefinable fashion as soon as they become aware of themselves. Self realisation, that is what creeps in. As she watched the sleeping face, the nose suddenly wrinkled, the tiny fingers flexed and he opened his eyes, staring straight up into her face. She had drawn back quickly, shocked. The eyes had taken her unawares. They were not what she had been expecting. Not the eyes of a new baby. This one was already fay. Full of himself.

Lydia's eyelids fluttered open. She lay still, staring up at the ceiling. 'It was Samhain. He was driven there by his own demons.'

There was a heavy silence and then she continued. 'I made a serious mistake, telling him.'

'Telling him what, Lydia? What did you tell him?'

'About the eyes. I shouldn't have said anything about the eyes.' she repeated, as if talking to herself. 'That was when he banned me. Wouldn't let me anywhere near. He didn't need me any more, you see. I'd outlived my usefulness.'

She became agitated and Rachel took hold of the bony hand.

'Why, Lydia? Why did he ban you? What did you tell him? I don't follow .....'

But it was too late. Exhausted with the effort, Lydia had closed her eyes again and appeared to be asleep. Rachel watched her for a while and then, as she got up to leave Lydia stirred.

'I'm going now.' said Rachel, gently. 'Thank you for seeing me, Lydia.'

'I became interested in the past, the distant past.'

Her voice had grown so faint that Rachel had to bend closer.

'When the world was young and magic.' whispered Lydia.

'You mean once upon a time.' said Rachel, smiling.

Lydia looked at her so severely that Rachel shrank back, inwardly cursing that she could have been so stupid, so flippant. Suddenly, Lydia's face changed and she started to laugh.

'Pass the pouch - the hessian one, over there, on the bookshelf.'

Lydia struggled to pull open the draw strings, and dropped the missing rune inside before holding it out to Rachel like a bag of sweets.

'Shake it around. That's it. Now pick one out.'

Rachel shook her head. 'I'd rather not, if you don't mind. Not now. Another time, perhaps.' She put the pouch back on the shelf.

'Not scared are you? Next time you come we'll do you a proper reading, with the full set. Have you got a cigarette?'

Rachel shook her head. 'I'm sorry, I don't. Do they let you smoke in here?'

Lydia produced a crumpled tissue and wiped the corner of her mouth. When she looked up again Rachel detected a subtle alteration. It was something in her demeanour. Rachel thought it might be fear.

'I don't think they'll make a great song and dance about it. I won't be able to drag on a fag for much longer. Well, you'd better bring some with you next time - and an ashtray. I do need an ashtray. I think you and I might become friends, if I've got sufficient time. And fetch those Korats. I would dearly like to see them.'

'I don't think the staff will allow it.' said Rachel

'Don't let that bother you. You bring them. Soon as you can. Don't leave it too long.'

On the way out she knocked on the door marked Reception.

'Come in.' Sister Renshaw looked up and smiled. 'How did you get on?'

'All right - she wants me to come again.'

'You are honoured. It's strictly by invitation only. It would be nice if you could. She doesn't get any visitors, apart from the woman from the MN support group, who calls to see if she needs any comforts. She refused to see anybody when she arrived, so it wasn't long before people stopped bothering. You can hardly blame them. She said she would ask if she wanted anyone to visit. I was very surprised when she agreed to see you today.'

'And has she ever asked for anyone?'

'Only once, a few weeks ago, when she was very poorly. It turned out to be a chest infection, but I suspect that Lydia thought she was dying. So did we, to be honest. It would have been a blessing if she had, poor old thing.'

'What exactly is the matter with her? She's very shaky, isn't she?'

Jane Renshaw looked even more surprised 'You don't know? Rachel shook her head. 'Is it cancer?'

'No, she's suffering from motor neurone disease.'

'Oh - what is that, exactly?'

'It's a degenerative illness. The messages from the brain can't get through to the muscles. It eventually affects everything except the brain itself. In the end the patient becomes trapped inside the body - unable to eat, unable to swallow, unable to move, and unable to communicate. Totally dependent, but not vegetative. Still fully aware.'

Rachel looked shocked. 'How long will that be?'.

Jane Renshaw shook her head sadly. 'They say it's rare to survive for more than two years. It's not my place to make such predictions, but in Lydia Pendle's case it's started to advance quite rapidly. That's the reason she's in here. She struggled on at home for as long as she could, but there was no one to look after her. Once she started losing her balance and falling down she had to concede defeat. I don't think it will be a great deal longer - if she's lucky. A terrible, cruel thing it is and as yet there's no cure.'

'Does she know?'

'Oh yes, she knows all right. She's read everything she could find on the subject. She gives the doctor a hard time. She's a fighter, is Lydia. It would be better for her if she wasn't. She's just prolonging the agony.'

'That's terrible. Just out of curiousity, who did she ask to see? Was it a relative?'

Jane Renshaw shook her head. 'No, she hasn't got any. She's completely alone in the world. It was a young lad called Ben. Can't remember his second name. She got very distressed about it. Insisted that we telephone for him. His mother brought him in the next day. It seemed to do her good. She started to get a little better after that.'

'Poor Lydia. I think she's a very proud woman. I was surprised when she wanted me to come again. I don't get the impression that she's in the habit of asking favours. I have to go now, but I will try to come back soon.'

15
Baby Talk

After he had dropped Rachel off at the nursing home, Julian Whitehead drove on to Medlar Hall.

'I hope I'm not disturbing you, Mrs Jackson. I've brought you this - from Rachel.'

Susan Jackson smiled and took the huge white azalea from Julian's outstretched hand.

Oh, it's beautiful! What a lovely surprise - but she shouldn't have. There was no need.'

'She had to work this afternoon, so she couldn't bring it herself and we didn't want to be bothering you on a Sunday evening. She's really upset about the computer. Worrying herself in case she's done something dreadful to it.'

Susan shook her head.'That's a shame. Poor Rachel, you must tell her to stop fretting - it wasn't her fault. The computer doesn't matter, it doesn't mean a thing to me. Anyway, Ben has had a look at it. He's quite good with computers. Seems to know all about them, they use them at school. He even opened the back and checked the inside. It was caused by a sudden power surge, some of the - whatever they call them - boards, I think that's what he said. The boards are burnt out and that's the reason it crashed, whatever that means. It was an electrical fault. It had nothing to do with what Rachel was trying to find.'

Julian nodded. 'That's what I told her, but she feels responsible. She asked me to apologise to you.'

'There's no reason why she should. I'm sorry she's been blaming herself. Be sure to tell her there was no need to worry. She's not to give it a second thought.'

She unwrapped the plant, almost in full bloom. He stood

watching while she put it in a blue and white pot and set it in the centre of the mahogany half moon side table in the entrance hall.

'Azaleas like to be cool. It will last longer in here. That's beautiful, Julian. Do thank Rachel, it was a very kind thought. And explain about the computer.'

'Doesn't Ben get lonely around here?'

'No - he's happy with his own company.'

'How's he taken the news about Uncle Vinney?'

'Never mentions him.' said Susan, 'Anyway, I've tried to keep him out of it, as much as I could. He's far too young to be exposed to things like that. It was such a relief when they told me he didn't have to go to the inquest. They just read out the statement he gave to the policeman. None of it was very pleasant for any of us. It brought back Brian's inquest. Things I thought I'd managed to forget. All sorts of stuff I never ever talked about. Ben never asks me anything about his father, either. He's a strange boy, even though I say it myself.'

As Julian, embarrassed, took his leave she looked as if she was about to cry.

Postnatal depression didn't really exist in those days, although there was something called the Baby Blues. Nobody had ever set it to music. It wasn't a song. It meant that you sat around, exhausted and weepy, dreading the next feed because after a week of struggling you'd got abscesses for nipples. The next verse got worse. It was all about feeling guilty because you'd given up on your breasts and resorted to bottle feeding and didn't dare to tell anyone at all that you'd entertained a despicable, unnatural thought about putting him up for adoption because you didn't love the baby the way you were supposed to. You hadn't bonded with him and you didn't know why or how that could possibly be. All you knew was that the poor little thing had got a monster for a mother. It meant your husband starting to get seriously pissed off with you. Being told to get a

160

grip. To pull yourself together. Draw tight the strings on the soggy little dolly bag of your soul so we don't have to see what's really inside.

It had started in the hospital. The ward contained ten beds, all occupied. She was older than all the others, even the ones who were nursing second or even third babies. They all seemed enviably relaxed and confident, almost blasé about the whole business. Unaware that she was in a state of shock after a really bad time in the delivery room, where it had taken so long that she lost track of time, she had lain in silent misery, listening to their horror tales of Caesarean sections and forceps and ruptured stitches and unfaithful husbands. Now she felt shaky and kitten weak and acutely aware that Brian had failed to put in an appearance on the most important day of her life. When the nurse came to her bedside, she finally plucked up enough courage to ask.

'Do you happen to know if my husband has telephoned, nurse?'

The nurse looked up from checking the chart at the foot of the bed and smiled. 'Mrs Jackson - Susan, isn't it? He did come up here late last night, but you were sleeping and Sister thought it best not to disturb you.'

She deftly shook a thermometer and popped it under Susan's tongue. 'I think he'd been - wetting the baby's head.' she added. 'Sister told him to come back today. I'm sure he'll be along at visiting time.'

The auxiliaries were beginning to wheel in the cots.

'Baby Jackson?'

The nurse nodded, plumped up the pillows, and helped Susan to a sitting position. She watched as the baby was lifted from his cot and suddenly found herself dreading the next moment, the moment when she was supposed to take him in her arms.

'Now, let's see about getting him to feed, Susan.'

As the nurse took the little face in her hand and steered the shell pink toothless mouth towards his mother's breast, he had turned his head away, spurning the offer. The nurse pushed his head back into position and Susan stiffened uneasily.

'You're not relaxing.' said the nurse, reprovingly. 'He can sense your tension. You need to be very calm to breast feed successfully, you know.'

'I don't think he wants me.' she said, close to tears.

'Nonsense!' replied the nurse, briskly. 'We've seen it all before, haven't we, little man? What are you going to call him?'

'Ben.' Even the name sounded wrong, stupid. Some figment that didn't really exist.

'Right, young Ben, give your poor Mum a break, will you? Listen, my dear, it does take time. You've got to get to know each other. To begin with, you just have to persevere. I'm going to draw the curtains round the bed, so you feel a bit more private. Just relax and get used to the feel of him. Give him a cuddle. It will come, you know. In a day or two you'll wonder why you ever worried about it. I've not seen one yet that deliberately starved itself to death! You must not worry so much. The more you do, the harder it will be. Worry stops the milk from coming in. I'll look back in on you in a while, when I've finished my rounds.'

Left alone behind the curtains, she took a closer look. His fingers, dark purple against the shell pink nails, stretched outwards. She watched as they opened and closed, grasping at nothing. Long nails, already in need of a trim. As she pushed her index finger into the minute palm, the tiny warm fingers closed round it. Next she inspected his feet and the hard, smooth little heels that had kicked at her insides. She found the Identitag. It was fastened round his left ankle. Complete with the date of his arrival. Baby Jackson. Ward 6. Proof that he existed.

She wanted to talk to him, she really did, but could think of nothing to say. Not yet, not out loud. Not here. It was as if he really belonged to the hospital and they'd handed him over for a little while. Asked her to babysit him. How awful, she

162

thought, guiltily, to have to remind herself that she was his mother. Shakily, frightened of dropping him, she turned him over onto his stomach, so that he was lying across her. Slipped her hand inside his clothing, feeling his warmth, sliding her hand up his back, stroking the smoothness of skin against her finger tips. Her expression changed. Shaking, she fumbled with the ties on the back of the little white gown until she got the vent open. A thick pelt of reddish down extended across the shoulders and down the backs of the forearms. As it neared the tiny elbows it petered away to nothing. She pressed the call button.

After a while the nurse popped her head through the grey curtains. 'Mrs Jackson? Why, whatever is the matter?'

Susan pointed at the baby's half naked back in agitation.

'Look - look at him. There's something wrong. He's - he's covered in hair. Oh, I knew there was something wrong. I knew there was something you were not telling me. Tell me what the matter is - you've got to tell me.'

The nurse picked up the sleeping baby. Cuddling him close, she sat on the edge of the bed. 'Susan, there's nothing wrong with him, not a thing, believe me. He's a lovely, perfect baby, aren't you, Ben?' She turned stern eyes upon Susan. 'Now, you've got to stop this nonsense. You're getting hysterical.' she said, rather harshly. 'This is called lanugo hair. Very soon it will rub off. It's there to protect them while they're growing in the womb. Sometimes babies still have it when they're born.'

Susan stared at the fine pelt in distaste. 'Are you sure? I've never heard of it. No one ever told me about it. Have you seen it on other babies?'

The nurse nodded, reassuringly. 'Yes, of course I have. It really isn't anything to be worrying about. Ben has got rather a lot and I've not seen a baby with quite this much, but it will soon disappear. Really it will. It's probably nature's way of making sure that he keeps warm while he's so tiny. We don't have it anymore because we wear clothes. Probably all the winter babies were born with a good thick protection of hair, in the olden days. Their own little fur coats!'

'Like monkeys.' murmured Susan, miserably, wondering what terrible thing she had permitted.

'Now you can stop that immediately.' said the nurse, sternly. 'Just take a proper look at him. Can't you see that you've got you've got a beautiful baby? He's perfect, Susan and you should be thankful for that.' She leant a little closer and lowered her voice. 'I'll tell you something now that will put this into perspective, Susan. There's a poor girl in the next ward and her baby was born yesterday, too. A little girl, with a hare lip and a cleft palette, the poor little mite. A baby that can't feed properly - and she isn't going to be able to talk properly, either. The poor thing is going to need at least two operations before she's three month's old. You've got nothing at all to be getting upset about. Anyway, like I said, it will have all rubbed off in a few week's time. Here, take him.'

'I'm sorry.' said Susan, scarlet and ashamed.

The nurse handed him back.

'I panicked. It was a shock.'

'It's all right. You need to calm down. Now, no more nonsense. Let's wake him up and see if we can get him interested in his breakfast.'

Coming home had been a dreadful anticlimax. Just a blur, with Brian hovering somewhere in the background. The first few days had been spent in chaos, struggling to cope with the haphazard routines of the baby and her own exhaustion. Only the daily visits of the district nurse had prevented her from going completely crazy. Nurse Hunter had seen it all before and her brisk, no nonsense approach was exactly what was needed.

'Now, don't forget. If you have to leave baby, never leave him lying on a bed or chair or anywhere he could roll off. If you do have to put him down in a hurry, the floor is the safest place.

Always remember that, Mrs Jackson, it's important.'

She did remember and the following day, when the telephone rang in the middle of changing him, she laid him down on a blanket, on his stomach, in the middle of the floor. When she returned to the room a few minutes later it had been a nasty shock. So sudden, so unexpected, to see him there, lying quite naked. She stayed in the doorway, arrested by this shock of alienation. Intimidated by the twitching, the jerky, uncoordinated movements of that fleshy thing upon the pink and blue checked blanket, she stared in disbelief. Something awful, something primitive, something she had struggled to push out into the world.

Now, still purple and mottled from the birth, it was lying on the floor, heels and buttocks floundering. Her eyes travelled to the fuzz of red hair covering the shoulders. Something which she had felt slithering hot from her own insides. Pushed forth by her, from her own body, had come this strange demanding creature. Alive. Twitching and quivering and tensing and pulsing, there on the floor all by itself. Independent. Striving, struggling - trying to LIFT itself, trying to get up. Not strong enough yet. But already trying. Sickened by a great wave of estrangement and disgust, she felt her heart sink.

The feeling had passed in a trice and she hurried across and wrapped the blanket around his nakedness. Picked him up, held him close. Tried to be a mother. Two more sleepless nights, and she had been reduced to an irrational, weeping heap. Nurse Hunter took one look and summoned Brian.
'Now Mr Jackson, it's time we had a little chat. It would be a good idea for your wife to get a proper night's rest, so she's going to make up a bottle for baby and you are going to do the night feed for her. What that poor girl needs is a good night's sleep. You see to it that she gets one. He's your baby too, you know.' she added, severely.

Brian had rallied, made an effort. Tried to help more. For

the next few nights, Susan nudged him awake and he stumbled out of bed to attend to the crying infant. Way down the corridor, undisturbed, Vincent Rush slept quite peacefully.

Towards the end of the week, Brian decided upon a change of tactics. He would sit up and wait until the child awoke for his feed. 'You get yourself off to bed, Sue. I know what to do for him now. There's a late film on the telly. I'd rather stay up and wait till I've done the feed than have to crawl out of bed at that time in the morning.'

The luminous dial of the clock told her it was two thirty. She lay for a moment, listening to the muffled noise. The baby, she thought, sleepily. The baby was crying. She lay there, listening for it to stop, but it didn't and after a few minutes she got up to investigate. Opening the door of the sitting room she was greeted by the smell of beer and a haze of tobacco smoke. Brian was slouched in his chair. The baby lay across his knee, howling lustily. Around the chair lay a litter of empty beer cans. A cigarette, still smouldering, dangled from her husband's limp hand.

She stood over them, staring down at Brian's peaceful, stupid, drunken face and wanted to punch it viciously. Instead, she removed the cigarette and carefully extinguished it before lifting the screaming infant. She carried him back to the bedroom. Unbuttoning her night dress she began to suckle the poor, hungry mite. Watching him intently, watching his tiny cheeks move, seeing his eyelids flutter, she felt the milk rush down and saw him begin to swallow. Slowly, feeling him drawing the nourishment from her, she began to relax.

Everything was down to her. She knew that now. The entire responsibility was hers and hers alone. She would never trust Brian again. Never rely on him, never try to lean on him. Never ever. Her face had suddenly taken on a harder, less pliant look, but she felt stronger. Much stronger.

**

After Julian Whitehead had gone she made herself a cup of tea and carried it upstairs. It didn't take much to set her off lately. Everything reminded her about Brian's death, making her think about all those miserable years leading up to it. Things she thought she'd forgotten. Opening the precious Building Society book she checked the date of the opening deposit again. She could recall every tiny detail of that hot and sultry Thursday afternoon with perfect clarity. Wandering up and down the street, trying to choose a Building Society. Avoiding the one that had repossessed her home. Trying to make her mind up which one to enter. Sweating as she waited in the queue, growing increasingly nervous as her turn drew nearer. Trying to look cool and composed, trying not to think about the incredible bargain she had struck and the terrible chain of events which had brought her to this cashier's window.

16
The Deal

Financial problems finally over, Brian Jackson now had ready money passing through his pockets, with predictable results. During the long, dark evenings of January, his nightly consumption of strong drink doubled. By February it had tripled. The beginnings of belly flab now bulged uncomfortably over his waistband, whilst his expanding buttocks strained against the constraints imposed by his trousers. When Susan finally commented on his changing shape he patted his expanding beer gut with jesting pride.

'That's a very expensive piece of flesh, Susan!'

The next time she voiced concern, he turned upon her sharply.

'Leave it out, will you? A man's entitled to his pleasure after a day's work. I've earned my drink.'

She lapsed into silence, afraid that he might turn nasty. He was always short tempered these days, especially in the mornings, when he crawled out of bed with yellowed eyes, body glistening with sweat. Occasionally he tried to paw her in a show of drunken affection which she found extremely disagreeable. She always pushed him away.

'You stink of beer and you look terrible. Have you seen your eyes? Here, look!'

She picked up a mirror from the dressing table and held it out to him.

'Go on, take a look at yourself.'

That was when he had slapped her for the first time. Hard in the face so that she heard her teeth jar. They spent the remainder of the day in silence and it was the next morning before he came to her in the kitchen and attempted to apologise.

'You're going to lose us this job if you carry on.' she responded, tight lipped and unforgiving.

'Oh, Sue, don't be so silly. You always have to exaggerate, don't you? I do the job all right.'

'Only just.' she flared. 'You don't show one scrap of enthusiasm We're on a good number here, Brian. Why do you want to put it at risk?' She turned towards him, pleadingly. 'Please, Brian, please don't let us down again. I couldn't stand it.'

He drank two long glasses of tap water, one after the other.

'You worry too much.' he said, wiping his mouth on a tea towel. 'Never happy unless you've got something to whine about, are you? You'd drive any poor sod to drink, the way you go on. Rush wouldn't know if I was on the piss all day long - and then you would have something to complain about.' he added, warming to his theme. 'I never touch a drop during the daytime. Go on, tell me, when have you ever seen a drop pass my lips during the day? That's more than you can say for a lot of blokes I know. You don't know when you're well off, my girl.'

'That's because you daren't. That's the only reason, so you needn't bother trying to make a virtue out of it.' she said, quietly.

'Daren't?' he exploded, indignantly. 'What do you mean, daren't? I can take my drink. If I wanted a drink, I'd have one. I know how to control myself.'

She stared at him coldly.

'Do you? You daren't because you know damn well that once you start you can't stop. You'd carry on till you fell over. That's the reason you never drink in the daytime. I'm not stupid, you know, so you can stop trying to make some big deal out of not drinking during the day. You're hardly sober from the night before till lunchtime, anyway.'

'You talk a load of crap.' sneered Brian, walking towards the door. 'And you needn't worry yourself about the boss. He doesn't even know what bloody day it is. When he is around he's either shut up in his study or on the phone to that daft old trout. Just lay off me, do you hear?'

He slammed the door hard and escaped to the tack room, where he lit an old paraffin stove and settled down to read the morning paper in peace.

A few weeks later she had come to realise that Brian had made a big mistake in his assumptions about their employer. Vincent Rush was only too well aware of the state of play beneath his roof, but for some reason he had chosen to remain silent on the matter.

As winter gave way to the spring, bringing lighter evenings and improving weather, Brian began to go out every night, away from the critical, counting eyes of his wife, to take his drink with like minded cronies in more congenial surroundings. Each night he risked the breathaliser, driving home very slowly along the quiet back lanes. By then she had reached a state of near despair. The more she complained, the more time he spent away. If she said nothing he would sometimes settle down for the evening, sitting opposite her. No fun any more, no more joking, no little laughs together. Just the television set and the tiny gassy explosions of the ring-pulls as he worked his way silently through the cans, until she almost came to prefer it when he did his drinking away from the house.

One Friday evening, as they sat down together in the kitchen to eat, she had tried to talk to him again. She had thought about it for days, deciding what to say, waiting for a good moment. It was no good rowing with him, no good at all. This time she would be sympathetic, get him to see sense. She'd been handling him the wrong way, she could see that now. This time she'd do like the magazine article suggested. Explain to him that it was a sort of illness, talk to him gently. Persuade him to get help.

'Brian, I want you to listen to me.'

He glanced up from his plate, disturbed by her tone.

'What's up?'

She cleared her throat and hesitated for a moment. 'Well, the thing is, I think you've got a real problem love, and I want you to see someone about it. I can't just sit back and do nothing, watching you wreck your life - both our lives. You're an alcoholic and you're going to need help to overcome it, Brian. I'm going to see that you get it.'

The kitchen chair grated against the tiles and then it fell over with a loud bang and he was towering over her. There had been a moment while she had waited for him to hit her and then, as he hesitated, she backed away. A second later he swept the dinner plates along the length of the breakfast bar and they crashed to the floor, splattering vegetables and gravy up the doors of the units as the dishes shattered. His face darkened with rage.

'That's it. You've done it this time, you moaning bitch. I don't have to take this from you. Don't rile me any more - do you understand? That's it - finished. I've had it with you,'

He stormed out of the kitchen and a moment later she heard the car engine revving furiously. And then he was gone.

Feeling slightly sick, she bent down to pick up the broken pieces of crockery. She dropped them into the bin. She scooped up the food and wiped and polished the floor and the kitchen units until they shone again. The other mess was way beyond her cleaning powers. The most that she could do with that was to try and contain it.

Later, lying in bed, miserable and wakeful, listening fretfully for the sound of the car, she had half made up her mind to leave. It had been long past midnight when the tyres squealed on the drive. The wave of relief had only lasted for an instant, obliterated by that dreadful moment when metal collided with brickwork. The ensuing silence was even worse, then the car engine jumped back into life, revving noisily, followed by another loud crash. By this time she was running down the

171

corridor. Peering through the landing window, she looked down upon the roof of the car below. It was standing across the drive at a crazy angle, wedged between the wing of the stable block and the main wall of the house. The outside lights went on, illuminating the full extent of the damage. Her eyes widened in horror as she surveyed the creased side and crumpled wing of the new Ford. She watched as the driver's door opened slowly and Brian emerged from the vehicle. He hesitated, one hand on the roof of the car, his other arm raised to shield his eyes from the light. She saw him swaying, placing one leg hesitantly forward, testing the space before his foot made contact with the ground. As he lurched towards the passage door like some monstrous piece of clockwork she had raced down the stairs to let him in.

He almost fell inside as she opened the door, regained his balance and collapsed heavily against the lintel. Swaying towards her, frightening and ugly and unfocussed, she had retreated in alarm.

'Sorry - Sue, wanna say sorry.'

He suddenly doubled forward and expelled a foul stream of vomit. When he had finished he straightened up again, smiling idiotically. She backed away as his hands clawed towards her.

'Stay there. Don't come anywhere near me.' she said, desperately.

Brian continued his advance.

'Bit of a prang. Misjudged. Nothing much, soon fix it.'

'Keep away.' she repeated dangerously, backing down the corridor.

'Leave this to me, Susan.' Behind her, Vincent Rush was leaning casually against the wall. With one stride he brushed past, gripped Brian firmly by the arm and led him upstairs. Susan rushed after them and then watched helplessly as Dr Rush closed the bedroom door on her husband.

'I should sleep in the other room tonight, Susan.'

Suddenly she found her tongue.

'Oh, Dr Rush! Oh, dear God, whatever must you think of us? I don't know what to say. We'll pay for the damage. It was an accident, honestly, an accident, we'll see to it, we'll put it right. I'm terribly sorry about it. We'll see that it's fixed .....'

He held up a hand and she fell silent again.

'Not now, Susan. Explanations can wait until the morning. Just get that filthy mess cleaned up and then try to get some sleep. I'll see you in my study at ten o'clock. On your own. I don't want him anywhere near me until he's dried out.'

He turned abruptly, leaving her shivering in the corridor, utterly defeated, afraid and ashamed. Knowing that it was the end of everything and horribly aware of the nasty, bitter taste in her mouth.

It was still there the next morning. Her eyes were dreadful. Reddened and still moist from all the weeping, she had tried to improve their appearance by smoothing green eye shadow over the swollen lids and had brushed thick layers of mascara onto the lashes. Her reflection stared back at her, cheap and painted and with a wave of miserable self loathing, she rubbed it all off again. When she crept into the bedroom to retrieve her clothing the room stank of him. She stood over the bed and stared down at her husband. Still fully dressed, he lay prostrate, one glistening smear of saliva dribbling from the corner of his slack mouth. She left the room, closing the door softly behind her.

There was no defence, nothing she could say in mitigation. Maybe she should beg, plead for another chance? Until the next time, till it happened again, as she knew it surely would. No, better to tell Dr Rush that they would be leaving today. That would be the dignified way to handle it, if it was possible to retain any self respect in such humiliating circumstances. Least said, that would be best.

Pausing at the head of the stairs, looking down, she had suddenly realised just how fond of the place she had become.

Started to think of it as home, to take it for granted, to let herself settle and belong. How she had cared for it. Now it had taken Brian just a matter of months to ruin their wonderful opportunity. Outside the door of the study she hesitated. There was music playing.

Vincent Rush had timed everything carefully, conducting this important scene with the same metronomic precision with which he had orchestrated the rest of the piece. The slow movement, vaguely familiar and veering towards the mawkish side of sentimental, commenced at the precise moment that poor distraught Susan Jackson steeled herself to knock. When he opened the door she was greeted with a slow arpeggio of heartbreak from violins in a minor key, exactly as he had planned. Tears welling, she steadied herself, holding them so that her throat became an aching lump instead.

'Ah, Susan. Good morning, do come in.'

He crossed to the cassette player and pressed the off switch, beckoned her into the sudden loud silence and indicated the chair. She sat down. Taking up his position behind the desk he rested his chin on his hands and looked at her without speaking, until she wanted to squirm. Unable to hold his gaze any longer she bent her head and contemplated her shoes.

'Is there anything you wish to say, Susan?' he asked, at last.

She had forced herself to look up at him, knowing that he could read everything from her face, and cleared her throat nervously. He stared back at the wretched, vulnerable girl impassively, waiting for her to speak.

'I'm terribly sorry, Dr Rush, so very sorry. There isn't really anything else that I can think of to say. We've let you down and I know apologising will never make up for what's happened.'

As her eyes brimmed he took up a pencil and began rolling it between the palms of his hands whilst she fought to gain control of the tears. Next he drummed the pencil against the edge of the desk, a tiny, irritating noise which escalated the tension. Finally he spoke.

'I would be perfectly justified in throwing you out.'

Susan nodded and bowed her head.

'I know. We'll go today.' she whispered. 'If you could just allow me a bit of time to organise it.'

More pencil tapping and then he rolled it aside. Leaning his arms on the desk he began his speech.

'Brian is one of the world's parasites, Susan. A likable fellow, but a parasite, drink being his downfall. I have known that almost from the moment you moved in to Medlar Hall.' He paused while she blew her nose.

'I have no complaints about you, Susan. On the contrary, I am well aware that you are the one who does the work. I've watched you, covering for him, carrying him along.'

He leant forward, pale eyes staring intently from behind cold lenses. She looked away instinctively. 'In his present condition your husband is virtually unemployable. Does his father have a drinking problem?'

Susan nodded. 'They all do. The whole family. His father and his brothers, they're all heavy drinkers. They boast about it, like it's sign of manliness. Mum did warn me.'

Her employer leaned back a fraction. 'And you should have listened to her. This is obviously an inherited problem, my dear. Some people can take it or leave it, whilst others become addicted very rapidly. It depends entirely upon one's genetic makeup. If Brian is consuming on a daily basis the number of units that I suspect, he's on the road of no return. And you - well, you're going to end up a very unhappy woman.'

She blew her nose again, knowing he was speaking the truth. 'But he's my husband, Dr Rush. I've tried talking to him. I want to help him, but he won't listen. He just gets very angry. Please don't sack us.'

She bit her lip in embarrassment. She had never meant to beg. Vincent Rush's shoulders eased down a fraction. When he

175

next spoke there was a subtle alteration in his tone, which Susan was far too distraught to notice.

'I've considered dismissing you both. Considered the matter very seriously, very seriously indeed. It is only because of you, Susan, that I am going to suggest one further option. I feel that you have already suffered enough. Because of this I am prepared to make you an offer. There is a way out for you, if you want to remain here.'

At that point he had waited in silence, trying to gauge her reaction. When she looked up at him again she had known that he had spotted the tiny flicker of hope.

'Now, before I go any further, let me make one thing perfectly clear. The rest of this conversation is strictly private. It is between you and I and no other person. I am going to divulge - to tell you about - certain information which is highly confidential, connected with my work. Look at me, Susan. Do you understand what I am saying?'

'I think so,' she said slowly, puzzled, 'but what has it got to do with me? Why tell me about it?'

'That will become clear in a moment.' His tone was brusque. 'Do you promise never, under any circumstances, never ever to speak of the things I am about to tell you? Neither to Brian, nor your mother. Not to anyone at all?'

Susan nodded. 'If that's what you want, Dr Rush. You're the boss.'

He was staring at her closely now, concentrating, willing her. 'I mean it Susan. One word to anyone and you're finished - the pair of you.'

She experienced an unpleasant ripple of alarm. Before it had finished his next question hit her like a hammer and she felt her heart thump.

'Would you like a child?'

She stiffened, straightening up against the back of the chair as if trying to rebalance herself against this disturbing shift of ground. This wasn't an employer's question and it certainly did not deserve an employee's answer.

'That's very cruel, Dr Rush.'

He stood up and came to her side of the desk, leaning against it in a more relaxed manner. 'It was never intended that way, my dear.' He spoke very gently. 'It is a very direct question and I would like you to answer it honestly.'

For the first time ever she looked him straight in the eyes. 'I would have loved to have a baby, oh, I can't tell you how much I longed for a baby. It would have meant the world to me. Four years I spent, trying to get pregnant. And after all that time on the pill, so we could wait until we were good and ready before we started a family. Well I needn't have bothered. In the end I managed to get the doctor to send me for tests at the clinic. Brian wouldn't come with me. He wasn't that interested. He's just happy to drift along from one day to the next. Anyway, as things turned out it wouldn't have made any difference, even if he had come along. The fault's with me, not him. They said the only way I could ever have a child would be in - I've forgotten what they called it. A test tube baby.'

'In vitro.'

She nodded. 'That was it. Well, I knew Brian would never agree to anything like that. That was over two years ago. And since then, things haven't gone too well for us. My mum says it was a blessing in disguise, us not having any children.'

Dr Rush nodded understandingly. 'I see. That's what I thought. Now, Susan, I think we may be able to help each other. I am prepared to ....' he hesitated and she studied him questioningly. 'How shall I put this? I will make a deal with you.' He watched her eyes widen as she moved forward in the chair, startled.

'What do you mean?'

He went back behind the desk and sat down.

'I can make it possible for you to have your child.'

Susan's mouth fell open. 'How?' she asked, incredulously. 'I'd need an operation, wouldn't I?'

He shook his head. 'No, nothing like that.' he replied, soothingly. 'The procedure is quite simple and involves no risks. This is precisely the type of problem with which my research programme is concerned. At the present time it is highly confidential. What we call classified information. However, it is still in the experimental stage.'

'You can't use me for an experiment.' There was a note of outrage in her voice.

'Calm down. I did not explain myself properly. What I meant to say was, the method is not yet freely available and is unlikely to be for some time. Now, do you remember the blood samples that I took from you and Brian at the time of your interview?'

She nodded, her thoughts turning back to Brian and the way he had joked about it, afterwards.

'I still have those samples. At the laboratory. From them I could extract all that is needed, using your blood and Brian's blood, to create a fertilised egg. So you can have your child, your own child, from your own blood, fertilised in vitro, just as they would do at the clinic. Then, I merely have to implant it in your womb.'

He paused, waiting for his words to sink in, trying to gauge her reaction as she continued to stare at him in stunned silence.

'It would actually take about three minutes of your time.' he added, casually.

Finally finding her voice she asked, doubtfully, 'Why should you want to do that for me?'

He smiled. 'As I said, Susan, to help us both. It would be a perfect partnership. You desire a child and I need to test my work.'

'So you're asking me to be a guinea pig?'

He smiled again, but only the trace of a smile, this time.

'I don't really think that's a terribly apt way of putting it, Susan.

I would prefer to say that you could provide the environment I need to take my work to its next stage. Think of it as a service to others, my dear. You would be helping the advance of science. In years to come, perhaps other childless women will profit from my work.'

'Then why is it so secret? I don't understand.'

Dr Rush gave a long and exaggerated sigh. 'Because, Susan, you are not my patient. I am not your doctor. Therefore, it is against the law for me to conduct this programme of .....' he paused and cleared his throat. 'Susan, try to concentrate. Should anyone find out that I had performed an act of assisted fertilisation upon you, my career would be finished.' He held up a hand, silencing her interruption. 'Please allow me to continue. If you agree to undergo this procedure, I will guarantee the roof over your head. Brian as well, if you wish him to remain here. That would be entirely up to you. You would have long term security for yourself and the child. And in addition, once the pregnancy was confirmed, I would invest the sum of ten thousand pounds in your sole name. In return, all I would ask is that you remain here, at Medlar Hall, and allow me to monitor the child's growth and development.'

At this point he spread his hands, palms down, flat upon the surface of the desk.

'That's all.'

She sat in silence, pulling at her bottom lip with her fingers.

'I don't think Brian would agree to it.' she said, eventually.

Rush stiffened and when he spoke there was a sharp edge to his voice. 'Brian is not to know, not to be consulted. I've already explained that no one else is to be told. There is nobody for you to confide in, Susan. You have to understand that this is one decision you must make alone. Brian has forfeited his rights here. It would be quite simple. You just have to tell him that the miracle has finally happened, after all these years. He would have no reason to disbelieve you. Now, this is entirely up to you. Your choice, nobody is forcing you into anything. You can have a child, security, a substantial sum of money and this roof over your head. It would be a dream come true. What more could anyone ask for?' He paused, watching her face as she struggled to conceal the complex mixture of emotions as they began to torment her. 'Or you can walk away from this room, pack your things and take your chance out there in the world. You and Brian. You'll probably be able to get your old job back.'

He stood up and crossed to the window, staring out over the garden, silently willing her to comply. When he turned back into the room, she had not moved.

'Right, Susan, I need your decision by Monday. Consider everything. Think about it very carefully before you decide. Personally, I would not have thought it a difficult choice. In the meantime, discuss it with anyone, anyone at all, and that choice no longer exists. Do you understand?'

'Yes, Dr Rush. I understand.'

She crossed to the door and then appeared to change her mind. She came back over to the desk, where he had started to write something. He looked up.

'What is it now?'

She sat down again. 'I can't spend the rest of the weekend wondering what to do. It will drive me crazy. I'd rather make my mind up now, one way or the other. First I need to ask some questions.'

'And I will do my best to answer them.'

'Where would you actually do it?'

He looked at her in surprise. 'Do what?'

Well - the implantation. Is that what you called it?'

Simple questions. He gave a small sigh of relief.

'Why, here at home, of course. It's absolutely nothing to worry about. I've done it many, many times before.'

'On other women?'

'Well, no, I'll be perfectly honest with you. Not on women, Susan. You would be the first. I've never done a human implantation, but I have done a vast amount of work on primates.'

She gave him a puzzled look.

'Monkeys, chimpanzees. It's all the same to me. You have to trust me. I am a scientist, but I'm also a doctor. What you would undergo would be no different than a gynaecological examination, and you must have had those before. There's nothing at all to fear, it is quite painless. Everything would be perfectly simple and straightforward. It would take up just a few minutes of your time - and think of the rewards. It would be the most important few minutes of your life.'

He must have been amazed at how easy it had all been. No cliffhangers, no agonies of suspense over the weekend, no dangling at her mercy whilst she made up her mind. None of that. She had just sat forward in the chair, with a hot flush of colour in her cheeks, and asked when he would like to do it, watching in silence as his eyes closed against the sudden surge of gratitude towards her. When he picked up his pen she had seen the hand tremble.

'I'm sure you've made the happiest choice, my dear, for you both. Now I need to take some details from you. We have to be absolutely sure about the timing. It has to be precise. As you probably know already, there is a certain point in your cycle when the lining of the uterus is ready to receive the fertilised egg. It is vital that we select the correct day. In the meantime I will proceed with the necessary preparations in the laboratory. I'll press ahead and get everything organised.'

Afterwards he came round the desk to her and held out his hand. As she stood up he pulled her towards him and kissed her cheek. 'Thank you.'

When she shrank back in alarm he must have realised immediately that she had misinterpreted the gesture and hastened to reassure her.

'It's all right, Susan, relax. I'm not here to exploit you in that way. You have no need for any fears in that direction. That was just my way of saying thank you.'

She stared at him with large eyes.

'You're thanking me? After what happened last night? Surely I should be the one —'

He put a finger against her lips, silencing her, and shook his head.

'Leave everything to me. You can just concentrate on enjoying motherhood, like any other woman. I will organise the transfer of the money. It will be invested in your sole name. Now, I won't be able to let you have the full amount all at once. It will have to be paid over in three instalments. The first as soon as the pregnancy is confirmed by your own GP, the others at the beginning of the next two tax years. That way there will be no tax liability for you to worry about. And Susan?'

'Yes, Dr Rush?'

'Get some driving lessons organised for yourself. Right away. I don't want Brian anywhere near that car again, once it's fixed. It really would be better if he stayed home at nights.'

She closed the door quietly behind her and he sat listening to her footsteps on the linoleum, growing fainter as she walked back down the corridor to the kitchen.

**

'Good afternoon, Dr Rush.'

Sarah Chalfont treated him to a pleasant smile which did not extend to her eyes. He was waving a receipt at her impatiently.

'I need to collect this from cryonic archives. I'll take it now, if that's convenient.'

She took the receipt from him and keyed the details into the computer. The file number appeared on screen.

'Just the one sample. Is that correct, Dr Rush?'

He nodded, tapping his fingers on the polished surface of the counter and Sarah watched with distaste as the smear of clammy finger prints began to evaporate.Very nervous, she thought, but then, he always was.

'Do you want to wait? It will take a few minutes to retrieve. I can have it sent over to the lab, if you prefer.'

'No, I'll wait.'

He paced the reception area carpet restlessly, one eye on the swing doors. He had picked his moment carefully, correctly anticipating that mid afternoon would be the slackest time. Eventually she reappeared with a small polystyrene container. She placed it on the counter and proceeded to remove the lid. He watched intently as she took out the phial.

'E3.' she said, reading the label. 'Intact. Seals unbroken. Is that the correct sample?'

He nodded, curbing the almost overwhelming desire to snatch the precious phial from her well manicured fingers. Instead he forced himself to crawl through the the red tape ritual, countersigning all the documentation in triplicate. Only then did she permit him to take possession. He thanked her brusquely and started for the doors. He was almost there when she called him back.

'Dr Rush, I think you've forgotten something.'

He turned, startled.'What is it? Is something wrong?'

'The receipt, Dr Rush. I need the receipt. I have to file it in the day book. You know, as proof that the sample has left our keeping. To absolve this department from any further responsibility.'

His annoyance did not show as he made his way back to the desk.

'Of course, how very remiss of me. So much paperwork attached to everything.'

After leaving the cryonic department he made his way across the site, past the main kennel blocks to the large warehouse beyond. He nodded abruptly to the man sitting up in the security box beside the entrance, who watched intently as he inserted his card key into the main door. Once inside the building he made his way quickly through a confusing maze of corridors until he reached the central site stores. Here he requisitioned several steripacks containing a selection of gynaecological instruments.

'Oliver tied up, is he?'

'I beg your pardon?'

'Oliver - Dr Tindall.' repeated the file clerk, pleasantly. 'He usually collects all your equipment.'

'Oh, I see. Yes, he's busy just at present. Now, I also require a minibator. I may as well take it with me, since I'm here.'

'Right. Let's see what we can do.' He leafed through the pages of a huge stock book, found what he was looking for and ran his finger down the list.

'Now, how about the Glo'n-grow 7? Or perhaps you'd be better with a 12?'

'The smallest you can find.'

The clerk went away and Rush listened to him as he rummaged about at the rear of the storage units. He returned bearing a small package.

'Brand new. Never even been opened. I'd better just check it's in good working order for you, sir.'

He removed the tiny machine and checked out the plug.

'Testing, testing.' he joked, flicking on the power switch. They peered together through the tiny door of tinted glass, at the dull red glow.

'There we are - all systems go, sir. We have lift-off! What is it this week, pigeon's eggs?'

Rush forced himself to grin at the man's feeble jokes as he began to pack the instruments and the machine into his case. The clerk hastened to his assistance as he struggled to fasten the clasps.

'You'll be ruining that case, sir. I can have it sent over within the hour. It would save you carrying it.'

'No, no, that really won't be necessary. I can manage.' said Rush, hastily, heaving the heavy case down to the floor. 'We need these things immediately.' he added, by way of explanation.

'Oh dear, bit of a panic on?' asked the clerk, sympathetically. 'We all get days like that. It's the same down here, some mornings.'

'Quite. Better dash - many thanks.' Rush made his escape.

Later that night, Rush locked himself inside the study and began his lengthy preparations, making copious notes as he worked. It was not until thirty six hours later that thermal checks put him out of his misery, confirming that the phial's contents had reached room temperature. At this point he placed it into incubation and, for the first time in his entire career, rang in sick. Work would have to wait. The delicate balance between time and temperature factors played an increasingly vital role during this tricky stage of the operation.

He checked the graph again. Each morning Susan had left a note of her temperature reading on his desk and over the preceding days he had carefully plotted her cycle. Assuming that she was accurate about her dates, as the temperature readings appeared to confirm, he had planned the implantation for seventy two hours hence.

During the interim he feverishly monitored the progress of the cell clump, which was dividing rapidly now. He sat for hours, immobile and transfixed, staring down the lens of the microscope at the haphazard cluster grazing in its dish of nutrient jelly. At this point he had a terrible yearning to share his astounding success. To gloat a little. Although not boastful by nature, it would be enormously satisfying to have his colleagues gasping at this particular sight. He had toyed with the idea of showing Lydia, but her remarks about that stupid glass legend still rankled, so instead he contented himself with a solitary toast. One generous glass of whisky held ceremoniously aloft in front of the inky doors of the incubator which temporarily housed his precious blastocyst.

'To us.' he said. 'To me and to you - whoever you are.'

On the final evening he summoned Susan to the study. When she came through the door she looked so pale that he got up and came over to her, concerned.

'Are you feeling all right? You're not ill or anything, are you?'

'No. I'm OK. Well - I'm a bit queasy, actually. It's nerves. My stomach's been churning all day. The thoughts of - I don't know if I can go through with it. Letting you - touch me. It's so awful, I can't even bear to think about it. It's too embarrassing.'

'Susan, calm down. Just lock the door behind you.'

When she sat down, he handed her a thick green bag made from recycled paper. She peered inside at the bottle of brandy and looked at him quizzically.

'For Brian. Just to make absolutely certain that he sleeps tonight. Tell him I gave it to you because I never touch the stuff. He won't ask any questions.'

Susan bit her lip. 'It all seems so underhand. I feel awful.'

'Don't. There's no need. You're doing this as much for him as for anybody, Susan and don't you forget it. You're keeping the roof over his head as well as your own. Now, as soon as he's sleeping soundly, you must come to my room. Everything is prepared and I'll be waiting for you.'

She shivered. He patted her cold hand reassuringly. 'Listen, I know you're feeling extremely nervous, my dear, but there's absolutely no need. Everything is under control and there's nothing for you to be worried about. I can understand that this is something of an ordeal for you, but I've explained the whole procedure. We've been over it step by step. There's nothing I've left out. You know exactly what I am going to do. We are going to be completely professional about this.'

She nodded and he patted her hand again.

'Good girl. You only have to relax and trust me. Trust me as you would your own doctor. You do trust me, don't you?'

She made no reply, fidgeting instead with a small piece of tissue, shredding it and crumpling it in her hands.

'Is something the matter?' he asked, sharply. 'What is it, Susan? Tell me.'

She cleared her throat.

'You remember when we were talking about - things. And you said that Brian's drinking was inherited. I'm worried in case his baby will have the same tendency. Is it just the boys that get it, or girls as well? It's been worrying me all week, Dr Rush. I don't want his drink problem being passed on to the baby.'

He intervened, quickly. 'I've already checked for signs of any genetic defect. That's my job, Susan. I'm as sure as I can be that this baby is going to be perfect. These characteristics can skip generations. This particular child has inherited the best qualities from both parents. Just get up now, and come over here. Would you like to see?'

Reverently, he removed the phial from the incubator and took it to the microscope.

'Now,' he spoke so very softly that it was almost a whisper, almost as if he was afraid of disturbing something, 'this is actually no larger than the head of a pin, but if you look down the lens - ' he grabbed her arm and pushed her forward, ' - there we are. Now just use this little dial to bring it into focus. Tell me what you see, Susan.'

She stared down at the mulberry cluster. Nothing moved.

'Is it really alive?' she asked breathlessly, not taking her eyes from it.

'Oh yes, very much alive. In another week or so it will begin to reform and within a fortnight it will be quite recognisably a human embryo.'

Susan shook her head in wonder. Turning to him, questions began to pour from her.

187

'Is that how we all were? Like that? Is that how we started off? It's hard to believe, hard to imagine, seeing it, that we were all once - oh, it's incredible! Don't you find it amazing, Dr Rush? I suppose you're used to it.'

He shook his head, delighted by her reaction.

'No, you are quite right, Susan. It is incredible. A fantastic, extraordinary achievement. A miracle. The creation of life itself.'

'And do you know if it's a girl or a boy?'

'Of course.'

'I don't want to know. Promise you won't tell me?'

'As you wish. I had better put - it - back in the incubator. There we are, nice and snug. Just another few hours. Now, down to the practicalities. In about six weeks time, you will go to your own doctor and tell him that you think you are pregnant. Ask for a test. At that point, once it's been confirmed, you will be channelled into the National Health system, just like any other expectant mother. I would be more than happy to pay for you to have the baby privately, but unfortunately that would arouse suspicion. Your baby will be born around the second week of March. You've got a great deal to look forward to.'

She nodded, unable to speak.

'Whatever happens, you must keep to our arrangement. The timing is vital. There will be no second chance.'

He patted the top of the incubator.

'Come on, Susan, cheer up. Tonight is Baby Night. The very beginning of a new life. That tiny miracle is in urgent need of you now. Without you, it cannot survive. It will die.'

Susan picked up the bottle of brandy from the desk.

'I'll be there, Dr Rush. You can count on it.'

It was after two in the morning when he returned to the study. He removed a battered notebook from the desk and wrote two words on the final page;

May 27th 1984: Seed planted.

He locked the book away in the drawer. Next he arranged the instruments neatly on the desk, counting and checking them carefully before wrapping them in the cloth. He unplugged the tiny incubator and put it back in its box, then packed everything away into the case, to be returned to the stores in the morning.

17
June 1984

Once he had absorbed the totally unexpected news of his impending paternity, Susan Jackson had been both surprised and gratified to find her husband behaving in a more considerate and protective manner. He even attempted to change his drinking habits and one evening took the gigantic step of consuming nothing at all. For the first time in years he retired to bed completely sober but his reward was a tormented night of restless insomnia. Perseverance never featuring highly on Brian's short list of virtues, he decided the following morning that nature had not intended that he should lead a life of total abstention. Instead, he settled for a dramatic reduction in his consumption, permitted himself one grand lapse on Saturday night, the result being an immediate improvement in temper and finances.

'We've got something to save for now.' he would tell Susan frequently, patting the swell of her stomach. 'He's going to need all sorts of things.'

'It might be a girl, you know. Would you be disappointed?'

'A girl?' he repeated, as if the idea had never crossed his mind. 'Well, I suppose not. It would be a fine thing to have a son, though.' He lit a cigarette and flicked the spent match into the ashtray. 'I still can't really believe it, Sue. Me - a father!' He drew hard on the cigarette. 'And that Rush's not such a bad bloke, is he? I thought he'd fire the pair of us when he found out about it. No kids, he said. That was part of the deal. I just hope he doesn't change his mind later on, when you've got lines of nappies all over the place.'

'I don't think we need to worry.' said Susan, reassuringly. 'He

190

promised - and he is a gentleman, after all. Not the sort to go back on his word, Brian.'

The effect of Susan's pregnancy upon her employer was something which he had totally failed to anticipate. It left him wrestling with a new and strange mixture of emotions. The idea of some national health service obstetrician now monitoring the life within her brought floods of frustrated jealousy. Such bitter irony! The greatest of all his achievements, the very apex of a lifetime's devoted research, now having to remain unacknowledged. And if that was not torment enough, the child's development was now under the stewardship of a total stranger, whilst he, Vincent Rush, the creator, had to bear silent witness to Brian Jackson, suddenly lionised by his spurious paternity. Dripping with pride and strutting around like a bloody stallion, he thought, peevishly.

The whole episode was proving unexpectedly painful. His disquiet peaked on the day that Susan returned from a trip to the ante natal clinic and came shyly along to the study, clutching an ultra-sound print of the growing foetus. He stared silently down at the grey, watery image and saw deeper, beyond the growing flesh, beneath the newly formed rib cage, to the tiny viscera and the perfect heart. The size of his thumb nail and beating. Flip. Flap. A newly landed fish. Out of his reach, beyond his control, safely tucked inside this young woman. Beating and pumping and developing. Susan watched his Adam's apple travel up and down twice as he gazed closely at the picture, confronting the daunting realisation that he had started something it was now quite beyond his power to halt. These feelings lasted but an instant and his hand was quite steady as he returned the photograph with a wintry smile.

'Everything appears to be going splendidly, my dear. You look wonderful. Pregnancy obviously suits you.'

As the weeks passed, he watched her closely. Out of the moss, out of the centuries, out of his laboratory. Here she was, stomach swelling, standing at his own kitchen sink. Eating and breathing for the microscopic parasite he had implanted, while it grew. Gathering power, heartbeat by heartbeat. Gaining strength. Overtaking him. He was beginning to find the torment almost unbearable.

He confided his anguishes to the waiting pages of his journal. This gave him little comfort and did nothing to alleviate his sufferings. The stress remained, lodging like great stones somewhere within the cavity of his chest. The weight of it slowed him, dulled him and finally altered his appearance.

Colleagues began to notice and to wonder. It was not unknown for men of Rush's calibre to suffer nervous collapse. Frank Newbolt finally elected to have a word with him and turned up at the laboratory on some flimsy pretext.

'Isn't it time you had a break, Vincent? Why not take a couple of weeks off - longer if you like. Surely the research programme can wait a while?'

Rush turned upon him sharply. 'What exactly are you implying?'

'Why, nothing, nothing at all.' said Newbolt, surprised by the reaction. 'Look, we can all see that you're a bit below par, that's all. Take a holiday, recharge the batteries. Get a change of scene. Have you had a check-up recently?'

Rush tossed his head in irritation. 'There's nothing wrong with me, I'm fine. Now, if you don't mind, Frank, I need to get on.'

'Oh, come on, man. You've got to slow down. Take a look at yourself - you're going to be ill if you carry on. Get away from it for a while.'

Rush gathered up a small collection of phials, inserted them with care into a holding tray and handed them to Tindall.

'Return those to incubation, Oliver.'

He turned back to Newbolt. 'I cannot leave my work. 'Thank's for the concern, but there's no need. No need at all. I'm all right.'

Newbolt stood up and shrugged. 'You take care of yourself, Vincent.' he said, making his way to the door.

Looking up, Rush read genuine concern in the man's expression. He followed him to the door and opened it.

'Later, Frank. I will take some time off, later on. I'll organise something. In the spring.'

'If you don't have a breakdown in the meantime.' thought Newbolt as he walked back down the corridor to his own lab. He never raised the matter again. There was not much point with someone like Vincent Rush.

During the winter months he took to turning up at Lydia's cottage unannounced, to sit hunched before her open fire. While she talked, the two cats settled next to her on the settee, he would sometimes listen, sometimes not. He just sat in silence, winding down, going into neutral, glad to be away from his own territory for a while. For weeks she waited, expecting him to speak, to unburden himself, but it never happened. Finally she raised the matter.

'Vincent, you'd better tell me about it. I know something's wrong. What's troubling you?'

He turned away from her in something that may have been embarrassment, but she could not be certain. Her questions hung on the air for a moment and then died for want of an answer. She escaped to the kitchen.

Left alone, he stared moodily into the flames, dwelling upon his resentments. The mother that he had selected, glowing with the thrill of it all. There, happily keeping house for him; breathing the air of the twentieth century, whilst the born again iron age flourished inside her. When Lydia returned with the coffee she found him bent forward in the chair with his head in his hands. His shoulders were racked with silent sobs. Filled with alarm, she hesitated and then hurried across to him. Her hand reached out towards him. Then she remembered herself and drew it back quickly. He never knew.

'Come on, Vincent, talk about it.' She spoke briskly. 'Don't crack up now. You can't allow it to do this to you.'

There was a sharp intake of breath and as he straightened up she knew the moment had passed. He had retreated back into himself.

Readjusting his spectacles, he took the proffered cup of coffee. 'I'm all right, Lydia. It's nothing I can't handle.' He gave a thin smile. 'I think it's something like - like you had with the garotte.'

A shadow darkened her face. 'Then God help you.'

Which one?' asked Rush lightly, attempting to defuse the intensity.

'Your choice.' she said.

18
Dawn Raid- July 1983

Shortly before four thirty the little silver car turned out of the drive, invading the greyscale world which precedes daybreak. Dipped headlights slicing low through the stillness of that July night, with Rush alongside, a dark, nervous shadow in the passenger seat. Co-conspirators now, locked into mutual silence. The whole thing a wild implausibility.

They had talked all night. He had feigned disinterest when she first told him. Playing for time, betraying nothing. Playing a game, she had later come to realise. Raising objections, forcing her to persuade him.

'You could try again.'

He had yawned, inclining his head so that the light reflected off the thick lunettes of his spectacles, accentuating the impression of sightlessness. She sat and watched, waiting for him to say something. Eyes of too pale a hue, framed by colourless eyelashes and a skin so fine and bloodless that the blue veins showed through.

'Are you quite certain that it's fully fleshed?'

She nodded. 'Well yes, according to the boy. From his description it's obviously tanned by the peat acids. Kippered was the word he used.'

'I see. Even if I got as far a obtaining a sample, it could prove a disappointment, certainly as far as you're concerned. There's no guarantee that the same peculiarity would be present. It could have been a fluke. A one-off, peculiar to that individual.'

'Give me some credit, Vincent. I know enough about genetics to realise that there's a high degree of probability that the same characteristics will be shared, to a greater or lesser degree, amongst a close knit tribal community.' said Lydia, with a touch of pomposity. 'They were probably suffering from in-breeding.' she continued. 'Two bodies from the period. From the same patch of land. Surely there's a good chance? Anyway, what have you got to lose?'

He had laughed. A short, bitter sound.

'Only my career. My reputation. The prospect of being hauled up and sacrificed myself, on the alter of the ethics committee. Do you really have the slightest conception of what you are suggesting?'

Lydia lowered her eyes.

'I'm sorry.' she apologised. 'You're right. I haven't thought it through. It only happened a few hours ago and I let myself get carried away by the idea. Forget it ever happened. I should have stopped to consider the implications. I realise your work is monitored very closely.'

The remark had struck at an old, raw nerve. Quite inadvertently, she had manipulated him, eliciting the desired response. Anger had provoked him. He stood up and began pacing, filling the room with his restlessness.

'No one is even capable of monitoring my work.' he exclaimed, arrogantly. 'No one else has sufficient knowledge.' A tirade of long harboured resentments began to spill forth. Lydia listened in silence, alarmed by the depth of feeling in his voice.

'I have carte blanche at Forensic Industries. Am I to permit red tape to stand in my way?' He had been almost shouting by then. 'They might start to query expenses after a while, like they always do. But I can lose them elsewhere. The work would be completed long before the accounts department picked up on it.'

In the boot were rubber boots, a coil of strong rope and the lightweight set of ladders which he had unearthed from the back of the coaching sheds, together with a sharp spade. Behind them, on the rear seat, lay a small navy morocco case, into which the FINGERS monogram had been discreetly impressed. This case contained a complete set of autopsy instruments, surgeon's fine gloves and sterile packs of slides and phials. Beside it was an unopened roll of Size Fives (small mammal), which were veterinary body bags made from heavy duty pink plastic.

The sky was growing steadily lighter as she turned off the road into the single track lane. After a few minutes it reverted to little more than a bridleway, vanishing away into the neglected tangle of undergrowth. She parked up on the rutted verge.

'I don't think I can get any closer. We're going to have to walk the rest. It would be too awful if the car got bogged down.'

Rush started to unload the boot, grumbling. 'It's a long way to carry all this stuff.'

Lydia went to help. 'We can manage, between us. But I don't know how we're going to get it back to the car afterwards.'

He straightened up and looked at her sharply.

'What do you mean, 'it'? Are you referring to the corpse? We're not going to remove the body. Good God, is that what you thought? Are you completely mad?'

He slammed the car boot shut. 'I intend to remove the tissue samples in situ. And if that proves impossible, we can forget the whole thing.'

Ignoring the bitter disappointment on her face, he picked up the ladders and slung the coil of rope over one shoulder. 'It's no use looking like that. You can't add this to your Celtic collection. What exactly were you planning? To put it on display in your front parlour?'

Lydia collected the autopsy case and the bags in offended silence and locked the car.

They set off down the trackway, which continued long and straight, hemmed on either side by deep culverts. Within the undergrowth unacknowledged, nameless things felt the vibrations of their transit and skittered into the banks and ditches. Some unseen bird, flustered, gave a loud chatter of alarm as the strange pair disturbed his awakening dawn. As they travelled further along the path, others began to respond, greeting the day, but when they reached the beginning of the moss they walked into silence. No awakening, no dawn chorus, no suggestion of life. Everything appeared dead, especially the deep, uninviting pools of black water, framed by rigid reeds and cotton grass. As they entered the violated land they, too, fell silent.

Freshly excavated, the peat was stacked in black heaps high alongside the trenches, following a strange, dark geometry towards some distant vanishing point. As they trudged onwards the sun slid up onto the eastern horizon, casting new shadows over the diggings, and the flat grey sky was suddenly embellished with streaks of carmine and gold.

Rush shivered, buffeted by an unexpectedly bitter gust. 'I hadn't anticipated the chill factor. Is it always this cold around here?'

Lydia nodded. 'I've never known it any different. Even on a good day.'

'Well I hope I'll be able to work in it.'

Following the narrow metal tracks they headed deeper into the moss, accompanied by the sound of running water, spilling as fast, frothing streams down into the drainage ditches. His rubber boots clumped against the wooden struts and he stumbled forward, cursing as the edge of the ladder jarred against his thigh. He stopped.

It looked like someone's nightmare. A post-nuclear landscape. An arboreal necropolis of excavated skeletons. Square and dreadful furlongs of long dead trees stretching out before them. Stumps and roots littered the ground. Fractured limbs and twisted torsos, dry and brittle, rearing against the skyline. Relics of the primeval forest exposing their handsome violet lustre to the rising sun. A sheen imbued by their buried centuries. There was no other way to achieve it.

'This is an awful place.' he muttered, staring around in awe.

'You're feeling the evil.' she replied, with a trace of something which sounded like satisfaction. 'Ancient evil. Only to be expected. These were the sacrificial groves. Carefully chosen. It's one of those places, you see. A conduit where the foulness surfaces.'

Rush experienced a sudden wave of nausea. 'You can't seriously believe in all that psychic nonsense. Come on, you're an intelligent woman, Lydia. It's only because you know about the place - just an association of ideas.'

Lydia shook her head. 'Not true. The moss has always had bad vibes. I grew up just down the road from here and I felt it even as a child, decades before they began any serious digging. I've always known, instinctively I suppose, that this was a bad place, long before anything was found.'

His eyes travelled beyond her, following the surface of the ravaged terrain. Forcing back the rising sensation of disquiet he continued to taunt.

'Sorry, but I can't let you get away with that one, Lydia. It contains no logic. Scientifically speaking, there's no such thing as a good or a bad place - certainly not in the way that you are implying.'

They walked on until the silence was suddenly rent by a distant rumble. It grew steadily louder.

'That will be the Manchester to Montreal.' said Lydia, checking her watch.

Low but rising fast, a silvery aircraft penetrated the dawn sky.

'We'd better walk a bit faster. You have to believe me, Vincent. It is here. All around. We're completely surrounded by it. Surely you can sense something? You will, I promise. Let me try to explain. There are certain places which carry a predisposition for evil. They attract it. It flourishes, clings, becomes imprinted. With the passage of time the badness gathers strength. It's as if

199

the land feeds from it, succouring itself. Or maybe it's the other way round. Two way traffic, a bartering system. Like attracts like. Giving and taking.'

Rush tried to smile. 'That simply isn't possible.' His voice sounded strange, hollow, not like his own.

'Oh but it is.' she countered. 'Take any site where some evil has occurred. Battle grounds. Places of execution. Killing fields where massacres have taken place. Concentration camps. Do you think you could walk through any of those places and feel nothing? I very much doubt it.'

'That's just preconditioning.' he responded, lamely.

They had turned off the main track and were walking straight into the sunrise, along a flattened corridor of compressed peat where wide caterpillar tyres had created solid ripples. The walking became easier.

'Fortunately I don't possess your journalist's imagination. I'm trained to deal in hard fact, Lydia.'

'You will see it.' she had predicted. 'One day. You will come to understand. Oh, look, I think we must have arrived. There's a tag on that post. Over there - do you see?'

They came to a halt at the brink of the pit. It was about eight feet deep. Rush pointed at the solid walls which banked the sides of the excavation.

'Take a look at this. It's possible to read down through the various strata. See those bands running through the peat, the different widths, the way the colours change? Each level represents an alteration in the water table.' He sounded excited. 'It's absolutely fascinating.We're looking at a geological map that has recorded every climactic change and variation as it has occurred, over thousands of years.'

Lydia suddenly gasped and clapped her hand across her mouth. 'What is it? What's the matter?'

She pointed, transfixed. He followed her horrified gaze.

Grotesque, sliced, twisted, a petrified creature. A dreadful wizened homunculous leering out from the earthen wall. They crouched down on their hunkers and stared. A bat like thing with wings and a tail, deformed limbs leading to the frozen claws. All neatly pinned out against the sheer, perpendicular surface. The devil's emissary, reduced by the excavator to a two dimensional gargoyle. Lydia drew back.'It's monstrous. Like something out of a horror film.'

Rush suddenly began to grin.

'Get a grip, Lydia. It's just a tree root, in section.'

'It can't be. Can it? Is it? Are you sure?'

He nodded. 'Quite sure. It's a perfect example. Provides a good insight into the foundations of all your Celtic myths and superstitions. That's precisely how your ancient chums were duped. Clever stuff, mind you. I suspect the powerful Druid priesthood used it to their advantage to keep the tribes under control. Now you can see for yourself how easy it is to let the imagination run away with itself. What time is it?'

'Just after a quarter to six. You've got about an hour. I don't think we dare linger around beyond seven o'clock. Does that give you sufficient time?'

'Not really.' He was already lowering the ladders carefully down against the side of the pit. 'It's deeper than I'd expected. Good thing we brought the ladders. I'm going in now.'

She peered over the side. 'Can I do anything to speed things along?'

'It would help if you could pass down the rest of the equipment when I ask for it.'

He was already starting to sink.

The trench had accumulated several inches of water and he swore softly, dragging his boots free with difficulty. 'You're better off up there.' he called. 'I've found it. Just stand guard, tell me if anyone is coming. And don't try to watch me. This isn't going to be terribly pleasant. Not for a lay person.'

He sloshed his way along the pit to where a large slab of peat lay, already partially submerged. The acidic water rippled, a frothy yellow scum protesting at the disturbance. When he finally reached the slab he felt his way around it carefully, trying to gauge the dimensions. It was just a massive, anonymous cake of peat, with nothing to indicate its strange contents. He looked up to the place where the dark outline of Lydia's trilby filled the sky.

'Just before I make a start - are you quite certain that this is E3?' The trilby bobbed in assent.

'This has got to be it, then. There's no sign of anything else around here. I'll have to try to turn it over. Pass the spade down.'

It was proving impossible. He lacked physical strength. Several times he lost his footing and overbalanced into the sticky slutch. After a few minutes he was soaked through, covered in debris and extremely cold. Eventually he managed to force the blade of the spade beneath the slab and heaved the handle downwards. Nothing happened. He tried again and again, each time straining until he thought his stomach muscles would tear. His glasses began to slip forward and he removed them, slipping them into his pocket. Lose those and he'd lose everything. He rested for a moment, weighing up the problem. Trying a new tactic, he extracted the spade and moved to a slightly different angle. Exerting his full weight on the handle he made another frantic attempt to gain some leverage. This time the massive block slowly began to rise.

Suddenly he lost his balance and the great bulk fell back with a resounding splat, covering him in the filthy bog water. Half blinded by sweat and slutch, at the next attempt he managed to raise the block to its fulcrum. Letting go of the spade he placed both hands underneath, attempting to support it whilst desperately trying to maintain his balance. It took one final, shoulder wrenching heave before the block slowly rolled back and came to a shuddering halt against the smooth wall of the pit. The disturbed water rippled against his legs like cold and indignant slaps of recrimination.

He took a handkerchief to his smarting eyes before turning back to the slab. A blink, followed by a sharp intake of breath. He stood motionless, gazing down upon the face. It glistened, dewed with water droplets, just like his own. Dark skin, toughened to leather, each pore clearly visible. Male, beard and moustache still intact. A sleeper. Eyes closed, a calm expression. Serenity? How would Vincent Rush know?

The wound told a different story. A terrible laceration had opened the top of the skull. Jagged flaps of skin poked from a caked, tarry mass, an ancient, obscene scab that had started out as hot blood, matting into the hair.

'Looking promising.' he called up to Lydia. 'Pass me the autopsy case.'

Unrolling one of the body bags he spread it out on the peat block before carefully laying out the implements, counting as he did so. Three scalpels, two fine probes and a small, wide bladed saw which flashed, catching the dawn sunlight as he turned it over.

'How's the time?'

'Flying.' Lydia's voice had an anxious note.

He wiped his hands down the front of his already filthy anorak and began pulling on the fine gloves with some difficulty. Working far faster than he would have recommended to anyone, he began to lift back the head until the throat was fully exposed. More black tar cratered the long gash which had severed the jugular vein. Here he noted the slight traces of clotting which informed him that the corpse had been bled prior to death. Above the neck wound his gloved fingers encountered the garotte, which appeared to be made from a strip of thin sinew. It had bitten deep into the flesh. He gave a knowing smile. The reversed tourniquet. Small wonder that the blood had gushed forth in such copious amounts.

He picked up one of the scalpels and began to take scrapings, carefully transferring minute particles of tissue into the glass phials. Completely absorbed in his task, he started in alarm when Lydia called out.

'I can't hear you. What is it?'

'There's someone coming.' Her voice was stage whisper low. 'A long way off, but heading in this direction. Someone with a couple of dogs. The dogs have spotted me.'

Rush straightened up. 'How long before they get here?'

'Two or three minutes. It's a woman. I think she's seen me. I can't just carry on standing here. Vincent - quickly, tell me what to do.' Panicky now.

He stared around helplessly. On their peat table the autopsy tools glinted. Anyone approaching the trench would have a bird's eye view. There was no possible way of concealing his activities. 'You'll just have to head her off.' He thought fast. 'Listen, start walking towards her. Now. Right away. Keep her talking, think of something - anything - to keep her away from here. Wait for me in the car.'

'But you'll never get back on your own. There's too much for one to carry with the ladders and the spade and all your equipment. How are you going to manage? We daren't come back later.'

'I'll worry about that when I've finished. Is there any other route back to the car? I can't follow you back across the moss, not if she's walking around.'

'Hell - I've got to go right now. The dogs are racing towards me. She's trying to call them back and they're taking no notice. Now she's tearing after them. Listen - get yourself back to the main trackway and bear left instead of right. After a few minutes you'll come to a metal bridge. It leads over the main culvert. Cross over and get into the woodland. Follow the sandy path till you get back to the bridleway, then turn right. I'll be at the car.'

He crouched low in the pit, listening. Dogs barking. A shout carried on the wind, followed by more barking. The sounds began to recede. After a few moments of silence he stood up stiffly, and decided to risk the first few rungs of the ladder. To his great relief the view was obscured by tall peat stacks, which also meant he was well hidden. 'Thank you.' he said out loud, and clambered back down into the pit. Ignoring the fading sounds of dogs and the voices carried on the wind, he returned to his task.

When he picked up the scalpel his hands shook uncontrollably. He found himself quite overcome by the waves of weakness now rising from the pit of his stomach. Aftermath of the adrenal surge, he told himself, fighting desperately to regain control of his hands. It was useless. He couldn't even hold the scalpel steady. Panic stricken, just like some greenhorn student on his first day. Totally impeded by the shakes he set the instrument aside in disgust and acknowledged that he was in no fit state for precision surgery. Ripping off the surgical gloves he flung them aside and began to tear away large chunks of peat with his bare hands, until he had exposed the entire neck. Beginning to feel calmer, he inspected the area closely and carefully dusted away the remaining fibres of peat. After a moment of further contemplation he picked out the largest of the scalpels and set to work, thrusting the head backwards, hard. Further and further until the neck skin was taut. One swift incision followed, long and horizontal, well below the original neck wound.

It was quite unlike cutting into any flesh he had ever encountered, alive or dead.There was no spring back, no quivering response travelling back up the handle. He drove in deeper, just hacking now. Plunging through the leathery tissues until the main vessels were severed, he paused for a moment to wipe the sweat from his forehead and then began to work upwards through connective tissue towards the larynx. With a murmur of satisfaction he finally sliced neatly through the windpipe. The head lolled forward as he let go of the chin. It was strange to see it suddenly in motion. Exchanging the scalpel for the saw he reentered the cavity, delving into the recesses until he located the occipital joint, grateful that there was no blood flow to impede his progress. The bone had degenerated to the point where it had become soft and crumbly and he was able to work quickly, the only sound a faint rasping as the saw worked through the vertebra. Afterwards it only took a moment to dissect out the remaining skin and tendons. His hands had stopped shaking. He stared down at the prize for a second and then quickly sealed it into one of the body bags.

**

Not until she was alone, back in the privacy of the car, did she inspect her leg properly. The blood, already drying, had glued her stocking to the wound. Wincing, she pulled the torn fabric away from the bite and tried to massage the rapidly swelling calf muscle. It was too painful to touch. From the glove box she removed a small first aid kit and rummaged for the little pack of painkillers. Dry mouthed from shock and fear, she had had great difficulty in swallowing the tablets. Many years later she would realise that she had failed to spot the moment. Missed because she had been too busy trying to remember when she had last had a tetanus shot. The first tiny intimation of her ultimate destiny.

The woman had been terribly upset. The incident, however, had served its purpose and curtailed her walk. It was probably because of the cats, thought Lydia. The Alsatians had bounded towards her and picked up the scent of the cats - that and the reek of apprehension. They halted, backing off slightly, two sets of hackles rising to untidy ridges. Two lolling pink tongues, white frothed, lodged between long fangs. Ugly growls rising from the deep.

Lydia had remained stock still, standing her ground, trying to calm them. For the first few moments she could hear nothing but the thuds of her own heart. She remembered moistening her dry lips as the woman rushed forward, yelling, screaming at her to stay put, not to move. That's what had triggered the dogs. The next instant she was down on the trackway, trying to protect her face. The first hot flash of agony came as teeth sank deep into her leg and then she was lost, smothering beneath a tumbling kaleidoscope. Coarse fur and dogs' breath, hot and meaty. White teeth and flecks of saliva. When she opened her eyes she was confronted by a pair of gloved hands and flashing silver choke chains.

The long walk back had been all tearful apologies and impassioned pleas for forgiveness. Lydia had forced herself to ignore the throbbing pain and concentrated her efforts upon reassuring the owner. It was her own fault. The dogs were not to blame. She had startled them and no, she had no intention of reporting the incident. Yes, she could see that they were not really nasty. Once she got back to the car she would sit quietly for a while, just to get over it, and then she'd be fine. Just a little nip, not worth making a fuss about. Really, nothing more to be said.

Eventually she persuaded the woman to go. After she had vanished towards the road, Lydia reversed the car as far as she could, until the bridle path became too narrow. She lit a cigarette and waited, watching anxiously through the rear view mirror. Almost half an hour passed before he finally appeared, weighed down with rope and spade and ladders, implement case in one hand. From the other dangled one pink body bag. As he staggered from the undergrowth she climbed out of the car and limped towards him.

Rush was virtually unrecognisable, his face well camouflaged with thick daubs of mud and peat, twigs and leaves adhering to his damp hair. Clothes ruined, he looked as if he was returning from some military manoeuvre. As she drew closer he peered out from behind smeary, splattered lenses.

'You look terrible. What happened, Lydia?'

She touched the side of her leg. 'Dog bite. Hurts like buggery. Did the trick though. That woman insisted on walking me back to the car.' Her eyes had fastened on the the pink bag. 'Did you get what you need?'

He nodded and began loading things in the boot. 'Are you going to be all right to drive?'

Lydia had already started up the engine. 'Yes, I'll manage. Get in. Come on, hurry. We need to get away from here.'

**

The sounds of cars arriving and departing marked the changeover of shifts. It must be six o'clock, she thought. Headlights raked across the ceiling, sweeping over the far wall as the driver reversed in the driveway beneath her window. Listening to the fading sounds after the car had pulled out into the main road she wondered whether it had turned left, in the direction of the airport, or right, towards the moss. She swallowed painfully, forcing time to dissolve.

**

When she returned in the late afternoon he was in the kitchen, with the blinds pulled down. She halted in the doorway, amazed at the transformation. All the mess of the previous evening had been cleared away and the kitchen was spotless. Every surface gleamed, sterile as an operating theatre, the breakfast bar crowded with a selection of glass slides and phials. The autopsy equipment shimmered, reflecting the brightness of two angle poised lights. To one side lay a small, powerful microscope. In the centre of this array stood the severed head, resting preposterously on a white linen cloth.

He continued working, ignoring her completely for several minutes. She stood in silence, too intimidated to interrupt.

'It was the only way.' he said at last, without looking up. He continued probing into the gaping hole in the top of the head with a pair of long forceps. With a small grunt of satisfaction he dropped a tiny fragment of bone into a glass dish. 'It was this blow to the head that actually killed him.' He dug out another splinter of bone. There was a tiny tinkling sound as it fell into the container. He finally glanced over to her.

'I couldn't work out there on the moss, not under those conditions. If this shocks you, you can wait in the study. I've almost finished.'

She sat down heavily on a stool.

'No, I'll stay, if I may. It was just - walking right into it like that - I had no idea -'

She indicated the bag which contained their meal. 'Shall I put it in the fridge for later?'

'No,' he said, hastily, 'don't open the fridge. You'd better put it out of the way somewhere- stick it in the larder. Come over here, I want to show you something.'

He directed the beam of the angle poise lamp right inside the scalp cavity.

'There's the brain. There's been a certain amount of shrinkage but it's still intact.'

Lydia stared down at the convoluted mass. Suddenly Rush tapped at a portion with the scalpel.

'If you look closely you can see the staining. It's a very promising sign. Can you see? Still pink. That's blood, Lydia, and it hasn't deteriorated to anything like the degree of the external samples. I just need one perfect red corpuscle. As long as the cell nucleus is still intact ...... stand aside now.'

She watched in grim silence as he carefully dissected out the stained section. Afterwards he proceeded to cut the tissue into several thin slices, enclosing each one between glass slides. Each sample was then carefully tagged. He removed the surgical gloves and straightened up, flexing his aching shoulders.

'Right, I've got everything I need. It's all taken a lot longer than

I anticipated, but I could hardly do it at the lab, under the circumstances.' He nodded ruefully in the direction of the head. Lydia cleared her throat. 'And what are you going to do with that?' she asked, staring at the head. 'It will have to be disposed of now. It's the most damning piece of evidence. We need to get rid of it.'

'Destroyed?' he interjected, aghast. 'Certainly not! I intend to treat it - to preserve it and then if -' The sentence tailed off and he began to clean the instruments.

'If what?' prompted Lydia, watching him closely.

'If this attempt ever reaches ultimate fruition it will be invaluable for purposes of comparison.' He glanced up. 'I almost forgot, that's for you.'

He pointed to a dark green operating cloth which lay on the draining board. She folded back the fabric to reveal the garotte. Thin, stringy and slightly menacing, it curled across the surface like the tail of a rodent.

'I've already checked it. It's well preserved and unlikely to deteriorate. Seems to be made of some sort of sinew. I thought you might like to keep it.'

She picked up the relic hesitantly, and studied it for some time. Then she closed her eyes, concentrating, and began to pass it through her hands like some ghoulish rosary, rolling it between the pads of her fingers.

'What on earth are you doing?'

Lydia opened her eyes. 'Psychometry. Have you never heard of it?'

'Not that I recall.'

'Well briefly, it functions on the principal that an object always retains some vibration, an emotional imprint given off by the individual with whom it was connected. I suppose it's the psychic equivalent of giving a tracker dog a piece of clothing which belonged to the missing person. Theoretically, the more intense the emotion, the stronger the trace - and you can't get more intense than the final moments of sacrifice. I'm not very expert, but it has occasionally worked.'

She continued to handle the garotte, trying to coax something from it.

'No, I'm not getting a thing - nothing at all. Wait a minute - it feels cold. Very cold. Yes, it's becoming colder.'

'Impossible!' scoffed Rush, 'if anything, it will become warmer as you handle it.'

Lydia opened her eyes again. 'I don't mean physically.' she explained, patiently. 'It's not a physical sensation. Nobody would expect a murder weapon to be psychically warm. It's difficult to describe, but try to imagine an emotional coldness. There's an ugliness about it - it's beginning to escalate. Something is coming across. I've never felt it like this, not like this. You don't believe me, do you?'

Rush had returned to the head and began to bandage it into the cloth before returning it to the pink bag. Satisfied with his package, he carried it to the fridge.

'It will have to stay in here over the weekend. I'll bring the necessary chemicals back from the lab on Monday and then I'll make a start on the preservation process. I wouldn't go so far as to say I disbelieve you, Lydia. At one time I would have scoffed, I suppose. Right up to the time I found the evidence of heightened perception.' He closed the fridge door. 'Now I retain an open mind. Lydia? Lydia, are you all right?'

All the colour had drained from her. Her face had become horribly contorted and her thin arms shook as she flung the garotte back down onto the cloth. Collapsing heavily onto a kitchen stool she began to rub her hands feverishly against her skirt, as if trying to rid them of the contact.

'What is it? What's wrong?' he asked, alarmed. 'Are you unwell?'

Lydia swallowed hard. 'An image - I got a terrible image. A woman. She's pregnant.' She buried her head in her hands, shuddering.

'It was dreadful. Nothing to do with him.' She glanced quickly towards the fridge. 'I could feel her, Vincent. I could feel the child inside her. I felt it move.'

Rush brought her a glass of water. 'Here, drink this. Was there anything else?'

She gulped down the water and still shaking, set down the empty glass.

'I had to let it go. I couldn't take any more. The power that started to come through was terrifying. The strength of feeling absolutely overwhelmed me. I couldn't take it.'

Rush hovered uncomfortably, slightly embarrassed. Barely capable of looking after himself, he was poorly equipped to take care of Lydia in her distress. He looked enormously relieved when the colour began to return to her face. She stood up.

'Perhaps you'd better rest for a while.'

'No, I'm all right. I'll be better in a few minutes.' she insisted. 'I think we both need to eat. Not in here, though, if you don't mind. Should I take it through to the study?'

She began to busy herself, reheating the takeaway, setting a tray, almost restored to normal. Rush finished clearing away his things in silence and then followed her through to the study. They were halfway through the meal when the sound of the doorbell created an unpleasant ripple of alarm.

'Surely you're not expecting anyone?'

He shook his head, motioning her to be silent.

The bell rang again, insistently. It went on for longer this time and he got to his feet.

'Don't answer it.' whispered Lydia.

'I'm not going to. I'll go upstairs and look through the landing window. I just can't imagine who it could be.'

Lydia set the food aside. She had suddenly lost her appetite.

'You don't think - it can't be anything to do with this morning?'

Someone was knocking now, round at the back door. Rush

exited the room quietly and a moment later she heard the creak of a stair tread.

Left alone to face the sudden realisation of what they had done, Lydia's nervous system took over. The events of the preceding hours had placed both of them firmly beyond the pale, morally and probably legally, as well. Everything had happened so fast that she had been carried along, overtaken by the exciting possibilities. Since then the thing had gathered a momentum all its own. The experience with the garotte had shaken her more than she cared to admit and now she was left feeling distinctly uneasy. An unease which stemmed from the certainty that their meddling would not go unrewarded. That much she knew.

The last forty years had turned Lydia Pendle into a hard woman with a strong stomach. There had been times when she had given way to the darker side of her nature. Dabbled a little. Hers was the old religion and she had always kept faith, maintaining an unswerving belief in the natural forces, forces to which man still remained subservient. But none of that had prepared her for today. Pendle and Rush, co-conspirators, locked together, having foolishly, thoughtlessly overstepped the parameters. He certainly had. He was something else and it was beginning to show. Cold and detached, the black magician, hiding behind his degrees and the string of letters after his name. It had all been so tempting, with his slides and phials beckoning like irresistible fingers.

He came back into the room, startling her out of the reverie.

'It was Frank Newbolt.' he announced, sitting down again. 'He's gone. I watched him from the landing window.'

'Did he see you?'

He shook his head. 'The glass is covered with creeper. He wouldn't have spotted me even if he had looked up. Anyway, he was too busy weighing up your car.'

'Should I know him?' asked Lydia in a worried tone.

'I doubt it. He works for FINGERS. We collaborated on a couple of projects in the past. He's not a bad chap. His wife is extremely friendly with my sister. I can't imagine why he should turn up here, though. Unless Barbara put him up to it. Of course - that's probably it. She likes to keep tabs on me.'

'I'll make some coffee.' said Lydia. 'It frightened the life out of me when that doorbell rang. Guilty conscience.'

She made her way to the kitchen. It was here, whilst preparing the coffee, that the full significance of an earlier remark finally struck her. What was it he had said? Ultimate fruition, that was it. 'If my work ever reaches ultimate fruition'. The words of a man who had no intention of stopping once he had extracted the genetic thread from that poor corpse. She returned with the coffee, wondering how to phrase her next question. She tried to speak and found herself unable to utter the word.

It was after seeing the head, ancient yet strangely young. She had been moved by the repose of it. The stillness of the features, the closed eyes. It could have been sculptured bronze, except that the facial hair retained a softness that was far too realistic. She tried again, forcing the word forward, out of her mouth, onto the air. There, she'd uttered it. It tumbled into the room. No lightening, no clap of thunder. Just heavy silence and Vincent Rush wiping the coffee from his mouth with the sleeve of his jacket.

'What I mean,' she carried on rather lamely, feeling forced to continue, 'is - well, would it be possible, theoretically?'

Rush was nodding. 'Once you've got the DNA structure, it's perfectly feasible to clone anything.'

'You seem very confident about it.' she said, rather quietly.

'I am. I've done it before.' There was a faint vestige of boastfulness in his voice. He took quiet pleasure in watching Lydia's jaw line drop a fraction.

'When?'

'You know. That time I told you about. When they vetoed me. I made the foolish error of feeding all my information into the main frame computer.' He stood up and began to pace around.

'They destroyed my greatest triumph, Lydia. But not this time. Not a trace this time, I never make the same mistake twice. There will be no record. Only you will know.'

He crossed the room and came behind her, bending over the back of the chair until his face was too close, invading her space. She stared into it uncomfortably and her eyes locked on to the clear beads of moisture glistening, clinging to his enormous forehead.

'Look at me, Lydia.'

His eyes were over bright and there was a new forcefulness in his voice. His breath smelt of the coffee.

'One thing you can count on. If you were ever to speak of this -'

She opened her mouth to protest but he did not give her the chance.

'If you were ever to speak of any of this,' he repeated, slowly, 'no one would believe you for a moment. They'd think that you'd finally flipped. You'd be whisked off for psychiatric counselling, at the very least. I'd see to that myself. Is that quite clear?'

'Crystal clear.' she said weakly.

'Good.' He straightened up and walked round to the front of her chair. 'Then you'd better decide, here and now. Are you with this, or do you want out?'

Lydia suddenly got up and started to put on her jacket. 'I've got to be going, Vincent. We're both exhausted. I think you'll feel better about everything when you've had some sleep. And so will I.'

He grasped her arm in a surprisingly strong grip. 'You're not leaving here until you've answered the question.' There was an ugly expression on his face. 'Well? Which is it to be?'

'You're hurting me.' She removed his hand from her sleeve, trying to shake off the intimidation. 'Calm down, Vincent. We're in this together, whether we like it or not. I'm with you, of course. We're going to see it through. I wouldn't want to miss it for anything.'

He followed her out to the car. Before she climbed in she turned and held out her hand.

'You can trust me, Vincent.'

She looked at him with clear, steady eyes and he thought that he could.

'You've forgotten to take the garotte.'

'I haven't forgotten.' she said, switching on the ignition. 'I prefer to leave it here for the moment, if you don't mind. I'll take custody of it later, when I've had time to - to adjust.'

She drove off, leaving him standing on the drive.

19
Walls of Glass - Spring 1997

The garden was slowly stirring into life. The fourteenth of April was etched into her memory. It had been a Monday, with the moon entering its first quarter. A day filled with the first intimations of time ebbing. In the early evening, as dusk began to creep forwards towards the night, she had wandered outside to sit on the bench at the rear of the cottage, watching the cats as they stropped their claws on the old conifer, the bark of its ragged trunk shredded by years of such abuse. Through the upper branches the moon, a silver sliver, rose higher against a clear, star filled sky. Suddenly chilly, she got up to go back into the cottage. She spotted it as she turned towards the back door. A pallid beam hanging low in the north western sector. The long haired star. Unmistakable. The milky smudge of doom. An opalescent, misty snowball of the night, trailing its strange bearded tail; Milton's burning comet,

'...huge in the Arctic sky and from his horrid hair
Shakes pestilence and war.' Paradise Lost

　　She went back into the cottage to fetch the binoculars. Beyond the vapour trails the universe stretched. Stars danced and glittered down the lenses, dizzying her. She sat down again on the bench and refocussed, unsure as to whether it was her shaking hands or the stars themselves which trembled. They were no longer pinpricks and not white. As she watched they whirled, glittering and dazzling in some magical tarantella. Electric pulsing jewels. Turquoises and emeralds and icy sapphire splinters. A quick flash of fire. And no longer beautiful, the moon was pitted and pocked, its quarter edge an ugly and encrusted rind. She turned her attention back to the comet, harbinger of death and disaster and felt the weakness travelling into her arms. Oh, the unkindness of April. The dice were thrown.

Towards the Welsh border, beyond the Peckforton Hills, Ben Jackson was on the edge of the playing field with a group of classmates and the science master. They were also watching Hale-Bopp. Ben was standing silent and alone, slightly to one side, which was nothing unusual. None of them, not even the staff, bothered trying to coerce him into joining in any more.

The boys knew almost everything there was to know about the comet. It was composed of rocks and ice and frozen gases and traversed its orbit at around twenty miles per second. A comet's coda always points away from the sun. Hale-Bopp's splendid, awe inspiring tail, all two hundred million kilometres of it, was just dust. An emptiness of cosmic dust and vapourising gases. At a deeper level Ben also knew that it was a source of dread. The long haired star, the star of ill omen which precipitates destruction and pestilence and death and fearful storms and it made him shiver. The die was cast.

**

1983: The most significant day of his career had been marred by the presence of Tindall, who was oblivious to what was going on the neighbouring bench. He had been getting on his nerves throughout the entire operation. Having tip toed through an ethical mine field, Rush had just accomplished, single handed, what would normally have been an impressive piece of teamwork. Although he had emerged unscathed, the strain was beginning to tell. He struggled on, trying to pretend that he was not shattered and made an enormous effort to mask his irritation. Suddenly aware of his aching shoulders he got up from the bench and crossed to the window, unbuttoning his lab coat. He stared out, his eyes travelling beyond the confines of the lab to the distant parkland, his gaze fixing upon a copse of trees. He watched the upper branches, swaying slightly. Fresh air. He stared, following the movements, lost in thought.

'Problems?' inquired Tindall, making him jump.

Rush returned to the bench.

'Not really.' he said, shortly. 'Look, would you mind popping across to site services for me? I ordered a batch of enucleated ova about two hours ago and they still haven't arrived. I'm held up until they come.'

'Sure.' Tindall made for the door. 'Do they have the details?'

'Here's my copy of the request slip. You'd better take it with you.'

Tindall glanced down at the form.

'Human? This stipulates human, do you know?'

'Human.' echoed Rush. 'Yes, that's correct. I'm right in the middle of a comparison study. If you could hurry, Oliver, I'm waiting for them.'

Most of the clones failed. The ones that didn't developed mutant chromosomes. After Tindall had gone home he worked on late into the night. This time he had remembered to dispense with the chauffeur, arranging instead to contact Lydia Pendle when he was ready to be collected. She was to wait on the main road, well beyond sight of the main gates.

It was long after midnight when he placed the final phial under the microscope. By this time he could hardly bear to look. Delaying, playing for time, he tidied the bench. Removed his spectacles. Carefully wiped the lenses. Blew his nose. Strolled round the laboratory restlessly. Finally forcing himself back to the equipment he switched on the image intensifier and sat motionless, staring down at the blurred image for a long time.

The scene before him was familiar. There, in its tiny petrie dish of nutrient jelly, the single cell had made silent history. His face remained impassive as he scrutinised the division. Eventually he ejected the phial and placed it down on the bench, hands shaking slightly as he checked the seals. He took a white label and smoothed it out carefully across the upper surface.

Labelled it. *Gave it a name*. It existed. He placed it reverently inside the heated storage chamber.

**

Oblivious to the cold, Lydia remained immobile on the garden bench, staring into the night sky, her thoughts elsewhere.

It had been almost one o'clock when he had finally phoned for her to collect him and approaching two by the time she dropped him off at Medlar Hall. She had been about to drive off when he came back and leant inside the car.

'I think you should come in.'

She took the keys from the ignition and followed him indoors. He led her straight through to the study.

'Be seated.' He indicated a small winged chair and stood watching rather abstractedly while she removed the stack of document wallets and three heavy rexine bound text books from the seat and placed them carefully on the floor.

'Do sit down, Lydia.' he said, impatiently.

He flopped into his own leather chair, leaned back and closed his eyes.

Lydia watched him. Eventually she broke the silence. 'I presume you've invited me in for a reason?'

He opened his eyes and stared at her, and then nodded slowly.

'Well? What is it?' she asked, concerned. 'Tell me. Is something wrong? You look done in. Come on, Vincent, don't keep me in suspense. Whatever is the matter?'

Sill he did not speak. She began to feel distinctly uncomfortable.

'Stop playing stupid games with me.' She sounded impatient. 'Have you done it?'

'Yes.'

He enjoyed seeing her lost for words, relished the tiny gasp and the fractional drop of her jaw line as she digested the information.

'I can hardly believe it. I had no idea - no idea. It's incredible, quite incredible, Vincent. Amazing. You must be over the moon. No wonder you look so exhausted. Well, I could do with a drink. Have you got anything?'

'There's some whisky in the kitchen.'

'You sit there, I'll see to it.'

When she returned a few minutes later he was staring into space. She handed him a glass. 'So you've actually managed to extract a sample of DNA? Congratulations!' Her voice had a breathless quality. 'This must be one of the proudest moments of your career. What a tremendous achievement! Have you had chance to conduct the analysis tests?'

He said nothing, but there was nothing remotely pleasant about his strange smile. It made Lydia's skin crawl. She shut up and lit a cigarette. They remained in silence while she smoked. She stubbed out the cigarette, wondering how to break the deadlock. 'You're not intending to stop there, are you? Look, if you've something to tell me, do get on with it.'

He leant forward in the leather chair, fingers interlocked, his chin resting on his hands.

'It's alive.'

He sat back, watching her face change. When he did finally speak, his voice had altered. It was, thought Lydia, rather dreadful. A chilling note of twisted paternity, proud and proprietorial, mixed with lofty exaltation. Behind their lenses, the eyes had taken on a bright, slightly manic glitter which she found very disturbing. He leant towards her. 'The culture medium won't support him for very long. He can only survive in vitro for a few days.'

More silence. The room had become oppressive. Lydia gave a sharp intake of breath. Her reaction, when it finally came, was not what he had been expecting.

'Oh - you -' She paused in pursuit of the word. He noticed that she was shaking. Finally a long reptilian hiss emerged, soft and slow, then the word landed like spittle.

'Malefactor.'

He winced.

What was racing through her mind, what she really wanted to say, was that a child should be conceived in spontaneity. Not from a laboratory as the result of detached alchemy, but as the fruit of the melding and blending of two human beings, created with joy and pleasure and enormous satisfaction. Although she felt certain that was the way it ought to be, not knowing for herself, not knowing for sure whether this really was the truth she did not feel entitled to pronounce upon such things. So she remained silent on that aspect of the matter and asked, instead, 'Don't you realise what you've done?'

'What do you mean?' He scrutinised her closely, intrigued.

The room waited.

''The glass legend.' She bit her lower lip. 'Ynys-witrin - the Isle of Glass. You've fulfiled the legend.'

He cleared his throat nervously and then shook his head. 'You've lost me there, Lydia. You'd better explain.'

'Celtic doctrine held that a departed soul spent the afterlife on an island. Running water was thought to create a shield through which the spirit world could not pass. Being such a superstitious race, this belief probably made them feel safer. At that time Glastonbury Tor, where the early La Tène Celts established a Lake Village, was an island, surrounded by the River Brue. Some sources claim that it was also the most likely site for their sacred Isle - the Isle of the Dead. Over the centuries, in the way that verbal history always does, the legend gradually evolved. The original ideas behind them become transposed. Anyway, in this particular case they eventually convinced themselves that the dead were shielded behind a wall of glass. By the ninth century the Glastonbury site was also reputed to be the location of the Holy Grail. It is still vaunted as the Avalon of Arthurian legend.' She paused, glaring at him with angry, accusing eyes.

'Now you've got the reduction. A Celt in the glass dish. Your own unholy grail, lying on the bench in your laboratory. The notion is preposterous. Glass shatters, Vincent.'

'Without a uterus he'll die. I can't let him die.' He sounded slightly desperate.

She held up a hand to silence him. 'I haven't finished yet. While we're about it I have another legend for you. This is a later one that even you must have come across. The one about St Christopher. He's the the patron saint of ferrymen and travellers, in case you've forgotten. On day a little child begged to be carried over the stream. As they journeyed through the waters the burden grew heavier and heavier, until St Christopher could hardly support the weight on his back. Finally he asked his passenger for an explanation. 'I am the Christ child.' explained his passenger. 'I have to carry the sins of the whole world.''

Rush was looking at her in surprise. He shook his head. 'I thought you'd be the last person to go religious on me.'

'You thought wrong then. I am very religious. More than most, actually. I think you may be confusing unorthodox with irreligious. That's not very scientific of you.'

She waited for him to say something. After another long silence he held up his tumbler mockingly.

'Here's to glass.' he said, gulping the remainder of his whisky. He got up and poured another.

'Are you seriously proposing to find a surrogate mother? You're unhinged Vincent.'

The mood swing was instantaneous. He was angry. Worse than angry. Enraged, beside himself. Frightening. He suddenly leapt to his feet, firing livid, incandescent bolts of fury at her.

'Don't ever speak to me like that.' The upper lip twitched, then curled. 'I know exactly what I'm doing. Once I've screened the embryo - pre-embryo actually, we might as well be accurate - I intend to freeze him. I'll hold him in cryonic suspension and he can remain there indefinitely, until the time is right.'

He rushed over to the desk in a frenzy and began to drag open the drawers.

'Here, take that away with you. I don't like it around here.'

The garotte dangled from his fingers until she forced herself to take it from him, half drawn, half repulsed.

'I'm disturbed by it.' she confessed, in a subdued tone.

'Then you must overcome that fear, Lydia. We're right on the brink now. I'm fulfiling my side of our bargain. We're in this together, and don't you ever forget that. There are going to be gaps, question marks. You're the researcher, Lydia, the one who must follow up the clues. There's no more room for fear and superstition, you must cast it aside. We're talking about serious scientific investigation here, not a lot of pseudo religious twaddle.'

When she finally responded there was a trace of derision in her voice. 'The Celts made no distinction between your science and my religion, Vincent. They were one and the same thing. No tidy little pigeon holes. Life wasn't like that then and it still isn't. The journey - chooses us. We don't decide it. The only choice that is left to us is what we make of it all. You're a cold fish. You scoff too easily - and that's where you'll go wrong. You can't leave feelings and emotions out of the equation. Not then and not now.' She fingered the garotte gingerly and sighed. 'All right, I will take it home. I'll carry on, see where it leads, if that's what you want. But you be careful, Vincent. Very careful. Go ahead, freeze your embryo, but for heaven's sake think seriously before you go beyond that. It could have the most terrible repercussions. And I don't just mean on you or I.'

Following her to the door, he grabbed hold of her arm. She shook him off.

'You're extremely overwrought. Get to bed. You're going to make yourself ill. It's important that you keep things in perspective.'

After she had gone he returned to the study and sat listening to music. Serious, powerful music. There was nothing wrong with his perspective and there were no more choices to be made. It was no longer his decision. It was going to carry on, of that he was certain. He had been selected, chosen to start it off, to recreate. Unable to stop now, even if he had wanted. He smiled to himself. It was a strange, anticipatory smile. For the first time in years he was beginning to relax. He could already feel the relief flooding through his body. It was the most comfortable sensation that he had ever experienced, hiving off free choice.

He fell asleep in the chair. A deep, dreamless sleep, fully restorative. At last, after all those years of loneliness and neglect, something was looking after him. It had taken over, lifted away all the strains, leaving him free to concentrate on the work. All his future rolled out before him, a long, straight ribbon. Not a crossroad in sight. All he had to do was follow it. Follow it and drag Lydia Pendle along with him.

The next day he had called to apologise. Smoothing things over, blaming fatigue for his outburst. Seeing that she had little choice in the matter, Lydia had to let him get away with it.

**

She returned indoors accompanied by a disturbing, uncomfortable thought and suddenly found herself wondering whether she might have lived out her life on a false premise. All those years spent delving downwards, into subterranean regions, when perhaps she should have been looking up and beyond. The following day, when she answered the telephone it had not been his receptionist but the great man himself. He had received her test results. Would she please come to see him at his rooms. Without delay. Tomorrow at midday.

Yes, she agreed softly, midday would be fine.

20
Monday Lunchtime

Rachel placed the file retrieval software on Trevor's desk.

'Oh, thanks. How did you get on?'

'I didn't - the computer crashed. No one is blaming me but I still feel pretty bad about it.' said Rachel, ruefully. 'Then on Sunday I went to see Lydia. She was so pleased with the book, Trevor. Asked me to thank you.'

'Good. How is she?'

Rachel shook her head. 'Deteriorating. There's nothing they can do for her. She's wasting away. I had a word with the Sister.'

'What exactly is wrong with her?'

'It's something to do with the muscles. They've started to atrophy. Sister Renshaw said it's called motor neurone disease and there isn't any cure.'

Trevor's face grew serious. 'What a wretched way for her to end up. Oh dear, Rachel, you have had a grim weekend. Tell you what, let me treat you to lunch. You too, Sophie. I'll take you both to the George.'

Sophie shook her head. 'Sorry, I can't make it. Thanks Trev, I'd love to, but I'm already booked.'

They ate at the pub next to the old church. After they had finished Trevor emptied his glass and got to his feet. 'Instead of sitting around in here, how about a little stroll before we go back to the office?'

Rachel slipped on her coat. Once outside, instead of walking back up Church Street towards the town centre, he led her past the church and on down the hill until they got to the bridge, where he halted. They stood in silence, watching the sullen brown ripples of the Bollin.

Long before the waters had been named, and for many centuries afterwards, nothing had interrupted the flow's inevitable journey towards its union with the greater river. The nineteenth century had seen silk and cotton mills blossoming throughout the north west. As the industrial revolution belched and thundered towards its blackened zenith, country hamlets gradually turned into small textile towns. Along with many other such tributaries harnessed for the power offered by their waters, the little Bollin had suffered the indignities of man's interference. In terms of river time this had happened just the other day and although it still coursed through the valley meadows it was no longer on the headlong rush to join the Mersey. Now it was on its way to feed the mill pool at Quarrybank, before being rechannelled into the mighty Manchester Ship Canal. Divorced and diverted. Could worse be yet to come?

'I'm very fond of this spot.' said Trevor, gazing out over the valley. 'I find it relaxing, leaning over and watching the river flow. Good place to think, this.'

'Rivers makes me sad.' said Rachel. 'I think it's to do with knowing that they're going to outlive you. They'll still be there, running their course, long after we've gone.'

Trevor laughed. 'I wouldn't put money on it. The section of the river we're looking at now was diverted to this very spot in 1862.'

'Really? Why was that?'

He pointed towards the church. 'So that they could extend the churchyard. I once came down here with Lydia and she told me all about it. Claimed it was to keep things under control in the graveyard. Insisted it was because of some old superstition - a belief that departed souls cannot cross running water. You never could go anywhere with Lydia without getting the entire history, chapter and verse. That's Lydia for you.'

He paused, waiting for some response. Met by silence he turned away from the river and looked down at her. She was blowing her nose.

'Are you all right, Rachel? You've been very quiet. Would it help to talk about it?'

'I can't stop thinking about her. She must hate being in that place.'

'I'm sure that she does.' said Trevor.

'I feel so sorry for her. She's asked me to go and see her again. Soon.'

'And do you want to?'

'I think I should. At one point she started to talk about Rush. I couldn't really make much sense out of it. Says he went to the nursing home the day before he died, and she refused to see him.'

They began to walk back up the hill in silence. When they reached Bank Square Trevor said 'It might be better if we forget about Rush. That's all done and dusted.'

Rachel glanced up at him, surprised. 'Has someone told you to drop it?'

Trevor gave an enigmatic smile. 'Let's just say that it wasn't an editorial decision. Shall we sit on one of those benches for a few minutes?'

It was mild for the time of year, with more people about than was usual for a Monday. Christmas shoppers crowded the now pedestrianised main street, milling beneath the decorations which had been strung between the buildings. The faint sounds of Christmas carols drifted through an open window. A lunch hour queue had gathered around the cash point outside the bank. A mother with two small children in tow came out of the public toilet, a claustrophobic looking capsule which had been plonked down in a corner of the little park. Rachel watched as the younger child was strapped back into his pushchair, then they disappeared back into the crowds.

'Tell me about your visit to the nursing home.'

'Well it was all rather strange. I spent about half an hour with her. It was quite upsetting. Those places are depressing anyway. Lydia was trying to be tough and bossy. I was a bit alarmed by her at first, then I began realise that it was just a pathetic attempt to retain some dignity. I could see that she must have been a force to be reckoned with, in her heyday.'

Trevor nodded. 'How right you are.'

'Anyway, on the way out I went to tell Sister Renshaw I was leaving and we had a bit of a chat. She told me a bit about Lydia's illness and explained what is happening - and the way that she's going to end up. She'll be a prisoner, trapped inside her own body, that's how Sister Renshaw put it. Her brain will remain unaffected, but she won't be unable to move or swallow or communicate. If that's true, then whatever time she has left is - well, when I was leaving Lydia said herself that time has become very precious. I didn't really understand the significance of the remark, not until later, after I'd talked to Sister Renshaw. Quite soon she's going to reach a point where she won't even be able to talk. I can hardly turn my back on her at this point in her life. That's how I felt about it when I got back home. I've never really thought about time before. Just taken it for granted, like we all do at my age. We just think about having to wait for something - crossing off the days, getting impatient, stuff like that. Not about waiting for death, waiting for everything to end. Waiting for nothing - it's horrible.'

Trevor nodded. 'It certainly is. And it's far too much for you to deal with. I'll go instead, if you like.'

Rachel shook her head. 'Sister Renshaw said that I'm the only person Lydia has agreed to see since she went into Larch Green, so I can't let her down. She wants to see my cats. She asked me to take them in, but I'm sure it won't be allowed. And the cats wouldn't like it. I was wondering whether to ask if it would be possible to take her out of the nursing home for an hour or two.'

'You're very caring for one so young. Why don't you let me

ring Sister Renshaw? If she says that Lydia is still fit enough to go out, I'll drive you to the nursing home and we'll take her to your place to see the cats. You can't manage that all by yourself.'

Trevor glanced across to the round clockface, set in the little red brick tower of the old Union Bank building on the corner and sighed. 'We'd better be getting back to the office. Listen Rachel, a word of warning. Be careful of Lydia. I know you mean well, but she sometimes battens on. I've seen her do it in the past, when it suited her. She was always a one to use people for her own ends. She's a manipulative woman and she can be a dangerous influence. Don't let her draw you in.'

'What do you mean? I don't understand.'

'And I hope it stays that way.' said Trevor, getting to his feet. 'Come on. Just listen to your Uncle Trev.'

Rachel blushed.

'It's all right.' he said, with a broad grin. 'I know that's what they call me. Just remember that I'm always there if you need to talk to someone. Don't try to cope with everything on your own.'

**

Lydia, who could not bear the touch of another human being, had managed to avoid such contact for almost half a century; Lydia, who had recoiled from the entreating embraces of her own dying mother, now reclined helpless in the chair while the young nursing orderly lifted each naked, wasted leg in turn onto the towel-covered foot stool. As the foot massage commenced she looked at the girl's bent head, observing the inch wide strip of dark regrowth which etched outwards from the crown and made its way along the parting. The girl was afraid of her, avoiding eye contact whenever it was not too obvious. Divested of autonomy to the point where she could not even attend to her own feet, the girl's fear gave Lydia a certain spiteful satisfaction.

Halfway through the clipping of the toe nails the phone rang. The girl abandoned Lydia's foot and went to answer it.

'It's Sister Renshaw, Miss Pendle. She'd like a word.'

The girl disentangled the cable and brought the telephone over, holding the receiver to Lydia's ear.

'Lydia, I've got Trevor Stephens on the other line. Would you like to speak to him?'

'No. What does he want?'

She heard Sister Renshaw sigh.

'He's ringing to see if it would be possible to take you out on Sunday afternoon. To visit Rachel, so that you can meet her cats. I think you would be all right to go for an hour or so, as long as you remained in the wheelchair. He's offering to come and collect you. Don't you think it would be better if you had a word with him?'

'No.' repeated Lydia, stubbornly. 'I don't want him here. I don't want him to see me and I don't want to see him. Rachel can come and get me herself, if she wants. Tell him I'll expect her at two o'clock, unless I hear otherwise.' She pushed the receiver away abruptly.

After the girl had finished messing with her feet and taken her leave, Lydia lay in bed, pillows propped, flirting with astronomy. Anything to avoid the drabness which surrounded her, because she had known for a long time now that the secret of survival was never to become a part of it.

Sunday would be the day of the winter solstice. Halt of the sun. That moment in the year when the sun stops vertically over the ecliptic, the Tropic of Capricorn. Lingering above the tiny wobble of the earth before moving backwards towards the equator. Sidereal time. Midwinter in the northern hemisphere.

The people gathering, hot breath steaming on the cold morning air as the stars and the moon faded, gradually replaced by a high winter sky of icy blue. Dawn breaking through the mist. Belenos rising. A sudden, blinding dazzle, rushing headlong down that vast corridor between the mighty henges of the Sun Temple, to ricochet off the vast golden lozenge which covered the breast of the priest. Heads bowing in supplication.

The precession of the equinoxes. Almost nine thousand stars, star clusters, nebulae and the entire Milky Way. She knew that this winter solstice would be her last. By midsummer, when the sun reached the Tropic of Cancer, she would have ceased to be. Come the summer, she would be gone. The earth's axis points towards the Pole Star, in Ursa Minor.

In thirteen thousand years it will be directed towards some point lying between Vega, in the Lyre, and the star gamma in the Dragon. After a further thirteen thousand years have elapsed it will have returned to its present position and Polaris will once again be the North Star. Except that, because of the precessional movement the axis will be tilted in the opposite direction and midwinter and midsummer will have exchanged places in the Northern Hemisphere. Twenty six thousand years hence. That put things nicely into perspective.

Over the past months she had pondered at length upon the next level of existence. Perhaps one exchanged individuality to fuse with something greater, to become wedded to the rhythms of the entire universe. That helped. A bit.

Rachel was coming to get her, coming to take her away from it. One last fleeting moment before her own tiny system shut down. Would she - should she - tell? Was it for this that she had waited?

After returning home from the vets and putting the empty cat baskets back where they belonged in the shed, she had lain on the bed for a long time. Having made her preparations carefully, she fully intended to kill herself. But things begin to look different when you lie down.

She listened the steady beats of her heart, down to earth and reliable. Doing its job. The Mr Plod of biorhythms. Simple, decent and basic, unlike the brain, which was a sophisticated and anarchic trickster. The nigger in the woodpile - which was hardly politically correct, but by then Lydia was beyond bothering about such matters.

In the end it had not been fear of death itself that had stopped her, but some indestructible shard of respect for the forces. She had found herself terrified of disturbing the fine balance of energies, upsetting the delicate inner cycle of circadian rhythms. That strange, abstract, flow which drives every living thing. Frightened to leave behind something dreadful and unnatural to float in the ether, spoiling her cottage, filling it with that same awfulness encountered on the moss.

When it actually came down to it she simply hadn't dared. Unable to thwart fate, she had been forced to allow the paralysis to continue its inexorable creep forward. To wait for the power cuts to get worse and worse until they would prevent the neurons from firing at all. Which was why she was here now, waiting until palsy finally extinguished her flame.

Sunday was the only available opportunity to take Lydia out before the Christmas holidays. Sister Renshaw had told Rachel that it might well turn out to be the last opportunity full stop. 'If you sure you want to take her? It's very good of you to give up your time like this. Sooner rather than later - just for an hour or so.'

Julian had tried to dissuade her. When she remained adamant he had offered to drive them, but Rachel declined, sensing that Lydia, having already refused to let Trevor get her from the home, would have no wish to encounter anyone else.

**

On Saturday Lydia Pendle was visited by a new dream. A white dream, back at the cottage in the kitchen, where the tall fridge freezer was covered in great glittering mountains of frost and ice. As she reached up to investigate she discovered another compartment, high up and out of sight. A compartment the existence of which, until that moment, she had been entirely unaware. As she began to drag aside the great sheets of ice, brushing and scraping at the crunchy frost drifts, a door finally came into view. This door was slightly ajar. On tiptoe now, she reached up again, and stretched forward to push it shut, but as she did so the door suddenly burst wide. Under pressure from the contents within, dozens of tiny frozen birds began to tumble out into the kitchen. Dark fleshed purplish pigeon, baby-pink spatchcock, their puny legs skewered into place by thin sticks, and skinny yellow quail, all plucked and drawn and dressed, ready for the oven. Neatly shrink wrapped, nestling on their little blue polystyrene trays. Frantically she tried to gather them up, to stuff them back into the overflowing freezer, but it was no use. As soon as she touched one she knew that it was too late. They had already started to soften. To thaw.

**

Rachel had left the taxi waiting at the front entrance. Lydia was already down in the entrance hall, in a wheelchair. She looked better in her clothes, more normal with the heavy winter coat and woollen trousers masking the ravages beneath. A nurse wheeled her down the ramp towards the waiting taxi. The driver got out to assist, helping to slide Lydia into the back of the taxi and then he collapsed the wheelchair and lifted it into boot. Rachel sat beside her. The nurse stood on the steps, waving as the taxi pulled away.

Lydia stared out of the window. 'Ask the driver to stick to the main road. Tell him to avoid Chapel Lane. I don't want to drive past my cottage.'

Rachel leant forward and relayed the instruction.

'I wasn't expecting a taxi. Don't you have a car?'

'No, only a bike.'

'Then you must let me pay for the cab.' said Lydia.

Rachel shook her head. 'No need. This is Trevor's treat. He offered to take us in his car, but I knew you wouldn't like that, so he insisted on organising the taxi.'

The blue eyes weighed her up sharply. 'You're keen, aren't you?'

'What do you mean?'

'Are you chasing a story?'

Rachel shook her head. 'Not any more. To be perfectly honest, I was. That's what brought me to see you originally, but it isn't the reason I'm taking you out today. I wanted to give you a change of scene and I know you'd like to see the cats. I haven't got you here to probe a story out of you. Honestly. I wouldn't dare.'

Lydia grinned. 'I know that's what you think, but you were sent. You found your way to my bedside. And the story - yes, there is a story, but even if you got hold of it, it wouldn't do you any good. You would never be able to use it. I couldn't even write the book I'd spent most of my working life preparing. You either stop prying of your own accord or you'll be stopped. That's the way it works.'

'Why are you trying to frighten me?'

'For your own good. It's a burden you would have to carry. Is that what you want?'

'I still don't understand.'

'I know you don't. You couldn't possibly. You never will unless I tell you. And then it would be too late. The damage would be done.'

'And are you going to?' asked Rachel gently, suddenly aware of something important. An inner truth, lying in wait, hidden beyond the surface, waiting to be acknowledged, to be shared and felt.

'Probably not. I haven't quite decided.' said Lydia, as the taxi drew to a halt.

Rachel's room was cosy after the nursing home. They were settled around the log effect gas fire, Lydia having opted to remain in the wheelchair. Between them they had managed to remove the overcoat. Tea and biscuits finished, Lydia now sat in contentment with a rug over her knees and both cats curled in her lap. Not yet three o'clock and it was already growing dark. Rachel got up and switched on the table lamp.

'Shall I move them? You must say if they're too heavy.'

Lydia shook her head. 'No, leave them. This is what I wanted. You've no idea how it soothes me. Could you get me a cigarette? They're in my coat pocket.'

Rachel lit it and passed it over to her.

'Thanks.' She attempted a smile. 'This is like being let out of school.' She took the cigarette in a shaky hand and raised it to her lips with difficulty. It was too painful to watch and Rachel averted her eyes. They sat in silence until Lydia had finished her smoke. She held the trembling stub up and Rachel took it from the bony fingers and extinguished it in the ashtray. Lydia watched without comment while Rachel brushed away all the spilt ash from the slumbering cats.

'It's a good thing they're grey.' remarked Rachel lightly, in need of something to say.

'It took me a long time to get anywhere near Vincent.' said Lydia, changing the subject. 'We'd met a few times, off and on, over the years. I mean, I can wring the truth out of the devil himself - I'm good at it. That was my job. But it didn't work with him. It was hopeless. And then one day, back in 1981 I found him sitting there, in my local. One lunchtime. Couldn't believe my eyes. I still don't know whether he gone there deliberately, whether he'd been waiting for me. There he was, all on his own, in my usual corner. Looked as if he'd been there for some considerable time. As soon as I spotted him I could see that he'd been indulging in some serious drinking. That much was obvious. Anyway, I got my own drink at the bar and took it over to the table. To begin with I couldn't get more than two words out of him. He was in a terrible state, but eventually he did begin to talk.

They'd taken away his research. Forced him to abort the programme. Stood over him and watched while he destroyed it. Central Office had sent someone to stop him and the poor bugger was in bits. That's how he came to pour it all out to me. He knew I'd keep it to myself. And I did. I have. This is the first time I've ever spoken about it. We were both after the same thing you see, albeit for very different reasons.'

She suddenly stopped talking and took a sip from the glass of water. Rachel watched as she struggled to swallow.

'Sorry, voice is packing in again. I need a break. Throat muscles playing up. Give me a few minutes.'

Resting back against the cushions, eyes closed, silently reliving that fateful encounter and Rachel once again watched information slipping away, further and further below the surface, beyond reach. Back into the darkness where it could be left undisturbed.

**

Although until then he had never done more than hint at the nature of his work, Lydia had already guessed. That lunchtime, when he had taken too much wine and started to unburden himself to a willing listener, she had been left to conclude that the majority of his experiments were conducted more for the edification of Vincent Rush than for the good of mankind.

Following the accidental discovery in the locality of a well preserved corpse, carbon dating results had established that the deceased was of pre-Roman origin. Once satisfied that the remains were ancient the coroner had released this unusual find, which had then been handed over to the museum people. Prior to preserving the remains for posterity, the Paleopathology departments had conducted every test they could think of, including the allocation of certain minute extracts of tissue. These were sent to Vincent Rush who, from one microscopic blood sample, had achieved the seemingly impossible. After many weeks he had finally succeeded in his quest.

For the first time in the infancy of genetic research someone had isolated the precious DNA print which would enable man to study the earliest known replica of that vital thread which travels down the centuries from generation to generation. The code of life.

There is a universal mechanism which is basic to the properties of all living organisms. Comprising thirty separate proteins and three different nucleic acids, the particles are known as ribosomes. They are the amazing components essential to the translation the genetic code, for when these constituents are dissociated they spontaneously regroup and become an exact replica of the original material. Vincent Rush loved playing with ribosomes.

The ripples this created had lapped far beyond the isolated boundaries of his own academic island. Alarmed at the potential implications, his work had been blocked. One dark winter morning an intimidating individual with a pinstripe suit and glacial smile had arrived unannounced at the door of Rush's research laboratory. This envoy had already spent long session in the privacy of the Director's office, where there had been a long and uncomfortable exchange, accompanied by several transatlantic phone calls to the parent company headquarters.

When the visitor finally confronted Vincent Rush, his politeness had been icily intimidating. The scientist had perused the sheaf of official documentation and looked on in dry mouthed silence as his data was removed. After supervising the obliteration of every trace of his work from the main computer, the official had returned from whence he came, taking with him the precious samples, months of dedicated work and the major part of Rush's soul.

Eventually he had lapsed back into his habitual silence and Lydia had taken her chance.

'May I ask a question?'

'You can try. There's no guarantee that I'll provide the answer.'

'When you isolated that DNA, I presume you embarked upon a series of comparative analyses with modern samples?' She leant a little closer

'Well I would, wouldn't I?' he replied. 'Otherwise what would have been the point to any of it?'

Ignoring the trace of sarcasm, Lydia continued. 'As you know, I've spent years researching the pre-Christian era. A challenge, I'm sure you'll agree, with so little evidence to go on, but I have gained certain insights. I have one particular theory which I've always assumed would prove impossible to confirm. Maybe you are the one person who can finally provide the answer.'

The pub was beginning to empty and she paused as the barman began to collect up empty glasses from the next table. When he moved on, lowering her voice, she continued. 'That DNA, that ancient, Celtic DNA, I would dearly like to know whether it was identical to your modern samples? And if not, could you tell me in what respects it differed?'

Vincent Rush had hesitated and then given a small, contemptuous laugh.

'It didn't.' he replied, in the slightly patronising manner he reserved for the layman. 'DNA is DNA. The same thread, carrying the same coded instructions from generation to generation, onwards up the centuries. Our ancestors carried the same requisite number of zygotes and chromosomes as you or I. That body had the same blood group as around seventy percent of today's endemic population. By that period the indigenous Celtic tribes had evolved - physically, that is - to the same stage as modern man. I've no missing links or throwbacks to offer, I'm afraid.'

'I know that.' retorted Lydia, sharply. Unaware that she was being teased she sprang passionately to the defence. 'The Celts were a wonderful people. My own researches have produced most impressive evidence relating to many aspects of their culture and tradition. I have an enormous respect for them.'

'And so do I, Lydia, so you can climb down of your high horse.'

'Sorry.' She gave a half apologetic smile. 'Anyway, let me come to the big question. What really keeps driving me on, what I desperately need to know is this; what have the last two thousand years done to us? All those layers of civilisation, the march of time, how has it altered us? For the worst, I suspect.'

Rush gave a sharp intake of breath. He was suddenly looking at her differently. After a long hesitation he decided to speak. 'There was one thing.'

Lydia sat very still and alert, not daring to intervene, willing him to continue.

'I've told no one. Didn't even feed it into the records - which is just as well, considering what's just happened.'

Lydia suddenly experienced what she privately referred to as her invisible antennae. It only happened very occasionally, but whenever it did something crept beneath the surface of her skin and the effect was electrifying. 'Go on.'

'When I had finally succeeded in isolating DNA, I followed my normal procedures. These begin with the dissembly of the various components. Each section governs a specific area, and contains the instructions - the pattern, if you like, - from which we begin to develop. DNA controls not only the physical characteristics, but absolutely everything in our makeup,.'

Lydia nodded. 'I know.'

'Well, the next step was to undertake a long series of comparative analyses using a wide range of given samples - human and primate. In virtually every respect the iron age material was standard. An almost identical match against the modern human samples, just as I had expected. Apart from one tiny detail in the area which is believed to relate to perception.'

He paused maddeningly, savouring the moment, but Lydia did not dare to interrupt.

'I expect you would like to know what interpretation I placed upon my discovery?'

Lydia could contain herself no longer. 'Would you like me to tell you?' She stared at him, suddenly staggered by her own audacity.

He removed his spectacles and studied her myopically, sandy eyebrows slightly raised.

'You could try.' He put the glasses back on.

'You found evidence of heightened sensory awareness. What we call a sixth sense.'

'That's very perceptive, Lydia.'

The sarcasm was lost on her.

'It fits beautifully. The last piece. I knew it! He was the shaman, the sorcerer, bridging the divide between them and the spirit world, interpreting the signs, communicating on their behalf with the elemental forces.'

'Hey, slow down. You're losing me here.'

'He would have been sacrificed at Samhain.'

'What is that, exactly?'

'Samhain. The festival of appeasement which marked the beginning of the Celtic year. It was celebrated on the first day of winter. The month we call November. The tribe knew that hard times lay ahead. The cold and darkness, sickness and food shortages. The long struggle for survival. Grain was rationed. The cattle were slaughtered. The time had come round again, the hour when the debts of summer needed to be settled. Samhain was the day of the dead, the day when the Otherworld became visible and the supernatural forces were unleashed. The greatest and most feared day in the whole calendar. Blood gifts were required so the terrible rituals began. There had to be a sacrificial death - a triple death. First the victim was garrotted and stabbed in the neck so that the precious life blood could be released. As it spurted out they collected it in the chalice of atonement for Esus - the major Celtic deity. Then came the axe blows to appease Taranis, god of thunder. Finally they cast him into the pool as an offering to their tribal god, Teutates.'

'A definite case of overkill.' Rush interjected flippantly.

Choosing to ignore the remark Lydia remained lost in thought, pondering the revelation. Tribal and superstitious, their world dominated by signs and seasons, they lived within a carefully constructed hierarchy of greater and lesser gods, upon whose conciliation survival of the tribe depended. A nervous people, who believed in a world of cyclic return. Closely attuned to every change created by the forces of nature, every sign would have been interpreted by their priest.

'Heightened awareness would have been regarded as a priceless asset, you see. Anyone with the gift would have been regarded as an invaluable member of the tribe. They would believe that he held the key to their continued survival.'

'So why would they pick him for the sacrifice?'

'Precisely because he was so revered for his supernatural powers. Only the most valuable, the most precious blood would appease the deities.'

Vincent Rush had laughed but it sounded hollow. 'Not very logical. We appear to have science and the old religion sitting down at the same table. Strange bedfellows, if you'll pardon the mixed metaphor.'

She glanced at her watch. It was long after two.

'I have to go, Vincent. I'm sorry, but I'm already late. You can trust me, none of this goes any further. I guard my researches with my life. We could help each other - pool our resources. Can I give you a lift somewhere?'

He shook his head. 'No, I'll walk. I need some time to think. Don't get too carried away, Lydia. I have never pooled my resources and I'm not about to start. Thanks for the chat.'

'It wasn't a chat. You should think before you mock.' she said, severely. 'Race memory is stronger than you suppose. Samhain isn't forgotten. When they failed to stamp it out the festival was rededicated by the Christian church in an attempt to take over control. It became All Hallows Day. The eve of Samhain is Halloween.'

**

Rachel looked at the clock. Time to wake Lydia. The taxi would soon be returning. She took a tissue and bending over the sleeping woman wiped away the dribble of saliva from the side of her mouth. Lydia stirred, opened her eyes.

'It's all right, Lydia, it's Rachel.' She gently removed the cats as Lydia changed position slightly. 'You dropped off to sleep. The taxi will be here in a few minutes.'

'I'm, sorry, I hadn't meant to.

'It's quite all right, I don't mind, not at all.'

'Well I do.' said Lydia. 'What a bloody state to be in. Manage to get out from that place and then waste precious time sleeping.'

'Would you like more tea?'

'No. If you could pass me the water - and light me another cigarette.'

'Can I ask you something?'

Lydia drew on the cigarette and nodded. 'Not saying I'll tell you though.'

'Rush - was he queer?'

Lydia began to laugh. 'Very, but not in the way you mean. Why?'

'I just wondered. His marriage failed and he had no children. He's left everything to Ben Jackson.'

'I always thought that he would.'

'Why?' Rachel leant forward. 'Is Ben his illegitimate son?'

'You could say that. Not in the way that you're implying, though.'

'And what was he doing at the moss? What's so awful that no one will tell? Did he kill someone?'

'No, Vincent wasn't a killer. I can only guess. The timing was very significant. I think he went there to put back what he'd

243

taken. That sounds like the taxi.'

It was already dark. The weather had changed and there was a trace of sleet in the wind. As Rachel manoeuvred the wheelchair down the path towards the waiting taxi Lydia suddenly shivered. The solstice was over

21
Dispersing Dr Rush

She had asked the nurse to turn off the light. When she was alone again she lay on her back, staring up into the half darkness, thinking about dying. Trying to imagine and failing utterly because as soon as she got anywhere close the mind shied away from it and fled elsewhere. She made herself concentrate, trying to focus and still found it impossible. Maybe it would work if one tried someone else's death instead. The first of November, 1997. His death day. She knew it well.

**

The sandy hair, long since faded to nondescript paleness, had receded, extending the bulge of his vast forehead towards the crown of his head.The last few nights had left their mark and his face had taken on a drawn, haggard look. Stepping out of his clothes, he lay down on the bed. Asleep or half asleep, made little difference, for his mind continued to leap, racing and bounding. Throughout the long nights he lay beneath the covers listening to himself. Hearing the snoring, knowing that it was his own and quite helpless to stop it. He could also see his own body - even worse see inside his own body, prey to all its vileness. As if it was his no longer, but the body of the entire world, helplessly performing its functions.

In the deepest hours of the night he watched the spontaneous beating of his heart, the steady rhythmic coursing of the blood. He followed the progression, working methodically through each section of intestine. The converting, discarding, retaining, the careful processes of selection as the last meal was digested. The liver toiled, collecting the detritus ready for elimination, keeping him going, keeping him alive.

On and on went the pipes and tubes, gathering together the waste products of another day of his life. And so they would continue, unless something put a stop to it. The gift of life, so casually bestowed, was no more than a terrible chemistry which left its possessor trapped within.

On that final evening he had paused at the top of the stairs, one hand clutching the bannister rail. Turning, he glanced down into the shadows of the hall. A dull glow reflected from the highly polished carcass of the long cased clock and a trace of bewilderment flickered over his thin features. Wearily, he began to retrace his steps, carpet slippers scuffing softly against the cold linoleum of the corridor, where a narrow strip of light slid from beneath the door of his study. He hesitated for second and then entered, blinking as his eyes adjusted to the scene.

The voice came from behind the desk.

'Close the door, Dr Rush. Come in and sit down.'

He glanced at the chair set in front of the desk. It had been cleared of the piles of papers and books which had littered it for years.

Rush's smile of greeting suddenly froze as his eyes travelled to the relic, the contours thrown into sharp relief by the light of the angle poise lamp. He sat down heavily.

'Trick or Treat, Dr Rush?'

His interrogator gave a frosty, controlled smile and Rush averted his eyes, recoiling from the coldness.

'Look at me.'

The voice was low, dangerous, and Rush slowly met the glittering eyes, drawing back in alarm as the oval mirror which usually hung on the wall beside the door, was thrust into his face.

'Look carefully. Take your time. Tell me what you see.'

A glassy blur. Something alien that must be himself. He peered into the reflection until the glass became misted.

'Who are you?' The voice had changed, grown soft, yet not

quite a whisper.

Rush swallowed hard, but said nothing.

'What are you?'

The words, louder this time, were accompanied by a tiny shower of spittle. Rush remained motionless as his inquisitor leant across the desk. Too close. Far too close. Invading him. Rush could not move.

The tone of the voice altered. It began gently, coaxingly, gradually building towards a controlled crescendo of pure hate.

'They are all in there, Vincent. Barbara's little brother. The clever schoolboy - can you find him? That lonely, brilliant student? He must still be there somewhere, too.'

The voice was growing harsher.

'Ursula's lousy husband? Lydia Pendle's one time friend? Susan Jackson's employer - or perhaps exploiter would be a more accurate description. And the Caretaker. Yes, the mask that covers the rest. Do you see them, Dr Rush? All in there, waiting. Hidden behind this terrible, twisted face. And that - what do you call that? The Head of Genetic Research?'

As his gaze returned to the relic Rush seemed to crumple forward in the chair.

The mirror was suddenly snatched back and slammed down hard onto the top of the desk. The questioner clenched his hand into a hard fist and punched. As the glass shattered, small scarlet petals began to grow from the back of the hand. The scientist cowered back as the fist thrust towards him.

'Blood. Take a good look. Hot and flowing and bright red. That's what you wanted and that's what you get. Here, have some.'

In one fast movement the wounded hand was drawn across his sagging face, blooding it.

'Leave it!' the voice shrieked as Rush moved to wipe the blood away.

The angle of the desk lamp was adjusted until it highlighted the

247

blood smeared face. His tormentor treated Rush to a thin smile. 'Good. Now we have to wait while it dries. Look at me, Dr Rush.'

Rush obeyed. As the eyes focussed upon him, Rush became rigid. Unable to move. Paralysed.

'Just beginning to understand. Starting to know.'

The stare contained the fire and the frost of the world. Eyes flaming with power, thrusting him deeper into his final journey, hurling him down the final stretch of the route he had been travelling for years.-

There were noises. Blood pumping, mouth curdling until the dry saliva mingled with the metallic flavour of old coins. The room began to fill with a bitter sweet stench. The noxious stink of decay. Eyes suddenly grew bloodshot as the intolerable pressure ruptured the tiny network of vessels webbing the eyeballs. Out of him and into Rush, who was starting to choke, clawing with weak fingers at the imagined ligature now tightening around his neck. The chair behind the desk creaked slightly and Vincent Rush suddenly rose unsteadily to his feet, took the dangling car keys from the outstretched hand and lurched from the room.

Reeling down the passage way to the back door, Vincent Rush gave a low moan. The very fabric of the house was pressing on him now, squeezing him out, away from his mess. Towards something worse. Dreadful visions etched into the remaining fragments of his mind and he struggled with the bolts of the back door. As he stumbled towards the car the last remnants of his brilliance finally crumbled, clearing the way for hallucination. He collapsed into the driving seat.

There was no chauffeur to escort him to this last appointment. Only the urging voices, grating until they distended the canals of his ears and the pain became unbearable. He clamped his hands against the sides of his head, trying to deaden the noises. It was useless, for the sounds came from within. He withdrew his hands, feeling the stickiness of thin trickles of blood. Small droplets collecting, quivering for a moment on the ear lobes before falling to his shoulders. Reverse. Forward. Track back. Feed back. Pay back.

Whatever it was had been there in the mirror. His own disease, staring back at him. Somehow he located the lights and crashed his way through the gears until the car leapt forward. Weaving down the long drive he veered on an erratic course towards the moss.

22
Visiting the Sick

The boy moved with infinite care, double checking to make quite sure that everything was back to normal. Normal! - that was a laugh. The room was restored to its usual mess. Satisfied that nothing untoward remained, he closed the door and and felt his way back along the passageway.

Twelve years old, small for his age and old for his years, Ben Jackson padded barefoot across the dark hallway. Don't touch the bannister rails. Avoid five and eleven, which have a tendency to creak. From the front hall the grandfather clock chimed, confirming the hour. Counting each riser in turn he crept silently up the wide staircase.

When he reached the galleried landing he sank to the floor, back resting against the panelling, and began to lick the dark dry blood from the back of his hand. Next he turned his attention to the wound, dribbling saliva directly into the gash. Ignoring the sharp throb of pain he nipped at the torn flesh in a series of fast little bites, as a dog worries its fleas, then sucked hard, coaxing a fresh issue of blood. Salty, sticky scarlet liquid, flushing out the tiny glass splinters. One by one he spat them out into his good hand.

**

Overnight frost had turned the leaves dry and brittle. They floated in the chilly stillness of an October afternoon, lingering on the air before collecting in crisp brown heaps along the edges of the road. Towards dusk the wind would get up and uplift the leaves again, scurrying them across to the opposite gutter.

Susan turned the car into the nursing home gates and

followed the signs to the car park. Beside her, Ben nursed the large bunch of deep bronze chrysanthemums.

'Such a lovely fresh autumn smell.' she said, for the second time. 'They should last well, even in this place. They always keep sick rooms so hot. Poor Miss Pendle.'

'I don't really remember her. Why would she suddenly ask to see me?' He was already striding towards the nursing home steps. Susan locked the car and hurried after him.

'I've no idea. I was really surprised when they rang. They wouldn't just telephone out of the blue. She used to be very friendly with Dr Rush when we first went to work for him. I can't understand why he couldn't have been a bit kinder towards her. I think they must have fallen out. She's ended up such a poor lonely old thing.'

Their footsteps echoed across the huge entrance hall. 'I never really took to her, myself. Haven't really seen her since you were a baby.There aren't many young men that would give up an afternoon to go nursing home visiting.' she added.

The woman on reception gave them a quizzical smile.

'Hello, I'm Susan Jackson. We've come to see Miss Pendle. It is all right isn't it? You rang me yesterday.'

'Oh yes. It's good of you could come.' She turned to the boy. 'You must be Ben. Lydia keeps asking about you.' Lowering her voice slightly she continued, 'She's not been too good this last couple of weeks. Turn left when you get to the top of the stairs. Room 16.'

Lydia opened sunken eyes as they entered. Masking her shock, Susan forced a bright smile. The old woman's skin was sallow and taut and her wiry hair formed an untidy grey halo against the white nursing home pillows. She bent over to kiss Lydia on the cheek and pulled back with indecent haste from the sweet waft of decay. She turned her attention quickly to arranging the flowers in an empty glass vase which stood on the window sill.

'There we are, Miss Pendle. These will brighten up the room. This is nice. And private, too. More like a hotel, isn't it?'

'More like God's waiting room. Next stop the mortuary.'

The voice was strangled, little more than a whisper. The eyes were on Ben.

'Oh, Miss Pendle! That's a dreadful thing to say.' Susan was shocked.

Lydia managed the trace of a painful smile.

'It's the truth. At least they've stopped badgering me to go and sit in that bloody awful resident's lounge, now that my condition is deteriorating. Doesn't do to go upsetting the rest of the inmates. Mind you, most of them are neither in this world or the next.'

Susan sat down and studied her finger nails, at a loss for something to say. Lydia watched her closely. Ben remained with his back to them, staring out of the tall window. When the sick woman next spoke the words were barely audible and Susan forced herself to lean closer.

'What is it, Miss Pendle?'

'Vincent - how is Vincent? Did he know you were coming?'

Susan nodded. 'He's all right. Very busy, of course. He asked to be remembered to you.' she lied.

Lydia shook her head wearily. 'You don't have to pretend, Susan. Vincent dumped me a long time ago. He'll be glad when I'm gone.' She closed her eyes.

Susan looked at the hands lying on the sheet, thin and transparent and unnaturally clean. Like new, she thought. 'Don't tire yourself by talking. I thought that he might have come to see you. I did offer to bring him, you know. Miss Pendle, may I ask you something?'

Lydia opened her eyes again.

'It's something that I've often wondered about.' Susan continued. 'I feel as if I need to know. Was it because of Ben?'

Lydia inclined her head a fraction.

'But why? Why should he mind about you spending time with Ben?'

'Jealous.' The word was scarcely more than a breath.

At that moment the door opened and a young nurse entered.

'Time for her injection.' she said to Susan, as if Lydia was not present.

Susan stood up.

'Right, nurse. We'd better be going now, Miss Pendle.'

As she bent to kiss the parchment cheek Lydia caught hold of her wrist, clinging to it weakly. Susan bent closer until she could smell the sickly breath again.

'Ben - the cottage - I wanted him to have it. To live there. You too. Now they've made me sell it to cover the fees here. Get out of Medlar Hall. Get him away from that place.'

'You really had better leave now.' intervened the nurse. 'I have to give her this injection and she'll sleep afterwards. If you want to have a word with Sister, on the way out ......'

Lydia was struggling to raise herself from the pillows. The nurse approached the bed.

'Now, Lydia, you be a good girl. Lie still for me, this will only take a minute or two.'

Lydia thrust her away with surprising force. 'No!' the voice was stronger. 'No. Not yet. I have to - I need time, time with Ben.'

There was a note of panic now and the boy finally came to the bedside, hesitated and then took hold of her hand.

'She'll be asleep almost immediately.' said the nurse, brandishing the injection. 'You must go now.'

Ben looked down at the pillow and met Lydia's pleading eyes. He turned to the nurse.

'I'll wait outside until you've finished and then I'll come back and sit with her for a while.' he said, firmly.

The nurse opened her mouth to protest, caught his glance and said nothing.

'Wait for me in the car, Mum. I'll just have a few minutes with her. I won't be long.'

She was still now. He sat and watched as the drug began to take effect and he knew she was trying to fight it. Gently he took hold of her hands. When she finally managed to speak the words were slurred. Her fingers tightened for a moment, but there was no strength left in the grip and one hand fell away, back onto the bed cover. She was rambling now, agitated, battling against the effects of whatever they had used to help her into oblivion. Soon the ravings subsided and he drew closer.

'Lydia, listen to me. Calm yourself. Don't try to speak. There's no need. Not with me. I understand anyway. You know that, don't you?'

Her eyes followed him as he took a tissue from the box on the locker and smoothing back her hair gently wiped her damp forehead.

'There now, that's better.' he told her, feeling the tension easing from her. She became still. He waited with her until her breathing grew slower, heavy. When he was sure that she was sleeping, he got up quietly and made his way towards the door.

He was almost there when something pierced his mind, cruel and hellish. Psychic leakage from a sick, drugged old woman. Quaking, he retraced his steps and took up his place beside the bed. Staring down at the face on the pillow he saw beyond the mask of jaundiced flesh. He sat immobilised, a helpless receiver gathering the trapped emotions that had tormented Lydia Pendle for years.

Caught a glimpse of Barry Doyle in the Drover's Arms and felt his fear. Watched Lydia talking enthusiastically in Rush's grimy study. Saw a long cobweb dancing in a draught of air, and looked at them trudging over Lindow Moss as the July dawn broke. A flash of steel as the scalpel reflected the first rays of sunlight. Forced himself to stay, to live out the whole ghastly story. An affront to mankind, to nature, to the great earth goddess.

Benjamin Vincent Jackson. An offence against humanity. He laid his head down on the bed cover and wanted to die alongside her.

All at once the thought transmissions became calmer. The stream of pain began to disintegrate, replaced by a great flood of sorrow. A new pattern surfaced, directed, this time, at himself. He stopped sobbing and listened.

'Rush cloned you and I did nothing to stop him. I let him do it. Watched it happen. Forgive me. Please. I'm begging you. Make this bearable for me, this terrible burden. Your mother, Ben - your mother doesn't know. Take care of your poor mother. Never tell her. Live this life, Ben - use this life that he forced upon you.'

Opening the bedside locker he felt around inside until he found it hidden at the back. Lifting out the small bag, he placed it on the bed. Nausea. Waves of revulsion. Stay in control. He drew the garotte from the bag and placed it on the bed. He stared at it, forcing his mind to remain clear, to quell the buzz of terror forever trapped within its coil.

Before he left he wrapped Lydia Pendle's bloodless fingers around it. 'Let them take that to the mortuary with you.'. At the door he turned round and stared hard at the sleeping woman. 'I forgive you, Lydia. You can go in peace.'

But Rush - never. When he got back to the car he looked at his mother so strangely that she experienced a surge of apprehension. She leant across and put an arm around his shoulder.

'Ben? Whatever's wrong? Tell me. Has she gone? Say something, Ben. Speak to me.'

He opened his mouth and then held himself in check. He stared out of the window, towards the nursing home steps and watched two nurses laughing together as they walked towards the entrance.

It was not her fault. She had been a good mother to him. Struggled on year after year, under miserable conditions.

Suddenly he leant across and, for the first time in his life, hugged her. Forcing himself to sound natural, he met her anxious eyes.

'Sorry Mum - no, she hasn't gone. It just upset me, seeing her like that.'

'Try not to take it so hard, love.' she comforted. 'She's old and it's her time. She looks like my Dad did. That's just how your Grandfather went, towards the end. A dreadful thing to watch, all that suffering. Serves no purpose.'

He shook his head. 'It does. It makes us understand ourselves.'

Susan stared at him in surprise. 'Oh Ben, how can a young lad like you come out with things like that? You've hardly lived yet. How much longer do you think she'll last?'

'Not long. A few weeks, perhaps. Look, Mum, I don't want to talk about it anymore.'

They drove back to Medlar Hall in silence, each lost in thought.

That night he lay in the darkness listening to the word as it continued to ricochet off the walls of his mind, stinging until the pain was almost physical. Clone. Small wonder he was different. All those lonely years wondering if everyone else felt as he did, trapped within themselves. He had sensed that they did not, but there was no real way of knowing. No one went around asking those sort of questions.

With the growing realisation came the beginnings of an understanding. The borders of Brigantia, Lydia had said. The ancient lands of the Brigantes. Were they his people? If so, he had no recollection of them. A mother, a father? Brothers and sisters, maybe? An entire tribe? His own rightful heritage was nothing more than question marks and nameless shadows. He tried to concentrate his thoughts upon the sacrifice. Still nothing. Just some painful half remembered moments that had haunted him since childhood. Five years old at the harvest festival, when he'd peed his pants during the service ......

On the final afternoon of term, the children filed into the

school hall, now brightly decorated with the wall friezes which they had been painting all that week. Against one wall, a long trestle table displayed a colourful collection of the fruits of autumn - purple bilberries and blackberries, crimson rose hips and boughs of bright red berries which Class 3 had gathered on a nature walk along the course of Sugar Brook. There were wicker baskets of apples and damsons arranged in nests of wispy hay. Marrows and onions, massive eggs from the ducks and geese and trays of dainty little bantam eggs, sent along by the wives of the local farmers, together with jars of jams and pickles. All the small chairs had been taken onto the stage and arranged in neat rows between the buckets of flowers. Along the front of the stage were the children's own gift baskets which they had excitedly brought from home that morning.

Susan slipped into her seat, eyes scanning the crowd of children up on the stage until she found him. There he was, in the second row, watching her. She gave him a little wave and he stared back impassively.

Lisa Marsden took her place at the old upright piano as Miss Turner came out onto the stage, waiting whilst a couple of latecomers found somewhere to sit. She smiled down into the audience.

'Good Afternoon, ladies. We would like to welcome you all to our Harvest Festival service. You can all see how hard the children have been working to decorate the hall. Our thanksgiving service will last for about half an hour. Afterwards, you may take the children home with you.' She turned to the children. 'Those of you whose parents have been unable to attend this afternoon will remain behind until the school bus arrives. Miss Marsden?'

Lisa Marsden got to her feet, signalling for the children to do the same. There was a scraping of chairs, some shuffling, followed by a moment's silence as Miss Marsden reseated herself at the piano. 'Right, children, after three! One, two -

three!' As the tinny notes sounded out across the hall, the children opened their mouths and began to sing loudly.

"We plough the fields and scatter,
The good seed on the land......."

Forty enthusiastic young voices swelled to the chorus. The mothers smiled to each other, exchanging knowing glances before turning their attentions back to the stage. Miss Marsden thumped out the tune on the piano, depressing the loud pedal in time to the music. Susan's eyes returned to Ben, half hidden now behind a tall girl on the front row. Had she been closer, she would have seen that he had stopped singing. He was standing quite still, eyes open but unseeing, in some sort of daze. Feelings, strange feelings, sensations that no small boy should be expected to understand. Broken fragments. Race memories from the recesses of his mind.

Wet groves of dripping birches. Season of sacrifice, season of tears. Seed in the woman, seed in the ground. Seed for the earth goddess. Samhain again. Time to pay the dues.

Solemn beat of the tympan, slow and repetitive, announcing their arrival. The thin mist from the Otherworld begins to rise and their feet are lost in the vapour. The dance begins gently.

They place the golden torque around his neck. Elder and Priest lead him forward, bound and naked beneath the old, bloodstained skins of the precious Samhain Cape. They drag him to the heart of the circle. The drum beat suddenly ceases and there is an awesome moment of heavy silence as they reach the edge of the pool. The dance resumes, wilder, faster, tribal hands and feet beating the rhythm. Weaving, chanting, circling him, echoing the torque. Already knee-high, the mist continues to rise.

The painted suck whore enters the cone of power, coppery red hair cascading wildly. The crowd chants as the splendid, savage looking creature begins her terrible dance, baiting her audience. As she approaches, the Priest removes the golden torque. The Elder replaces it with a long sinew strip, the ends left to dangle, for the present, down the back of the cape. She continues to dance towards them, ever closer, until she is kneeling before him, ready to perform. Ready to coax the first gift. She tosses back her hair so that her breasts are exposed. The Priest and the Elder step to one side.

He is staring at the spirals which contour her entire body, mapping out regeneration in the red and ochre pigments of the earth. Teasing fingers and carmine lips, anointing him with circles of saliva painted with a long tormenting tongue, gathering in the entire focus of his concentration. Holding out, making it last. The penultimate moments of his lifetime. Eyes shut tight against the final act. *Le petit mort*. The crowd roars in unison as his seed arcs and falls upon the mother earth.

The dancing continues now, wild and frenzied. The men are beginning to move in. Sensations fade. Blood drains. Spent, he clears his throat, opens his eyes. The fear takes over. In the final heartbeat he sees his own woman, proud and pale and ill, swaying on the edge of the circle. Their child heavy in her belly. Grief in waiting.

Shockwaves.

Then the hammer blow from behind.

As the piano played its last chords the mothers began to applaud enthusiastically. The scraping sounds of chairs brought him back. He suddenly looks around to find that he alone remains standing. His pants and and the top of his left sock are warm and wet and Miss Marsden is flapping her arm at him in a downward motion. He sits down quickly. Head bowed, emptying his mind, he comes back to school. Back into the hall.

**

Unable to sleep, he finally rose. He understood now. Knew for sure that he had been executed on behalf of his people and had gone bravely, honourably. One of the chosen. His killing had been a privilege, not a punishment. A courageous act of propitiation, desecrated by the ignorant Vincent Rush. A callous manipulator who had made a mockery of his atonement. Such deliberate profanity demanded an act of attrition. Once the malevolence of outrage had been unleashed, Ben could only loathe him.

Creeping downstairs he entered the study, carefully closing the faded curtains before switching on the desk lamp. For a few minutes he stood immobile, lost in thought. Long hours he had passed in this room. All his growing, all his developing thoughts probed by that twisted maniac. And for what? Because Vincent Rush wanted to enter the mind of a dead man from another era.

'And so you shall.' he said aloud. Dragging a chair over to the wall behind the desk he clambered up and removed the bunch of keys from their hiding place in the Leeches jar. A moment later he had the desk drawer open.

Only one trace of emotion had crept into this terrible record of his conception, birth and life, chronicled here in minute detail, and that was the author's own frustrations. At the opening of the journal, Rush's hand writing was an untidy scrawl. As he turned the pages the writing began to degenerate, developing loops and twists until it was so full of eccentricities as to be barely legible. It was almost possible to chart the progress of the writer's mania, reflected here in the steady deterioration of his script. Ben's dark eyebrows knitted in concentration as he struggled to decipher his own history, seeking one tiny shred of pity, one small vestige of remorse for the strange child that had been brought into being. All he found was a monstrous, proprietorial boasting. Not one shred of respect for his own inner privacy. Maybe a clone did not have any rights. A clone belonged to its creator.

The final entry was a curt and self-congratulatory observation that Lydia Pendle, sole witness to his act, was soon

260

to take her knowledge to the grave. It was almost daylight when he finally closed the journal and returned it to the drawer.

One entry led him hesitantly to the locked cupboard. Unable to find any key which would open it he crept out to the stables, returned with a long chisel and took some pleasure in forcing the lock, patting the tiny splinters of mahogany back into place as the door swung out on its hinges.

Unwrapping the linen cloth with trembling fingers, he compelled himself to look. It was unique in the history of horrible visions. As he stared at the preserved image of himself he began to realise the depths of Rush's depravities. There before him was the hacked neck and the top of the skull, cratered open like a crushed egg. Between these two outrages the face - his face - was peaceful. He touched the short beard shyly, tracing the jawline beneath with his forefinger. A life lived. A life finished, terminated more than twenty centuries ago. Until it was disturbed, interfered with, forced to reawaken. Save the hatred and the anger, let it simmer.

Lydia's final message flitted into his mind. 'Live this life, Ben - use this life that he forced upon you.'

He decided to wait. The eve of Samhain fell at the end of the month. He would get him at Samhain. That would allow enough time to work on him, to pour some acid bile into the chemistry of that over brilliant brain. Time to prepare him. Night after night of green and yellow nightmare would interfere with the metabolism, manoeuvring him into a very receptive frame of mind. Just long enough to prepare the brain for its death throes. And then he would be free of him, free to follow Lydia's advice.

**

When the cleansing was completed he got back to his feet and crossed to the landing window. After a struggle with the latch he managed to push it open with his shoulder. Leaning out over the sill he stared into the night sky, raising his fist of fragments to the new moon before letting go. Clinging determinedly to the sticky surface of his palm, the bloodstained slivers refused to fall. Gingerly he brushed them away, out into the darkness.

Afterwards he stayed at the window, listening. Nothing. Only silence. She'd get over it. They were going to be all right. He'd look after her. He pulled the window shut and tiptoed down the long corridor towards the bathroom in search of a plaster. Down in the hall the grandfather chimed the next quarter.

23
Pay Back Time

Rush looked up. A new moon surrounded by stars, with some broken cloud formations scudding across an inky canvas. Ahead, bare trees in silhouette and that dreadful trackway vanishing away into the blackness. The earache was becoming intolerable. As the surrounding air began to drone he could no longer differentiate. It was impossible to distinguish which were the genuine noises of the night. New strands of tension started to proliferate, accelerating his descent towards permanent adhesion. The network of energies continued to swell, sweeping him along to the final interchange. The marriage of mind and place. Oblivious to the distant orange glow which marked out the town on the nocturnal map, blind to the flickering light from some far off window beyond the bare autumn branches, he moved onwards, deeper into the howling void. Each shambling step drew forth a cold ooze of black moisture. The voices had stopped and the excruciating pains suddenly subsided to a dull throb. He paused, listening to the ensuing silence. Suddenly it was rent by a rush of air. He waited uncertainly.

A sharp crack brought a fresh surge of fear. A moment later the thin crescent of moon emerged from behind the clouds, faintly illuminating the contours of the moss. He glanced down. Beneath his feet the ground glistened, overlaid with trails of slime. Slime and decay. He tried to move forward but something was badly wrong. He found himself swaying and then collapsed to the ground. As he tried to raise himself his eyes focussed upon the crenelated circles. Suctioned to the peat, only dark gashes of primitive eyes broke the moist brown smoothness of the bloated bodies. Hermaphrodite couplings, united by the opaque blister of white mucus which rose from the midst of each pair. Cloacal lovers. *Slugs and snails and puppy dogs' tails.*

Sobbing uncontrollably he tried to crawl away and found their disgusting jelly webbing his fingers. As he struggled back to his feet the crushed bodies began to roll slowly down from the knees of his trousers, squelching beneath his slippers. His throat discharged a low howl, an unearthly, eerie sound that came down the centuries, taking possession of his vocal chords to thrust itself into the night.

Oblivious to the mist beginning to rise up from the moss, it was not until the temperature suddenly plummeted that he realised he had been engulfed. It slid over him, curled itself around his body. Filled with disgust he struck out, trying to part the strange vapour, only to shrink back in mounting horror. All around the air was filling with exploding showers of cells. Familiar cells, dancing and dividing. He watched as blastocysts became trophoblasts, as chorionic villi stabbed mean little fingers towards him in their relentless search for nutrition. Primary endoderm tissue drew towards the yolk sac, homing towards the embryonic plate. A thousand tiny, waving threads united in their commitment. Magic wands obeying the rules. The primitive streak formed.

Twitching clusters whirled towards him, a kaleidoscope of weird patterns floating forward, borne on the dense, frosted curtain. A terrified scream rent the night. Only when it echoed back from the surrounding woodland did he recognise it as his own. Sinking to his knees, he buried his aching head in his arms and remained in this position, rocking slowly, for a long time. When he eventually dared to look up again the mist had dispersed. He rose unsteadily to his feet. Nothing moved. He could not stop his eyelids from blinking and they began to ache horribly. He trembled, struggling to cling on to the final fragment of rational thought. Be calm. Think. Breath slowly. Clear the head. Oh, God, the head. Like Lydia had told him. Get rid of the head. Raving incoherently he veered off the trackway, peering across the blackness towards the direction of the main road. Recognising the noise of a distant car he fell silent.

When he turned back to the moss they were already rising. From out of the peat the Lindow dead worked their way towards him. A spectral file of withered flesh, smiling and beckoning. Preparing a welcome. The boggarts were accompanied by trails of green flame as marsh gases flashed phosphorescent wings from naked heels. He felt his gut tighten as the leather lips parted in each tanned face. The next moment a chorus of death cries reverberated down the ages.

Dark hands, raised in supplication, suddenly tearing at their garrottes, trying to prise loose the sinew bands. Blood leaking from slit throats, spilling in black rivulets down naked, concave chests. Others clawed wildly at their gaping head wounds, tapping the splintered bone, patting the jagged flaps of skin back into place before running thin, tapering fingers through flattened, peat encrusted hair. Tidying themselves up.

Eyes glittered in the cold moonlight as they began to circle, continuing to draw closer until he caught the mingling stenches of corrupting flesh and sour wet earth. The ground was spinning with them now, joining in the dance as it gathered speed, until the entire moss became a revolving cone, sucking him into the vortex of its embrace. Filled with a wild exhilaration, his eyes grew wide. Discovery! On the verge, the very brink. As they led him forward he moved along willingly, deeper into the moss. The pace accelerated, his head echoing with their voices.

All those years of dedication. Strange, the lengths that you went to when you could have taken the easy route. Come with us now, Vincent. Join us and then we can share it with you. We will reward your long apprenticeship. That final, precious knowledge. The mysteries, Vincent, belong to us.

Urgent and compelling, the chant gathered strength. The tightening around his neck grew stronger, until his throat became scorching pain. Warm life still coursed in the bloodstream, feeding the fibres. A moment later he was looking into his own scalding brain, awash, flooding, gushing, overflowing, shuttering his eyes as the dreadful carnival escorted him to the edges of the pool. At the brink they suddenly dissolved, leaving him to walk forward alone.

Bog water entering the body, filling the sacs. A hand clawing at the night. Growing limp. Sinking into the depths. Putting back. The final bubbles drifting lazily across the surface of the water. One last ripple lapping towards the perimeter. Repaying the debt. A semblance of peace. Only a semblance.

And even after all that Lydia Pendle still could not get beyond those final moments when the pool filled his lungs.

24
Mid January 1998

Lydia thought the nightmare had returned, but as the ascent began a quality of wonderment developed. When she arrived at the top no one was waiting. She glanced back briefly and then hesitantly let go to step bravely forward, straight and proud, head high, into a different kingdom. Clutching her bridal wreath she floated like thistledown on the gentlest of breezes. A tiny airborne seed riding the thermals towards the river of regeneration. Slowly unfolding, becoming magnificent. Understood, forgiven, raised and uplifted. Transfigured. Saved.

**

It was half past two on Friday afternoon. *The* Friday afternoon. Rachel peered though the office window anxiously. 'That's all I need. It's beginning to snow. Do you think it will delay the train? What if I miss the connection? Sophie, what do you think? Should I let him know? Ring and warn him, just in case? What if he gets to the station and I'm not on the train?'

'Rachel, just calm down. Stop panicking, the trains will be fine. Now, are you ready? We really need to leave in ten minutes.'

'Nearly. I've just got to wrap the present. Do you really think he'll like it? Tell me honestly Sophie. You know about these things far better than I do. They did say they'd change it if it wasn't right.' She stopped struggling to get the sleeves level and checked her watch again. 'I've just about got time, if we stopped off on the way.' She stared down at the sweater, which lay spread eagled on her desk. 'Oh damn and blast, I'm all fingers and thumbs - look, I'm making a real mess of it. It's your fault, making me open it.'

'Give it here.' said Sophie. 'Honestly. I don't know what you're flapping about.'

She took the sweater, inserted the layers of tissue and refolded it deftly while Rachel looked on in admiration.

'You're very good at that.'

'I should be. Practice makes perfect.' Sophie smiled mischievously. 'I used to have a Saturday job on the Pringle counter. Now, pass me that gift wrap. There we are. And now the tag. Didn't you get one of those little ribbon things to stick it on with?'

'No - I didn't want it to look too fussy. I thought it might seem a bit girlish. Oh, d'you think I should have got one?'

Sophie looked at her severely. 'Rachel, just chill, will you? It's a lovely sweater and far too expensive. In impeccable taste and obviously chosen with great care, as is the gift wrap and the card. He'll love it. You're spoiling him. Now will you please go and get yourself organised.'

'What was that all about?' asked Andy, after Rachel had gone out of the office. 'True romance. It's Julian Whitehead's birthday present and I'm giving her a lift to the station. She's going down to Oxford for the weekend. I don't think I've seen anyone that nervous. Love's young dream.'

'Well for God's sake hurry up and stick her on the bloody train. I don't think my nerves can stand much more of it. I'm trying to write here.'

'Don't be such a sour puss, Andy. It's really rather sweet. I think you've forgotten what it's like. Try and show a bit of interest. Anyway, what are you up to this weekend'

He almost blushed. 'Making a big effort. I'm just finishing this and then I'm leaving early, too. My wife's come back home.'

As soon as Rachel came back into the office Sophie began hustling her along. 'Come on, you don't want to miss that train. Here, give me that case.'

'You will remember to see to the cats?'

'Yes.' said Sophie, patiently. 'I won't forget the cats. That would be more than my life's worth.'

'You've got the list I did for you?'

'Yes, I've got the list. I just need the keys.'

'Oh, of course. Good thing you remembered. Here. The big one is the one for the front door and the Yale is for the flat. You know what time the train gets in on Sunday night? I've left the can opener out, it's next to the tins and...'

'That's quite enough.' interrupted Sophie. 'Say goodbye to Andy. Say goodbye to Trevor. Right, come on, we're off.'

**

There was gentle knock. Trevor glanced up as the door opened. Framed in the doorway was a tall middle aged woman, dressed in black stockings, low heeled shoes and a long navy gabardine raincoat. Beneath its damp haze of melting snow the rust coloured hair had turned frizzy, an uncontrolled bush framing a freckled face, now enlivened by a pleasant smile. Bright eyed and alert, she reminded him of a red squirrel, but he could see that she was nobody's fool.

'Hello, you must be Trevor. Trevor Stephens? We have spoken on the phone.'

He stood up and came forward.

She held out her hand. 'Jane Renshaw - from the nursing home.'

He shook the proffered hand. 'Oh, of course. How do you do. Do come in.'

'I'm really looking for Rachel Mackenna. The lady in the office told me to come up here.'

'I see. Well, I'm afraid you've missed her. Rachel finished early today. Can I be of help?'

Jane Renshaw looked at him. 'This is not a happy visit, Mr Stephens. It's about Miss Pendle - Lydia.' Then she shook her head slowly.

Trevor fetched a chair. 'Here, you'd better sit down.' His tone had altered. 'Has something happened?'

Jane Renshaw nodded. 'I'm afraid so. The end came suddenly, sooner than expected. Two nights ago. She died quite peacefully, in her sleep. A blessing really, everything was getting worse. It's always hard once they start deteriorating, but to see someone in the state that Lydia was reduced to - well, it was quite heartbreaking. That's why she wouldn't let you come that time before Christmas. I don't think she could bear anyone to see her in that condition. It was different with Rachel, because she hadn't known her before she was stricken down.'

'I'm sure you're right.' said Trevor. 'It's been hard on the girl, though. She's been very upset by it. Do you know about the arrangements yet?'

'The funeral is on Monday, if any of you wish to attend. I don't expect there will be many there, but I thought Rachel might want to go.'

'I'll be there.' said Trevor. 'There'll probably one or two other members of staff who knew Lydia, as well.'

'Before I forget. This is the main reason I'm here.' Sister Renshaw took an envelope from her handbag. 'They found this under her pillow. It's addressed to Rachel. Heaven only knows how she managed to write it, poor soul. It must have taken her hours, the state she was in. I promised Lydia only last week that I would see that Rachel got it, when the time came. Anyway, I was coming into town anyway today, so I thought I'd deliver it myself, just to make sure.'

'Leave it with me.' said Trevor. 'I'll take care of it.'

'Rachel's a nice girl.' said Sister Renshaw. 'Kinder than most. I think it meant a lot to Lydia, Rachel taking the time to visit her the way she did. That girl put herself out a good deal more than a lot of relatives, and I know what I'm talking about. You see it all in my job, Mr Stephens. It brings out the best and the worse in people and every degree in between.'

'Can I get you a cup of tea - or coffee?'

Sister Renshaw shook her head. 'No, thanks, I don't have time.

I have to be getting back. If you could just make sure that Rachel gets the letter.'

Trevor placed the envelope carefully in his desk drawer.

'I'm very sorry to hear about Lydia. She gave a lot to this paper. All her working life. We'll be giving her a good obituary.'

After Sister Renshaw had gone he reopened the desk drawer and looked down at the white envelope for a long time. It was addressed to Rachel, but not in Lydia's writing. This calligraphy, round and upright, was the product of a tidy, immature hand and he guessed correctly that it had been written by one of the young nurses. He shut the drawer again. Then found himself fidgeting, unable to concentrate on anything else. He grew twitchy and distracted. Deeply uneasy, he began pacing up and down the empty office. It grew worse and suddenly turned into a ripple of alarm.

He went back over to the desk and removed the envelope from the drawer. Lips pursed, he placed it before him on the desk. It was emanating some unpleasantness. Something almost tangible, rising towards him. Lydia, trapped within her own paralysed body, even dead, it seemed, still retained the power to disturb. His thoughts turned to Rachel. Sweet, caring Rachel, with all her life ahead of her.

Suddenly angry, he tore open the envelope and pulled out the single sheet it contained. There was something else. He shook out it out. A small terracotta square landed on the desktop. He picked it up, examining it closely. There was a strange mark impressed upon one face. He shrugged, mystified, and absentmindedly slipped it into his jacket pocket. Unfolding the paper, he smoothed it flat against the surface of his desk. As his gaze alighted on the open page he experienced a wave of disgust.

Before him lay clear evidence of the appaling, cruel mortification that she had endured. It was encapsulated here, where every painful stroke of her agony had been ensnared as she struggled to gain control of the pen. Whatever she was trying to convey made no sense, but he knew instinctively that it was something rotten. It was flaring off the page. One word and a travesty of that sign on the little tablet. Three distorted and distressed letters and a symbol. He clearly remembered Lydia's handwriting. He had worked alongside it for many years.

This tortured script bore no relation. The disease had wrought havoc. For some inexplicable reason he found himself wondering if it had really been the disease. It was a strange, irrational thought but - maybe something worse was to blame. That poor woman. He could feel the force of her sufferings, the pain of her anguish. He suddenly filled up and the message blurred as he stared down through his glasses. He blew his nose and continued to study the paper, trying to decipher, to make some sense of the twisted, distorted letters.

$$B\,E\,N\ =\ \text{ᚴ}$$

A disappointed woman. Frightened to live her own life so she had taken refuge in a sham existence, priding herself all the while on her self sufficiency. Waving it like a tattered flag down all those long years, flaunting her independence. Dragging all that pain around until it stopped hurting, then bravely trying to rechannel it so that it turned into scar tissue. And all emanating from one massive silent scream of loneliness. Still there, trapped, reduced, and finally distilled into three tortured letters and a strange symbol. Not quite brave enough to take it with her in the end, so in desperation she had tried to pass it on, to off load it onto Rachel. Trevor found himself wondering whether it might have been kinder if that crazed wretch had finished her off properly, all those years ago.

He left the office and went down to the next floor to get a paper cup of thin black coffee from the dispensing machine. That didn't help. He was still in the same terrible quandary when he got back to his desk. But of one thing he was certain.

He knew that he did not want to give that letter to Rachel. He needed help, someone to talk to. Edwin Nicholls came into his thoughts. What would he have done, confronted with this? Come on, Edwin, tell me what to do. I'm listening.

This position is all about responsibility, Mr Stephens. You have a serious responsibility here.

The sound of Sophie's stilettos clattering up the stairs brought him back to the moment and he hastily returned the letter to the drawer, forcing a bright smile as Sophie came into the office.

'Everybody abandoned ship Trev? Left you all on your own?'

'Did Rachel get off all right?'

'Eventually. Sorry I've been so long. The bloody train was late of course, and she was so nervous and excited that I didn't have the heart to leave her waiting there all on her own on that platform. Honestly, you've never seen anything like it! Talk about love's young dream. Quite sweet really.'

Trevor could tell that she meant it. For once Sophie had abandoned cattiness and was actually being nice. 'Rachel is sweet. I've got some sad news for her, though. I'm afraid Lydia passed away on Wednesday. During the night. I'm just glad that Rachel didn't get to hear about it before she went, it would have spoilt her weekend. She's going to be upset. I think she might take it rather hard. Rachel should never have been drawn into Lydia Pendle's sufferings like that. Anyway, it was a merciful release, from what Sister Renshaw told me.'

'I'm sorry.' Sophie said uncomfortably. 'But it was on the cards, wasn't it? Anyway, what have you been up to?'

Trevor smiled. 'Not much. Getting on with what they pay me for. Editing. Friday afternoon stuff. Putting things to bed.'

They worked on in silence until Andy Thrower came back in.

'I thought you were knocking off early.' said Trevor.

'I was, but I just found out about Lydia, so I thought I'd better come back to see about the funeral. I was wondering if you would like me to do the obituary.'

'No thanks, I'm going to write it myself.'

'Are we going to the funeral?'

'I think we should. We can't let Rachel go on her own.'

'I can hold the fort.' said Sophie. 'And I expect Keith will be around. When is it?'

'Monday afternoon at Macclesfield Crem. Come on, we might as well call it a day.'

'Right. Aren't you coming?'

'I've got something to finish off but I won't be far behind you. Oh, just one more thing, Sophie.'

'Yes? What is it?'

'For heaven's sake don't forget to see to those cats.'

She laughed. 'As if! Rachel's going to be ringing me all weekend to make sure they're all right. Have I to tell her about Lydia?'

'Not over the phone. No need to spoil the birthday weekend. Are you meeting her off the train on Sunday night?'

Sophie nodded.

'Well I should wait till then. And tell her about Monday and the funeral arrangements. She can come with us. I expect Dorothy Platt will want to come along as well. We can all go in one car.'

After they had gone he took out the letter. 'Sorry, Lydia. I'm still editor around here.' he murmured, shaking his head.

When the sheet of paper had been reduced to shreds he gathered them up and cremated them in Sophie's ashtray, watching the bits until they were pulverised, reduced to powdery grey-black curls of char. Trevor hung around for a few minutes, waiting until they cooled. When he deemed it safe to do so he tipped them into the bin, screwed the envelope into a tight little ball and tossed it in on top of them. End of story, he thought, putting on his overcoat.

Not quite. Towards the end of January, when the local dry cleaners were running their 'two for the price of one' offer,

Eileen Stephens began checking through her husband's jacket pockets. She emptied all the usual rubbish into a little pile on the dressing table, shaking her head in fond exasperation at the mounting pile of sweet wrappers, old tissues, bits of paper, one odd cufflink, various coins and accumulated fluff.

And a strange little terracotta tablet. When she had finished she gathered up the loose change and set it aside before scooping everything else into a black bin bag, which was collected later that week by the dustmen. They chucked it into back of the cart along with the rest of the refuse and at the end of the shift they drove back to Newgate to off load at the tip. The following day it was all bulldozed down into the landfill site. Another layer.

Appendix

A short manuscript, dated 1884, was found amongst Lydia Pendle's effects. Written in a fine copperplate hand, it was identified as the text of a lecture to be presented to the Lancashire & Cheshire Archaeological Society by one William Norbury.

The manuscript contained selected extracts from a series of articles written by Grant Allen. Underlining as it does the Darwin/Huxley - inspired Victorian preoccupation with ethnology, it is appended here as the reader may find it of interest. It may also, possibly, hold the clue to Lydia's lifelong quest in search of the 'darker elements'.

LINDOW COMMON AS A PEAT BOG -
ITS AGE AND ITS PEOPLE
BY WILLIAM NORBURY

A HINT was thrown out by our learned president, in his speech at the inauguration of our Society, that "it would be one part of our business to place on record the old before it disappeared utterly in the new." The peat bogs of Lancashire and Cheshire are fast disappearing, and will soon be things of the past. Our great Chat Moss is going rapidly from view as a bog; others are entirely gone. Lindow, the subject of my paper, is fast being cultivated, and in a few more years all that can be said will be - "This once was Lindow!"

I may remark at the outset that Lindow, in its structure and age, seems to be similar to Chat Moss and the other peat bogs of the locality; so that if we take this it will serve as a sample of all the rest - certainly of all those with which I am acquainted - and, therefore, after these general remarks, I shall confine myself to this moss.

Lindow Common, which is largely a peat bog, lies in the townships or hamlets of The Hough, Fulshaw, Morley, and Chorley, all in the parish of Wilmslow; in Great Warford, which is in the parish of Alderley; and a large slice of it lies within the parish of Mobberley. The moss was formerly very much larger than it is now, and it is not difficult to fix its original boundary. The area of the ancient moss, roughly measured from the ordnance map, was about one thousand five hundred acres. Fifty years back (when I first knew it) it was about half that and now it may be taken roundly as only one-fourth of the original amount.

By using our eyes, and by examining the levels, we find that it is the highest land in the locality. Not that the bog has grown until it is higher than the surrounding land, but the dish in which it lies is placed on the highest land; the bog is, in fact, formed in a shallow dish of clay lying upon an elevation. A shallow meat dish with a rim round about not unfitly represent the contour of the land, while a pie made in the dish, and raised up above the rim, with a slight depression running parallel therewith, is a fair picture of the bog. Through the rim of the dish the sluggish watercourses escape into the neighbouring rivers or brooks: on the northerly and westerly sides into the Bollin, on the easterly and southern sides into the Birkin and its tributary rivulets.

Under the bog is an original surface of soil, in which ordinary surface plants and shrubs have grown - a soil formed from mosses, ferns, and other vegetable matter, like other fertile soils. On this grew heaths, brambles, birches, alders and other brushwood, and at the time when these were produced this surface was comparatively dry; for the plants found are of kinds that only grow on comparatively dry surfaces; we have nuts, firbobs and other seeds, and even the remains of weeds in plenty that are now found on the surface in our cultivated fields, as the arsmarts and others. That this was an ordinary dry surface producing ordinary surface plants is as clear as anything can well be.

In a natural order, after the brambles, birches, and alders, came the pine forest - just what we should expect; and next in order came, to some extent oaks, yews, and other more advanced forest timbers, though these are rare in comparison with the pines. After a time, from some cause, the growth of the pine forest was arrested, and in the main the boles of the trees perished; for we find a hundred roots or stocks for one bole. The roots have remained in situ, and are generally found with the upper part ending in a spike of heart from which the bole has rotted and eventually broken off. In some cases the bole is found detached from the root, and lying in a partially rotten state, near the outside of it especially so; a sound bole, or indeed one with any considerable portion sound, being rare. In some few cases, in special localities, there are charred stocks, showing that the boles have been burned from them, but this is not by any means a common case. The fact we want

278